1

Fringe Ending

Emma Baxter's path crosses her father's more often than he would like as she directs an amateur musical at the Cambridge festival and he investigates a murder on the fringe of the university community. The elderly victim, Rupert Parsingham, a popular gardening adviser, was the great-grandson of a famous Victorian botanist. Suspects include Rupert's radical activist sister, the Director of The Parsingham Institute for the Scientific Study of the Tropics, his Filipino wife and two members of his staff, a jewel thief, and a playwright with bitter memories of the university city. Detective Chief Inspector Baxter does indeed track down the killer, but not without his daughter's active intervention.

MARGARET MOORE

Fringe Ending

THE CRIME CLUB
An Imprint of HarperCollins *Publishers*

First published in Great Britain in 1991
by The Crime Club, an imprint of
HarperCollins Publishers, 77–85 Fulham Palace Road,
Hammersmith, London W6 8JB

British Library Cataloguing in Publication Data

Moore, Margaret
    Fringe ending
    I. Title
    823.914[F]

ISBN 0 00 232354 0

Photoset in Linotron Baskerville by
Rowland Phototypesetting Ltd
Bury St Edmunds, Suffolk
Printed and bound in Great Britain by
HarperCollins Book Manufacturing, Glasgow

CHAPTER 1

Six inches of corduroyed leg—a left leg. To its right and in parallel, one green wellington boot.

Hardly the stuff of an identification that would stand up in court. But more than enough for Detective Chief Inspector Richard Baxter, who surveyed the scene through the kitchen window of his home in Kings Covert, Cambridgeshire. The coffee tray had already narrowed the possibilities: few of his wife's visitors rated Bernard Leach pottery. Fewer still would be allowed to rummage among the foliage of the Baxters' dear but decrepit mulberry tree, while Sarah held the ladder. Besides, on his way home, the Chief Inspector had spotted Rupert Parsingham's battered brown station-wagon in the parking space by the village green.

Richard turned away from the window and sought solace for the morning's frustrations in a mug of tepid coffee and the latest edition of *Collectors Guide*. Sarah's horticultural guru was much in demand on spring Saturday mornings, so with luck he wouldn't have long to wait.

Nor had he. In faded green dungarees and sweatshirt, with a triangular headscarf slipping off her reddish-brown hair, Sarah looked absurdly young. Typecast, he didn't dare tell her, for the rancher's helpmeet in a 'forties Western.

'Pear midge, cladosporium, clear-winged moth,' she muttered, evading his hug. 'Let me get that down, will you?' In large scale and felt-tip on the memo board her medico's scribble was just about readable.

'Sounds ominous. Have we got all of them?'

'Not yet, but I doubt if I'd recognize the early stages,

6

6
6
6## 6

and prompt treatment is essential. Wanted Rupert to run over the symptoms today, but it would have taken too long on top of the more urgent stuff. So I daren't forget next time round.'

'Why so? He'd fit in an extra visit, if you asked him nicely.'

'That's the snag.' Sarah scrubbed her hands at the kitchen sink. 'He's retiring in July. Quite cut up about it, poor man.'

'Lucky man, I'd say. So why's he going? *Ann. dom.?*'

'Partly.' Sarah flopped down in a basket chair. 'He's turned seventy, so he'd need medical backing to renew his driving licence. And his GP's warned him he won't play ball. Glaucoma's not responding to treatment, apparently. Already, he's lost some peripheral vision. Add that to arthritic hands—'

'And he's better off the roads? Take the point, darling. But surely mobility isn't essential for his job? I'd have thought he could've expanded his clientèle in Cambridge City, maybe even offered a 'phone advice service to his farther-flung customers.'

'Wouldn't be fair to his successor, he said, when I suggested something of the kind. Got quite shirty, as a matter of fact. Came across True Blue Camford for a minute or two—just like his sister.'

'Oh Lor'.' May was high season in Cambridge for protest demonstrations, and Eve Parsingham Wells featured colourfully and noisily in most of them. 'Maybe that's what getting him down—not being able to put a dozen miles between himself and Sis when the fancy takes him. Poor bugger. But there are worse fates, so don't let him spoil the rest of your weekend, love. More coffee?'

'*Our* weekend,' she amended as he poured it.

Their first shared free day-and-a-half in three months. He grinned. 'I hadn't forgotten.'

'Feel like a trip to Newmarket? 2,000 Guineas day, Rupert tells me.'

'Let's pick something we both like.' Sarah had no doctrinaire objections to horseracing, but it wasn't one of her favourite things. 'What say to a breath of sea air? Overnight stop in Aldeburgh or Sheringham?'

'Or Southwold? I really fancy Southwold. I'd say great, lovely. We could lunch on the road. But meantime let's slow down. Let me enjoy my cuppa. Besides, you know what rushing does to your duodenum. Your turn to off-load the mental baggage. How was the crime-busting pow-wow?'

Richard pulled a face. 'Funny, if you'd been a fly on the wall. Vic Highcroft's fancy new pattern-detection program has come up with the answer the rest of us arrived at weeks ago. On present evidence, there's no pattern to the jewel thefts, except that the merchandise is all top quality and the scenes of crime are in the Eastern counties.'

'So you reckon they're not the work of one gang?'

'I reckon we need more evidence. Doorstepping's getting us nowhere fast, so why not start at the other end, say I. Put tabs on the fences that could handle that class of goods.'

'Good thinking.'

'Ta. Highcroft's slapped me down every time I tried to implement it. This regional get-together was my first chance to side-step him, to fly the kite outside a Mid-Anglian forum.'

'So?'

'So the Norfolk lads cut me off in mid-sentence. Seems they'd got there first. The six fences they named coincided with my own first guesses. Three turned out to be in the slammer over the relevant period, one's gone straight, one's in a psychiatric hospital. But number six, who looked in many ways to be the best proposition, left the country in a hurry less than a fortnight ago. Day after the Norwich Ecclesiastical Museum job. Cross-Channel contacts suggest he's lying low in Holland or Belgium. On past form he'll dispose of the hot stuff long before he resurfaces. So we're back to square minus one—back to the doorstepping.'

'And what's wrong with that?' Sarah teased. 'Honest, labour-intensive employment. Keeps people off the dole. Speaking of which, here's a letter from Emma that should cheer you up.' She tossed it across the table and went upstairs.

The airmail envelope had, he noticed, a Leningrad postmark. The three scribbled pages began and ended with apologies for brevity. The rest was mostly taken up with a tongue-in-cheek précis of the Russian tour by the Merseyside theatrical company in which his daughter served as assistant director and dogsbody.

Then, almost as an afterthought, came the news that the company would be splitting up when their current tour ended in late May. Emma had a London-based job in prospect, but not before the autumn. Which was why she'd said yes to an SOS from a college friend—Paul somebody—the squiggly surname defeated her father. He'd persuaded her to take over the direction of a musical show in which he was involved, a fringe event at the Cambridge summer Festival. Since nothing more than pocket money was on offer, and if her parents didn't mind, she proposed to base herself at Kings Covert for June, July and August. *Mind!* Letter in hand, Richard went out into the hall.

'She'll be at home for her birthday,' he yelled above the hiss of Sarah's shower. For the first time in six years—no, seven. God help them, she'd be twenty-three.

Sarah made enthusiastic noises.

'Who's this Paul she's on about?' he shouted back, still unable to make out Emma's squiggle.

He didn't make out Sarah's reply either. But it could

wait. He picked up the East Anglian tourist guide from the hall table and began looking up hotels in Southwold.

Bang-clinkety-bang.

'Come on, Trickstep, COME ON! Give it to him, you dozy bastard—let him know who's boss. COME ON!' Bang-clinkety-bang.

Rupert Parsingham listened and loathed. *Look thy last on all things lovely*, De La Mare had urged, and Rupert Parsingham had come to Newmarket this May afternoon to do just that. Next to horse chestnuts in flower, he could think of few things more beautiful than thoroughbreds at full stretch. And thanks to the complimentary ticket passed on by his employers, he had a rare front-of-grandstand view of the races.

Bliss unalloyed, until the unspeakable woman on his left had started to shout and bang the railings. Thank God she hadn't edged forward until after the classic, the 2,000 Guineas. Bang-clinkety-bang above the roar of the crowd. OK, there was greed in that roar—open, childish greed. Greed, suspense, disappointment. But there was joy as well—collective joy in the spectacle of speed and grace and horsemanship.

Bang-clinkety-bang. 'Faster, you bastard. Get off your bum, can't you? Get stuck into him!' No joy there.

Half-turning, Rupert took in a pair of royal blue gaberdine sleeves, ageing scarlet-tipped hands, and the sapphire-and-diamond bracelet that was doing the clinking.

Bank-clinkety. Bang-bang. As he turned away something flashed in the left-hand blur of Rupert's visual field. He checked. Two blue sleeves, two scarlet-tipped fists. No bracelet.

Bang-bang! 'TRICKSTEP!' Silly bitch hadn't noticed a thing. Rupert wanted to laugh out loud.

He turned away from her again, swivelling clockwise for a glimpse of the row behind. His eyes were caught and held by a commonplace checked shirt collar and a commonplace Adam's apple. Above, a thin, tanned face set apart by black circumflex eyebrows and an expression of total concentration. The blue eyes focused on the front runners just as forty years ago they had focused on Rupert's diagrams of stag beetles. And twenty years ago on a sentencing judge at the Old Bailey.

'Simon! Simon Drinkwater!'

A frown. Then the quick, remembered smile.

'Bear! My apologies—Mr Parsingham.'

On the race-track below Trickstep had increased his lead from three yards to ten.

'All over bar the shouting, isn't it?' Drinkwater said. 'Any winnings to collect, Mr Parsingham?'

Rupert shook his head. 'And Bear—please. It's what all your lot called me, isn't it?'

The other laughed. 'Never knew you knew that. Changed monickers myself—for business reasons, you understand. I'm Dunnett now, Sam Dunnett. What say we get out of here, Bear, while the going is good? Fancy a jar?'

'Delighted.'

Dunnett, accelerating unobtrusively, reached the back of the stand before applause marked the end of the race. Above it, Rupert caught a screech of anger from the front row to which those in his immediate vicinity gave no reaction. Head down, he hurried after his ex-pupil.

'Out-of-town boozer might be more peaceful,' Dunnett said on the way to the car park. 'Any suggestions?'

Fifteen minutes later they were settled at a quiet corner table in the White Cygnet, Exning.

'Still schoolmastering, Bear?'

'At seventy? Have a heart. No, actually, I gave up that lark years ago, not long after your first—er—um—'

'My first conviction?' Dunnett's lips curved behind his brandy glass.

'Sorry—'

'Don't be. Boot's on the other foot, matter of fact. Your letter to me in prison, the offer of a reference . . . Bloody-minded of me not to reply.'

'Water under the bridge. You were eager to stand on your own two feet, I expect?'

Dunnett smiled again. 'Something like that. So you gave up teaching—for what, Bear?'

'Horticulture. Bought myself a nursery out Trumpington way on the strength of a small legacy.'

'Ah yes. Flowers were always your passion, weren't they? Though you did your duty by the horrid fauna we kids used to propagate in matchboxes. Was your degree in Botany?'

'Mmm, but a Third. A blot on the family 'scutcheon.'

'It comes back to me. Wasn't there a *Sir* Rupert Parsingham? Eminent Cambridge Victorian?'

'Yes, Great-Grandpa did pioneering work on the flora of the tropics. I love plants as much as he, I dare say, but I've no talent for theorizing about them—or selling them, for that matter.' Rupert contemplated the foam on his beer and was reminded of meadowsweet.

'So your horticultural venture ran into trouble?'

'Deep trouble. Luckily, I found a buyer with commercial flair but little specialist knowledge, who took me on as an employee. Phil tarted the place up, turned it into a garden centre, and the crowds began to roll in. He's learnt a lot about plants over the years. Might have given me the push long ago, I dare say, if his wife hadn't talked him into putting me on to after-sales service.'

'As for consumer durables?'

'More or less. Customers call me out if they're having problems with plants they've bought from us. Well, that's the theory. In practice, I try to answer any gardening question they care to put.'

'And you like that—nosing around your clients' gardens, pointing out the errors of their ways?'

'Love it. Can't face the prospect of packing it in in July—that's when I retire.' Rupert's face twisted. 'D'you know, Si—Sam, I've got the details of our regular clients' gardens mapped out in my brain. I could summon up any one at will and see it as clearly as I see you across the table—or that sapphire and diamond bracelet you nicked twenty minutes ago.'

'Now look here!' Dunnett reddened.

Rupert smiled wryly. 'I'm looking. At the man who was the boy I taught party-tricks in 'fifty-seven. Sleight-of-hand seemed a harmless therapy when you smashed your knee early in the cricket season. But I'm also looking at the boy who stole a wallet from the Chairman of the school governors the following Speech Day.'

'You can't prove that,' Dunnett whispered, paling.

Rupert shrugged. 'Who else had the chutzpah and the skills? You'd have broken down under police interrogation, I suspect, if I'd chosen to publicize your accomplishments.'

'Sir Archie Spooner wouldn't miss what he lost, the old bastard. And he *was* a bastard. His fault poor Stinks got the push for thumping the Fitzwinton kid.'

'So rumour had it.'

'One of the other Fourth Formers overheard the row at the Governors' meeting. Stinks was no great shakes as a teacher, but he was our form master and we felt protective. Besides, the way the Fitzwinton brat messed around in Chemistry, he could have got us all blown up. That kid was a born attention-seeker, real pain in the arse.'

'And a sadist. I remember the smirk on his face the time he told me the groundsman's Alsatian had got at the First Form hamsters. Cage door must have been left open accidentally, Fitz said. I knew he was lying and I knew he knew I knew. His smirk said it all.'

'Which is why you didn't finger me over the wallet business, I presume?'

Rupert nodded. 'Never could abide cruelty to animals.'

'Unattractive, I agree, even by proxy. So we'd both do better, wouldn't we, to forget the exhibition that bloodthirsty bitch made of herself this afternoon? If she did lose a few sparklers—*if*, please note—then by your book and mine, Bear, she had it coming.'

'Come clean, Sam. Evasiveness without good cause is scarcely more appealing than cruelty. I'm ready to forget what I saw in the stand—*everything* I saw—if you're prepared to be honest.'

'Now look here—' Another attempt at bluster.

Rupert sighed. 'You're cornered, dear boy. That barman over there's ex-Army, an old friend and a fitness fanatic. I know the number of your car. You've no option but to trust me.'

The younger man hesitated, then made a laughing gesture of surrender. 'OK, sir, Dunnett dunnit. That what you wanted?'

'I'd like to see the bracelet.'

'Why the hell?'

'A whim. *Look thy last on all things lovely*, the poet said. Apt philosophy for a man who'll be dead in three months, don't you think?'

'Dead? Good Lord! Awful sorry, Bear. You look good. What's the trouble? Something inoperable?'

'Nothing I want to talk about. But you'll indulge a dying man? One quick dekko.'

A handkerchief changed hands under the table. Rupert opened it on his lap and made a brief inspection of its contents. The sight depressed him. Two blue-eyed and diamond-spotted reptiles were intertwined in death or ecstasy. Sapphires and diamonds were lovely things: crowded into fanciful settings their beauty was dishonoured. As an ornament for day wear, the bracelet was absurd. Even by candlelight it would have been disagreeable. '*Un embarras de richesse*,' he punned, returning the handkerchief and bracelet to his companion.

Dunnett laughed—a little nervously, Rupert thought. 'Riches embarrassing? Wouldn't know about that, Bear. Never had much disposable cash. Anything I can spare goes back into the business.'

'The old business?'

'God, no. Horse-breeding. Strictly legit. Been running a stable near Buenos Aires for the past ten years. Steered clear of the UK up till now, but a fungus infection last year lost me my best stock, so I'm over here to raise replacement capital. Just enough to keep the show on the road, you understand.'

Rupert raised an eyebrow.

'Couldn't resist a trip to the Guineas. Don't know what came over me when I saw that bauble on Cruella's wrist. Challenge to prove I hadn't lost the knack, I suppose. A one-off. Put it down to the male menopause, if you like. And she deserved it. She bloody well deserved it.'

'Did your other victims?'

Dunnett grimaced. 'Below the belt, old man. I've paid my dues in the slammer.'

'For this season's activities?'

'I'm not with you, Bear.' Dunnett's blue eyes signalled injured innocence but his fingers tightened on the brandy-glass.

'Come on, Si—Sam. What the hell. You can put up with "Simon" from a man under death sentence. According to reports in the local media, which my dear sister is forever forcing on my attention, there've been a dozen or more jewel thefts in East Anglia this spring. Always top quality stuff, but assorted methods—con jobs, burglaries, simple dipping. The hacks' current theory is that more than one gang is responsible. But I've read the reports of your trials over the years, Si. Felt a mite responsible, to be honest. And you're nothing if not versatile.'

'Likewise non-violent. Never hurt or threatened anyone, have I? Never nicked anything the owner couldn't afford to lose?'

'Not to my knowledge.'

Simon rotated his brandy-glass. 'Speaking hypothetically, mind, if I *had* been playing my old game by my old rules, would you say I deserved to go back inside?'

Rupert considered, surprised that the other man had so nearly compromised himself. 'I'd need to know your motive.'

'Only way I can raise the wind to restock. Don't expect you to believe this, Bear, but horses are the be-all and end-all with me. Never had much luck with human relationships. Nags aren't as demanding as women, and to my eyes they're far more beautiful than overpriced baubles that spend ninety-five per cent of their lives in a safe.'

Rupert smiled. 'There's a flaw in your argument somewhere, but I shan't try to winkle it out. Life, as they say, is too short.'

'Look—about that—' the other man cleared his throat. 'Sorry if I'm speaking out of turn, but something you said earlier set me thinking. Retirement is on your horizon, you say. A time when most people could use a little extra cash.'

As if money mattered. Rupert was repelled by the other's insensitivity.

'Don't suppose you're one to spend much on yourself. But a little extra—five grand, say—could come in handy, couldn't it? For unexpected expenses or your favourite charity?'

Or a gift. A surprise gift to the woman Rupert loved. A farewell gift. That prospect pleased him. 'Am I to under-

stand, Simon, that you're offering to pay me for my
discretion?'

'Funds don't rise to that, old chum. Wish to God they
did. No, what I have in mind is a little business proposition.'

Rupert began to feel like a character in the schoolboy
comics he used to confiscate. The sensation was novel, but
not unpleasant.

'Spell it out,' he heard himself saying. With three months
to live, what had he left to lose?

CHAPTER 2

'Great—lovely—toodle-oo, my sweet.' Eric Finchley
watched in silent self-consciousness as his fellow-diner put
away his pocket phone and cleared his elbows from the
path of the approaching waiter.

'Yesterday's footage came out a treat, Corrie tells me.
And she's a hard girl to satisfy.'

Aubrey King's smirk suggested a joke. Not the sort of
joke Eric indulged in. Nor, even for the waiter's benefit, did
he propose to massage Aubrey's ego by inquiring further
into the relationship between the TV documentary maker-
cum-presenter and his senior camerawoman. Instead, he
witnessed in straight-backed silence the delivery of his duck
pâté and Aubrey's seafood mélange.

'Let's hope their bugs don't bite.' Aubrey jabbed a fork
platewards. 'And before I forget, Corrie loved the fishy
shots better than anything. Fishy—Her very word! Out of
the mouths of babes and sucklings . . . Hasn't a clue, of
course. Six years' collaboration and she hasn't seen through
me once.'

The waiter disappeared behind the service hatch, leaving

them, his first customers of this mid-May evening, alone in the stuffy dining-room. Eric grunted. Over the four years of their own professional relationship he had come to recognize Aubrey's expansive manner as a mask, an artifice.

Two hours earlier, Eric, as Director of the Parsingham Institute for the Scientific Study of Tropics, had taken a public farewell of the public Aubrey King and his team at the close of their third videomaking visit to Eric's workplace in Downing Street, Cambridge. On this, as on the earlier occasions, Aubrey had insisted that their private business should be transacted outside the Institute and the university city. The Ruffled Feathers, near Royston, which even in May was little patronized by tourists, was their usual rendezvous.

'You've a message?' Eric took the initiative and despised himself for it.

Aubrey's sharp-featured face softened into his screen smile. 'Several. First, as they say, the good news. Our friends liked your last batches of data, especially the gen on marine pollution.'

'A gift for Detoxicon, properly exploited.'

'There was, alas, one slight snag—'

'Not at my end, I can assure you. Went over that stuff with a toothcomb. Rechecked every crucial computation. Otley's work's outstanding—in a class of its own—'

'That, old man, is the snag. Term cognitive style ring a bell? Read any psychology?'

'Never had the occasion.' Not quite true. Once, a long time ago, Eric had tried. It hadn't helped. He had learnt to deal with his pain in his own way, but the memory distressed him. He reached for the wineglass.

'Pity. Good management course would give you most of what you need—'

'I am paid to administer, not to manage.' Eric faked anger to mask his unease.

'Really? Dear Camford! No business of mine, of course, but, given the mutterings I overheard from some of your younger staff over lunch in the Grad Pad, you and your Board might do well to drag yourselves into the twentieth century.'

The Grad Pad—the University Centre. So that's where Aubrey and half Eric's junior colleagues had sloped off to at lunch-time. *Carte blanche* was *carte blanche*, but all the same . . . Better not brood, though. 'Cognitive style?' he prompted.

'Ah yes.' Aubrey parted herring-bone from flesh. 'Cognitive thumbprint might be more accurate in this instance. I'm talking about a way of thought specific to one or a very small number of high-flying specialists in a given field of study, which would be instantly identifiable to other specialists in the same field.'

'Fuzzy sort of concept, by the sound of it,' Eric complained.

'As clear as most of the hunches we run our everyday lives by. And it can be quantified, if you know which features to select for a given discipline and how to weight them. In a science such as marine microbiology—'

A pause to let the penny drop. Eric focused on his bread-roll.

'Elements of experimental design would count, I'd guess. Plus features of conference and journal reports. Idiosyncrasies of syntax, imagery—'

'Imagery? Metaphors, similes, all that Eng. Lit. rubbish? For crying out loud, Aubrey. Sort of thing your TV fans expect, maybe, but unlikely to loom large in serious scientific communications.'

'No? Take a closer look next time you're in the library, old boy. You'd be surprised.'

The library? A veiled insult? Just what had the Young Turks been saying? 'Where's all this leading?' Eric asked.

Aubrey munched slowly and washed down his last mouthful before replying.

'To Julian Otley, I'm afraid.'

'The Pacific pollution project? You're saying he's let something out? Never. OK, he's an awkward customer, as you may have seen for yourself. Restless, too. But ideologically he's an infant. Believes in the potential of the UN, Third World regional collaboration, the lot. He's totally committed to that research programme.'

'Nobody's saying he isn't. But he's ambitious, isn't he? Goes to conferences—reads papers.'

'Nothing that matters on the Pacific project—nothing sensitive.'

'That's not the point. Among those attending the same conferences there's an Anglo-German bird called Dagmar Andersen—a marine toxicologist. Know her?'

Eric shook his head. 'Toxicology's off my personal wicket.'

'Since last April Andersen's been on the payroll of Detoxicon, Munich.'

'Oh my God.' Eric's butter knife slipped from his fingers.

'Seems she's been aware, for some time, that Otley was researching Pacific pollution. She also read two or three of his publications and heard him read a conference paper on some theoretical issue or other. Don't ask me what, but she was impressed. Emotionally as well as intellectually, perhaps. Impressed enough to request a transcript and his phone number.'

'No more?'

'She said not. I prefer to believe not. But taken in combination that was enough for her to guess he'd written the last experimental report you sent me—the stuff that hit her desk in Detoxicon six weeks ago.'

'Unmarked.' Eric's throat tightened. 'I'll swear that

report left my office unmarked.' But could he be a hundred per cent sure—of his secretary, for instance?

'My Munich contact assures me it remained unmarked, except for a *Commercial Confidence* stamp which was added by him. Nobody in Detoxicon knew its origin. All their local linkman has is a hot line to yours truly. Which he used pronto when dear Dagmar tried to check its provenance by ringing Otley at the Parsingham.'

'Christ.' Eric poured himself Malvern water. It tasted warmish, sweetish.

'Fear not, old chum. Her call was blocked, and it's highly unlikely to be repeated. Her impulsive tendencies have yielded—permanently, I feel certain—to arguments suggested by yours truly. Gentle art of persuasion and all that. You won't press me for details?'

Eric shook his head, sickening. *Oh, Mumsie. I never wanted anything like this, never. But I did it all for you. You know that, don't you? Tell me you know that, Mumsie.* No reply. Not to be expected in the Ruffled Feathers. There was only one place where she talked to him. And he'd never relinquish that. Never.

Aubrey repeated his small-screen smile. 'Accentuate the positive, dear boy. Consider the might-have-beens from which you have been delivered. All the same . . .' He leant forward, heavy brows knitting, as if inviting a close-up.

Eric dispatched urgent memos to his digestive system.

'All the same, my dear chap, you'll appreciate that this episode makes things difficult for Barney.'

'Meaning what, exactly?' Eric heard himself ask. The sort of inelegant construction he'd schooled himself for years to avoid. The Malvern water flowed uselessly over the greasy pâté in his stomach. Bile rose to his throat.

King reached forward to pat his hand. '*Nil desperandum.* Barney wanted you to know he isn't proposing a permanent rift—just a back-off. Keep the show on the road for another two years and he might well come up with something even better.'

'*Might?*' The word conjured forgotten yearnings for a spaniel, a waterproof watch, a bicycle. Eric's boyhood had been studded with aborted *mights*.

'Only one thing's certain in this life, old son.'

Eric shuddered. Mumsie had never liked to think about death, not even in the last long weeks in hospital. Neither did he. But sometimes you had to.

'In the meantime, how does this look by way of a consolation prize?' King passed over a long envelope. £300,000 was typed on the sheet inside. Nothing else. 'I'm authorized by you-know-who to make this sum payable to any offshore account you may care to nominate.'

'Money! Does Bryce really believe that's what I went out on a limb for? Do you, Aubrey? Bloody money!'

Eric's urge to vomit had been overtaken by a more pressing urge to weep. Rising, he pushed past the returning waiter and hurried across the still-empty restaurant to the men's room.

Three or four minutes later, he emerged from a cubicle and sluiced his blotched face in a basin. He reached blindly for a paper towel, patted the features that he'd never quite come to terms with. The strong nose and soft, off-centre mouth. Footsteps disturbed him. A second face was reflected in the cloakroom mirror. Thin, freckled, vaguely familiar.

Had they met before? Eric returned slowly to the dining-room, his self-control shaken anew by this uncertainty.

'Finchley didn't say anything about Friday night—didn't hint, even?'

'Not a squeak, love—I told you,' Valerie Gates murmured into the receiver and beamed reassurance at the photograph of Norman in his new blazer that she'd taken from her handbag. 'There's no way he could've recognized you, is there?' No need for Norm to know her boss might have caught one or two glimpses of that snapshot. He'd worries enough, and he was a born worrier.

'Can't help remembering the funny look he gave in the Gents,' Norman persisted.

'Fancied you, maybe?' She forced a giggle, fingering the cleft in his photographed chin.

'This'd be no laughing matter if it got to Trish, Val. Not after me giving her the overtime story to get out of supper.'

Trish, always Trish. Norm's only daughter and her late mother's champion, with Views on the indecency of early remarriage. 'No reason it should ever get to her, love.' Valerie's eyes slid from the snapshot to her wristwatch. She was already ten minutes into her lunch-break. Five minutes, it would have been, if that silly old fool in the outer office hadn't delayed her phone call. 'Listen,' she went on. 'If Doc Finchley didn't see us together, there's no way he could have made the connection. And I'll swear he never looked into that brasserie Friday night when we were there. Why should he? Stands to reason he ate in the dining-room, if his car was in the dining-room car park.'

When Norman had returned, grey-faced, from the men's room, she had slipped out—unobserved, she felt sure—to check the numbers of the parked cars.

'I keep telling you, love,' she went on. 'If the Doc looked odd when he saw you, I'll bet you what you like it was nothing personal. He was tense, wound-up all the time the TV crew were here. And he was like a bear with a sore head when I tackled him about my pay rise this morning. Money troubles, if you ask me.'

'D'you mean he refused?'

'Yes and no. Tell you when I see you tonight.' A Christmas wedding, they'd agreed. Thirteen months, that would be, since Enid's death. Val thanked God she'd her mortgage nearly paid, Norm being in a council flat. But there were things needed doing to the house before he moved in.

And she wanted a classy wedding dress this time round, informal but classy. Fine cream wool, she'd decided, like the one in last month's *Good Housekeeping* Look for a Lifestyle. 'You look good in cream, Val,' Norm had told her once. 'You've the skin for it. Most women your age haven't.' She loved the way he noticed things like that. If he wasn't up to much in the other department, well—she had her memories, hadn't she?

'Don't brood, poppet,' she urged. 'If the Doc gets sticky, I'll think of something. Val always thinks of something. 'Bye, now.'

This morning, when Finchley had hinted that the future of her job was uncertain, Valerie's thoughts had flitted back to the confidential tasks that had earned her those nice little Christmas and birthday presents and the promise of promotion. Then forward to the Friday evening meeting in the Ruffled Feathers between two men who had said a long goodbye in her presence earlier the same day. She hadn't told her lover that she'd recognized Aubrey King's car as well as Finchley's in the restaurant car park. She might never tell him.

Time to get moving. Valerie slipped Norman's photograph into her handbag and replaced the Institute Director's desk phone beside the jade statuette of his wife. Then she sprayed herself with White Satin toilet water and went into the outer office.

'No sign of your sister, Mr Parsingham?'

'Not yet, Mrs Gates. Punctuality never was Eve's strong suit, I'm afraid.' Rupert smiled apologetically above the copy of *Nature* he had taken from the magazine rack. Strange to realize that this dumpy, weatherbeaten little man in faded denims had anything to do with the oil paintings of the Institute's founder and his son whose portraits, in full academic fig, hung on either side of the entrance. Something about the faces, though. Teddy-Bear faces.

'Afraid I'll have to pop out now if you'll excuse me,' Valerie said. 'My lunch-break, and I've shopping to fit in.'

'Of course, Mrs Gates.' Rupert Parsingham beamed. 'Don't worry about me. Perhaps Dr Finchley . . . ?'

'Won't be back before three-thirty, I imagine. Going straight from lunch at Landers College to a Faculty meeting.'

'Another time.' Rupert began to grope in a pocket of his jacket. Valerie knew what he'd be up to the minute she'd left. That bloody pipe. But you couldn't ask a Parsingham not to smoke in the Parsingham Institute, any more than you could ask him to wait with *hoi polloi* in the entrance hall.

'Your sister will be on her tricycle, I suppose?'

'Most probably.' Another apologetic smile, almost as though he guessed about the trouble they had with the cleaners over the tyre-marks. Poor old bugger. You could almost feel sorry for him, living with a sister like that.

Whatever am I thinking of, getting sentimental about a Parsingham, Valerie asked herself, as she went out into the corridor. It's people like them that run this town, not people like Norm and you. Look out for yourself, girl. When Hardy comes to Hardy, their sort won't.

CHAPTER 3

The Vice-Chancellor and University Senators, still robed and manacled, clanked offstage. The sparse audience in the school hall applauded. The final dress rehearsal of *Spin City*, which had been protracted by a traditional sequence of fused lights, torn tapes, jammed zips, missed entrances and other last-minute crises, was finally over.

'So?' Stacey Caldwell, scriptwriter, prompted her left-hand neighbour in the front row.

'So jolly good show, my dear! Isn't that what they say in these parts?'

Shit.

Clive Sinton must have seen her face tighten. 'You've the makings of a good playwright in you, Stacey. But smart little scribblers scare the hell out of has-beens like me, if I'm honest. So you won't mind if I slope off to the boozer?' He was already on his feet, smiling apologetically. If it wasn't for the jaundiced complexion and the scar on his forehead, Stacey thought, he'd have made a good stand-in for Clint Eastwood.

Niggled by an incipient headache, she minded about his defection quite a lot. Two months ago, when Paul Sinton had first suggested inviting his playwright father to the preview, she'd been the sole member of the production team to oppose the idea. Now she'd a clearer idea of where she wanted to go as a dramatist, and a firmer belief in her own talents, she felt ready to use the criticism of a fellow-writer. Especially one with a reputation for straight talking. And Sinton was copping out.

Emma Baxter, who'd been sitting on their guest's other side, intercepted his escape. 'Are we good enough for Edinburgh, do you think?'

'So Cambridge Festival is second league!' Sinton flashed eyebrows in mock reproach. 'Bet you don't give that one to the local press.'

If Emma was irritated, Stacey didn't hear it in her voice. 'Edinburgh gets better media coverage,' she said sweetly. 'And their best fringe performance award would be worth having.'

'You're in for that with a chance, I'd say, but you'd do

well to rub down a few rough edges in the script and the production.'

'Such as?' Emma's clipboard was at the ready.

'Not now, my love. Get your local run over first.'

'And afterwards you'll lead a workshop session for us? Care to fix a date?'

'No diary on me. Bring it tomorrow night—OK, I promise.'

With that, Sinton squeezed past Emma and the others in the production team still seated in the front row.

'Eight a.m. swim, young Paul?' he called to the stage manager, now emerging from the wings, before hurrying out of the hall.

The Victorian paterfamilias role. As far as Stacey could gather, roleplay was the junior and senior Sintons' only means of intercommunication. How wearing. How sad.

'On stage, everyone!' Emma bellowed.

The Victorian dons, students, bedmakers, porters, shoe-blacks, city councillors, tradesmen, prostitutes and street urchins who made up the cast of *Spin City* obeyed with varying degrees of reluctance. The backstage team mingled self-consciously with the actors. Emma, successor to an apa-thetic director, who had been smitten with late-diagnosed glandular fever, had in past weeks taken a tough line with the amateur company.

Tonight, Stacey noted with relief, she was mostly dispensing reassurance. No last-minute changes were proposed to the spoken book, and only a two-word sub-stitution in the tongue-twisting lyrics of the shoeblacks' chorus.

Stacey didn't much care for the change, and she'd fight for its reversal before the Edinburgh run. But fatigue and her twingeing temple persuaded her to submit in the short term. As Emma turned her attention to the actors, she slipped thankfully into the wings and headed for the tiny backstage kitchen.

She was sitting there reading the fire emergency procedures and waiting for the paracetamol tablets to dissolve in a mugful of water when Paul Stinton joined her. He filled and switched on the electric kettle.

'Coffee, Stace?'

She shook her head. 'I'm checking out when I've downed this lot. Post-mortems aren't my scene at the best of times. Anyways, Julian's due to pick me up.' She glanced at her wristwatch. 'Overdue.'

'And he doesn't like to be kept waiting. You know, Stacey—'

'Lay off, Paul. Don't give me the Agony Uncle stuff tonight. Please.' *A one-track lab rat like Julian Otley's bad medicine for a creative type like you.* It had been some months since she'd heard the spiel but she'd sat through it a dozen times when she, like Paul, had been a research student in the University History Department. There had been some truth in the diagnosis, but her relationship with Julian had been more complicated and more rewarding than Paul could have guessed. Now that its end was in sight, she was in no mood for 'Told you so.'

It came as a relief, then, that Paul took her no for an answer. How little of his father there was in his appearance, she thought, watching his fair-skinned face and shock of straw-coloured hair as he cleared away the detritus of earlier rounds of coffee.

'Your dad didn't give much away at the end of the show,' she said. 'D'you think it got across to him—emotionally, I mean?'

'Your guess is as good as mine, Stace. I was backstage, remember.' Paul concentrated on the disposable beakers he was stacking.

'But you talked at the interval—I saw you.'

Paul laughed. 'About map shops. Dad's planning to see the sights while he's here. Revisiting the scenes of his misspent youth, I suppose.'

'Oh, great. Why don't you tag along with a tape-recorder and camera? Newspaper feature could get the show some good publicity.

'No go.' She watched Paul tip the beakers into the trash can and wash his hands at the sink. He turned back slowly to face her, paper towel in hand. 'We're not what you'd call buddies, Dad and I. Good thing, maybe. Blokes with big talents can overwhelm their offspring, if they come too close. We go swimming together, play chess now and then. But conversationally, there are quite a few no-go areas. And Dad's early life in Cambridge is one of them.'

'He's never written about it?' Stacey cast her mind back through those of Clive Sinton's black comedies she'd seen or read.

'Not yet.' Paul poured himself a coffee and sat opposite her at the formica-covered table. 'To the best of my knowledge he hasn't visited the place since he left in 'sixty-six. You don't know how I sweated to get him down for this show.'

'For which I for one am duly grateful.' Stacey, her curiosity aroused, recalled the glimpses she had sneaked of Sinton Senior in the course of tonight's rehearsal. The snorts of impatience at the assorted cock-ups, the barks of laughter when satirical lines came over the way she'd intended, the lacing of fingers in the few moments of unalloyed pathos. 'I think we got through to him. Thanks again.'

Stacey squeezed Paul's hand briefly before gulping down the dregs of paracetamol.

'So there you are!' Julian Otley was at the door, padded helmet in hand, his thin face pink and windblown from his motorbike ride across town.

Not a bad advert for her TLC, Stacey told herself, as she returned his hug. Six months ago it would have been a sarcastic 'Am I interrupting?' But maybe, if she were honest, he'd have said that six seconds ago, when she and Paul were tête-à-tête. The stage manager muttered that he had to see Props and departed. Julian pulled a chair close beside hers and sat down.

'Coffee?'

He shook his head, threw his arm round her shoulders. 'How was it?'

'Endless. Balls-up after bloody balls-up, so we overran. You'd have seen the last couple of scenes if you'd come when you said.'

Julian consulted his watch. 'Eleven-forty! Sorry, love. I was checking some calculations. I'd simply no idea!'

'Heard that line before some place, haven't I?' She kissed the tip of his elegant nose. 'Time was, you couldn't wait to quit the Parsingham. Now it seems like you'll never bring yourself to make the break.'

'Fair's fair, Stacey. You know my gripe was always against Finchley, not my research assignment.' He tweaked a strand of her short, curly hair.

'Go easy—my head hurts. Best if I crash soonish. Like to give me a ride back to Plumtrees?'

'Now?' The spaniel eyes registered dismay. 'Without stopping by at the flat, you mean? Oh, sweetie!' He buried his face in her T-shirt.

'Yes, now, Julian.' She pushed him away gently and stood up. 'Eve's expecting me before midnight. No reason why you shouldn't come too, though. She's told me often enough you'd be welcome.'

He jumped up to face her. 'At Castle Bloody Parsingham? No, Stace. No, thanks.'

He'd refused the invitation to sleep at Plumtrees several times before. The refusals and their bitterness had puzzled Stacey, hurt her. But she had put no questions.

Tonight, tired and needy, she asked 'Why not?', gripping

him by the elbows, forcing him to look her in the eye.

Julian flushed. He spoke softly, hesitantly. 'It's been so good between us these last few weeks, hasn't it?'

It! Sex, you mean, you dumb British bastard. S-E-X. So why can't you say it? Aching for him, she relaxed her grasp, let him pull her closer, talk over her shoulder.

'But I couldn't . . . manage . . . at Plumtrees, you see. And it'd be hell, wanting you the way I want you tonight and knowing we'd so little time left together, and not being able . . . Stay at the flat tonight.'

'Oh, knock it off, Jule.' She pulled away sharply. 'Snap out of the self-pity routine. Think of someone else for a change. Eve Parsingham Wells is an old lady who's been kind to me, who's got a hole in her roof, who's alone.'

'Not quite alone, surely? Why doesn't she root little brother out of his cottage to keep her company?'

'Fat lot of good Rupert would be in an emergency. He's eye trouble, plus arthritis, plus he's really depressed about retiring this month. But you know all that, Jule. Tell you straight, I don't like the way you talk about Rupert. After all—'

'After all what?'

'Nothing. It's just that I don't comprehend your attitude to that poor old man.'

'Dirty old man, don't you mean?'

Her anger flared. 'No I damn well don't. And if you know different, tell me.'

He shook his head. 'Forget I said it.'

'No way, Jule.' She looked up into his drawn face and wondered if hers was as pale. 'Mudslinging makes me sick to the stomach. Forget about giving me that ride. What difference does a couple of months make, anyway? Best if we made a clean break now, sorted out our priorities. I'll pick up my junk from your place tomorrow.'

'No, darling. No, please.' His fingers dug into her shoul-

ders. She held herself rigid. 'It's him, isn't it? That old
bastard Parsingham talked you out of coming to Karachi
with me, didn't he? Now he's put you up to this.'

'You're crazy!' The word came out before she'd time to
think, the word she'd told herself she'd never use against
him. Without daring to check his reaction, she wrenched
herself free from his grasp and ran out of the kitchen.

'Don't!'

Startled, Di Beresford let go of her nightdress and
stubbed her toe on the bedside table.

'Phil, you bastard!' She advanced on the bed threatening
her husband with her pillow. They tussled briefly, giggling.

'Oh sorry, sweetie.' Phil kissed the bruised toe. 'When
last did I get the chance to watch you undress?'

The question was serious and she answered it seriously
as she curled round him. 'February? In Madeira?'

Their holiday, their last holiday for how long? The Beresfords' home routine, imposed by the demands of the
Middlefields Garden Centre, was almost invariable. Phil
rose at six, Di at six-fifteen. At bedtime, she went up first
at eleven. More often than not she was out for the count
when he followed. They made love hurriedly, exhaustedly,
in the wee small hours, reminding each other of their need
for sleep.

Tonight was above par. Far above.

'Sure that film your mum took you to was a 'forties tear-
jerker?' he asked her afterwards.

'*Random Harvest?* Couldn't be weepier. And incredibly
relaxing. Just what you could do with, a weepie.'

Phil rolled on to his back. 'What I—what we could do
with right now, my love, is a Landscaping Services
Manager.'

'What about White, then?'

'Backed out, would you believe?'

'Oh no, not again. Not after the bloody interview.' On
the Beresfords' first two attempts to make the appointment,
candidates had withdrawn before they had selected their
short list.

''Fraid so. He rang around eight. Usual story for a
Northerner. He'd just got round to checking out Cambridgeshire house prices.'

Di groaned. 'Cheer up, love. Our fallback candidate
shouldn't present that problem. From Huntingdon, as I
recall. What was her name again—Stamford-Halley?'

'Stammer-Halitosis would be nearer the mark if her interview performance was typical. Rang her immediately White
hung up. Can't say I was sorry to hear she was now unavail-
able. Witchford Gardenplan signed her up the day before
yesterday.'

'She tell you how much they were paying?'

'Thousand more than we offered.'

Di wrinkled her sunburnt nose. 'Where do we go from
here, then?'

'Way I see it, we buzz the half-dozen local folk we fancied
who backed out last time round or the time before. Tack a
thou on to our salary offer and check their reactions. Interview those who show willing soonest—tomorrow for
preference—and on their own patches. OK?'

'OK, if we can afford it.' Even before the latest hike in
interest rates, they had agonized over the costs of launching
the landscaping venture.

'We'd have to cut the frills, certainly. Trips abroad. Sunday shop staff, now Chrissie's got the hang of the till.'

Di groaned. 'With her GCSE exams coming up?'

'I know, love, I'm sorry. But it's up or under. We'll be
in Queer Street if we don't recoup the building costs of the
new office pretty soon.' Di didn't know the half, thank God.
Left the books to him and their accountants—and Cam-
cross Financial Services.

'OK, Phil. You win.' Yawning, she snuggled back under the duvet. 'Oh hell!'

'Whassat?' Her drowsiness had infected him.

'Rupert's last day tomorrow.' Parsingham had been on sick leave for the last fortnight of his employment. 'I promised to see him. I was going to take him his leaving present, remember? But I can't go off base, can I, with you talent-scouting?'

'About that present—'

'We can't afford it? That what you're going to say, Phil?'

'You know we can't. Not with this latest development.'

'We've got to—we owe him. Think how much he's taught us.'

'Taught me, you mean.' Di, the daughter and grand-daughter of college gardeners, had had little to learn from the old man whose instruction Phil had so bitterly resented and despised himself for resenting.

'What have you against Rupert? Can't you tell me, now he's retiring?'

He felt her eyes on him. 'Nothing, don't be silly.' How could he make her understand that learning from her kindly, self-mocking Rupert had felt like learning from Granddad. Granddad, fifty years a cabbie, who had night after night drummed into him the names and locations of the several thousand streets of London. The Knowledge, he and his mates had called it. Granddad who knew every way under the sun of humiliating a kid whose skin was several shades darker than anything in his pattern book.

'Nothing personal,' he said in the careful voice in which he'd always spoken of and to Rupert Parsingham. 'Thing is, the old boy said himself he owed us for baling him out when he went on the rocks, for keeping him on all these years. He's not on his beam ends. He's got his State pension, if nothing else. And I don't suppose he pays rent to his sister.'

'Not the point.' She was sitting bolt upright now, brown arms folded beneath her little white breasts.

''Course it's the point, Di. OK, we give him a prezzy. Prezzies. A cheque plus that picture your dad wants him to have. Deliver them myself between interviews tomorrow. No problem. But a cheque for £50, not £500.'

'Oh, come on, Phil. £500's less than his month's salary.'

'And more than we can spare. Bet he wouldn't take if he knew how we were placed—'

'And you're not telling him. If you do, I'll find out, Phil, and I'll never forgive you.' Her face puckered.

'OK, OK you win. 'Night, sweetie.' He couldn't bear to see her crying. But he couldn't bear to part with half a grand either. There had to be another way. Pretty soon he'd hit on it.

CHAPTER 4

'Should see her right for you, love.' The photocopier engineer hauled his bulk to a standing position. 'Lend me a brush and pan and I'll leave everything shipshape before I push her back.'

Valerie Gates stopped typing. 'I'll sort that out, thanks.' New man, or he wouldn't have made the suggestion. You'd never believe how careless some people were about the stuff they let fall behind that photocopier. Checking up on that sort of thing was one of the little extras Dr Finchley appreciated. Her next boss too, Valerie hoped. She glanced at her wristwatch. Three-thirty. The Board meeting would be well under way. Maybe Finchley's appreciation wouldn't count much longer, if things went the way the Chairman's secretary had whispered they might. Still, she wasn't one for crossing bridges . . . 'Cup of tea?' she offered.

'I'll not say no.'

The way the engineer's eyes homed in on her V-neck as she cleared her desk, Valerie guessed there were other things he wouldn't say no to either. Get a grip on yourself, girl, she warned her reflection in the cloakroom mirror as she filled the kettle.

Heat did this to her. Couldn't settle her mind on her work in this dull, sticky July heat. Every window in the Director's suite shut. And she didn't dare open one in his absence, not at this time of year. Tough luck on his wife to live in a hermetically sealed house, but the air-conditioning at Appletrees was probably a sight more efficient than the three miserable office fans.

Valerie rinsed her face. Only Tuesday. Three-and-a-half days before the weekend. Feel better when she'd got home, maybe, had a shower and a change. Madrigals on the Backs tonight if the rain held off. Best part of the Festival, as far as Valerie was concerned. Norm wasn't so keen but he'd come to please her.

No more worries about being seen together, now Trish had been told. Last Saturday they'd gone shopping for the engagement ring. Valerie gave it a peck to cheer herself up on the way back to the office with the kettle. But what she saw in her mind's eye was that tapestry three-piece suite in Eaden Lilley's sale. Outside their price range, she and Norm had agreed. A good four hundred outside. Dare they, daren't they?

Afterwards, when the mechanic had left and she'd washed up the cups and saucers, Valerie hauled out the Hoover from the cupboard under the stairs and advanced on the photocopier.

*

Eric Finchley couldn't wait to get away after the Board
meeting. A swim had been his first thought, but he felt too
frazzled, too weary to brave the crowds in the pool just yet.
Better go home to Appletrees first for a shower and change
of clothes. Then to Parkside by bicycle. He risked cycling
on summer evenings. Then the swim, a small snack and
straight back to the Parsingham.

I tried, Mumsie, I tried, he assured his invisible companion,
as he steered his Volvo into the rush-hour traffic. He had
indeed tried his damnedest to win the Board over. And
almost won. The senior members, holders of established
Chairs and Professorial fellowships in the colleges that counted, had a sentimental affection for the name of Parsingham.
Few would wish to go down in the annals of the University
as traitors to the memory of the late, great Sir Rupert and
destroyers of the Institute created in his memory.

Eric's rhetoric had delicately, oh so delicately, mined that
sentimental vein. Then half way through his speech he'd
heard the sound he'd feared for longer than he could
remember. A buzz, now rising, now fading, as its maker
circled first near the window and then homed in on the
sugar bowl.

His language generators had stalled. A mere bluebottle,
as it turned out. No cause for alarm from that quarter. But
the spell had been broken. He had stumbled through the
remainder of his prepared text, exposing the thinness of his
argument, his disbelief in it. His hearers' eyes had avoided
his. The brief ensuing discussion was dominated by the
younger, tougher-minded Board members. They argued
that nostalgia was a luxury beyond the University's present
means, and not one of their seniors spoke or voted against
them. None was prepared to fight for a higher grant from
central sources. An axe hung above the Institute polished
and ready to fall—in one year, or two, at most, unless a
seven-figure benefaction materialized.

Don't worry, Mums, I haven't finished yet. Tell you later, Eric reassured, as he waited for the lights to change at Northampton Street.

As he turned into his drive, he remembered the invitation he'd refused to his next-door neighbour's garden-party. A couple of months ago he'd have fought his physical dread of such functions and accepted, for fear of offending a Parsingham. Not now. Not since he'd gone cap-in-hand to Eve and been turned away empty-handed.

He hoped to surprise Dolores, to catch that lovely, idiosyncratic startle response he'd married her for. But because she was at the kitchen sink, she'd seen him park the car and greeted him calmly, with her ready Filipino smile. It irked him to find her, floury-armed, in the butcher's apron that reached almost to her ankles.

'You made all this?' he asked after the ritual kiss, his eyes ranging over assorted sweets and savouries.

'Not all today. I raided the freezer. Eve rang me in a panic at lunch-time—caterer's let her down. One of her lame sheep, I think. And with her electricity off—'

'Surely Stacey could have made herself useful?'

'Eve felt it wasn't fair to bother her, not before the first night.'

'So it all falls on you.'

'Don't fuss, Eric. I've nearly done. Like me to pour you a drink?' There was already a half-full tumbler on the working surface beside her.

'No, thanks, Dolly. I'm perfectly capable . . .' He helped himself to a gin, ice and lime from the dresser. 'It's just that—you know I hate to see you overdo.'

'In case someone should take me for a mail-order bride?'

The words stunned him. He'd given her so much in the eight years of their marriage, asked only tact and good humour and a comfortable home in return. Until a few months ago, he'd had all in good measure. Now, every so often, she'd come out with something like that. Something disturbing. 'You're tiddly, Dolly,' he said.

She shrugged. 'If you choose to think so, Eric. When do you want to eat?'

What had got into her this year? Six months ago she'd have asked what kind of day he'd had. He'd have known she didn't care, would have told her nothing that mattered. Even so, the anodyne exchanges had been comforting. An assurance that they were a couple, as nearly normal a couple as made no difference.

'Thought we might have a late supper after the noise has died down next door,' he said. 'Haven't had my swim yet, and I'll have plenty to keep me busy at the Institute after that. Don't put yourself out. Just wrap me up a bite of something to eat at the pool. Leftovers will do nicely for supper.'

'Oh, I think we can do better than that, Eric.' She raised her brows as if mocking his frustrated martyrdom. 'Let's have a leisurely supper, shall we? There are things I need to say to you.'

Things . . . About her life or his? His professional secrets were safe from her, surely. So too, please God, the personal. Eric checked that everything was in order in his darkroom before going upstairs to shower.

Fifteen minutes later he descended, refreshed and strengthened with a new resolve. He fiddled about in his study until he heard Dolores's bath water running overhead. Then he left the house by the back door. He strolled uphill across the lawn that Dolores had replanted with flowerless evergreens, under Rupert Parsingham's guidance.

A somewhat futile gesture, given the jumble of flora in the old man's own fenced-off plot. As he walked, Eric surveyed the west-facing front of Rupert's cottage. Its curtains were drawn as they often were in summer against the setting sun. The notice on the door was a rarer, but not unprecedented, phenomenon.

Eric left the grounds of Appletrees by the back gate that opened on a service road. A few yards took him to the garden gate of Plumtrees Cottage, a few more to its front door.

The message on the door was what he had expected. PLEASE DO NOT DISTURB. He knocked, all the same.

'And another.' Clive Sinton waited for the second black coffee and scowled at the mirror in the public bar of the Signal Box. His reflected face scowled back. Scarred, yellowish from things he'd done to his liver, puffy-lidded from things he'd done to his kidneys, in need of a shave. Who'd want a monicker like that in a first-night audience? But Paul did or said he did. Hence the sobering-up routines.

They wouldn't quite work—never had. 'Why the binge?' Paul's eyes would ask. He'd long ago given up asking that question out loud, thank God. For Clive, a wordsmith by trade, couldn't begin to frame an answer.

To say he couldn't face the Second Court of Princes' College or the Northside caravan site stone cold sober would have prompted other questions. Questions he could never have answered, not even at one of those rare Scrabble or chestnut-roasting sessions when he and Anne and Paul had functioned like your five-star, impregnable nuclear family.

His lunch-time alcoholic anæsthetic had worked this afternoon—or maybe it hadn't even been necessary. Maybe what had counted was the recollection of Anne's words from '66, repeated like a mantra under his breath this afternoon as he walked through the housing estate that had been built over the caravan site, trying to work out the spot where their van had stood. 'He didn't touch me. That's all that matters, isn't it, love? He didn't touch me.'

No one had built over the Second Court of Princes',
which he'd skirted in one of the few bright intervals of this
dull, sticky day. A-24 had caught his eye as it had when
he'd worked on the scaffolding outside it in '66, but for very
different reasons. Today each of its windows glinted silver
with a grotesque metallic artefact, and other objects of the
sort lurked in the interior. Sculptures, people still called
them. Daft name for things that hadn't been carved, but
rather sliced and twisted. From what? Steel? Aluminium?

Then he'd spotted the raw materials on the shelves that
had once held Eric Finchley's books—or rather, Eric Finchley's uncle's books. Row upon row of beer cans.

'Look, Mother,' an old Suffolk voice had croaked behind
him. 'A-24. Ms B. Selwick. Fellow-commoner in Creative Arts.
That's what it says on the little old notice board. Creative
bloody arts!' Clive had turned, and was included in. 'Have
to laugh, don't you, mate?'

And he had—oh, he had. Finchley's image had been well
and truly exorcized from his old lodgings. If it lingered
anywhere thereabouts it was surely overhead, among the
petrified and powerless gargoyles.

The Dining Hall of Princes' was something else again,
the focus for Clive's worst guilt and his worst shame. But
it drew him nevertheless. He would go there tomorrow.

He sipped at the second coffee, muddy and probably
carcinogenous. His head was clearing, but slowly. When he
leafed through the *Cambridge Evening News* that someone had
left on the counter beside him, the small print looked blurry.

The headers were clear enough, though. Typical provin-
cial menu: COMMUNITY CARE PROTESTS, FESTIVAL BUDGET
ROW, CHANGES AT MIDDLEFIELDS GARDEN CENTRE.

And the photographs. Straightforward shots of local
faces, mostly. Nothing arty-farty. He made a child's game
of it, spotting animal resemblances, checking names. Councillor Vera Potterswade, vixen. The Vicar of St Peter Paul,

crocodile. Then a Teddy-bear face—called Rupert, for God's sake. Rupert Parsingham. Clive laughed out loud.

Then he looked again. It wasn't possible, he told himself. It didn't fit. *The retirement of Mr Rupert Parsingham, horticultural consultant (left) coincides with major organizational changes at the Middlefields Garden Centre, Trumpington. Mr Parsingham, who is the great-grandson of Sir Rupert Parsingham . . .*

It fitted. The old man was one of Them, with God knew how many rights to a place at the High Table of Princes' that night in '66. But no right at all to get out of his seat and stare at Clive the way he'd stared that night. The way he stared still in his nightmares.

Tomorrow, you bastard. Why couldn't you leave me in peace until tomorrow? Clive gulped down the dregs of his coffee, and checked his watch. Plenty of time before the curtain-up of *Spin City*. The dress rehearsal had moved him almost to tears more than once. And tonight the image of Parsingham's stupid, bearish face would be among those of the clownish dons on stage, staring down at him as though he was subhuman. He couldn't face it, not without something to kill the pain. But he'd promised Paul, and he couldn't let Anne's son down either. Not here in Cambridge.

With no thought but to distance himself from alcohol, he left the pub and turned right into Mill Road. A stale, warm breeze blew dust and litter in his face. He walked faster, hoping to wear himself out, for exhaustion was also an anæsthetic. Already he could smell his own grime and sweat. He'd have to stop soon, freshen up.

Then he remembered that the pool where he and Paul had swum that morning was only yards away. His togs were still in his shoulder-bag. He crossed over.

CHAPTER 5

Eleven-thirty. The first-night garden-party at Plumtrees was warming up. Not so the Stage Manager of *Spin City*.

'It wobbled, I tell you. The minute Larry put his weight on it, that bloody pinnacle wobbled.'

'OK, Paul, if you say so,' Emma soothed. 'Point is, though, the audience didn't give a monkey's.'

'Absolutely not!' Their hostess—a short, sturdy figure in a striped caftan—bore down on them. 'Everyone, but everyone, who saw that show has been praising it to the skies. Hear me, Stacey?' Eve beckoned the scriptwriter, who obeyed the summons a little wearily. 'A smash hit. Just what I prophesied at dress rehearsal.'

Stacey's face lost some of its strain. 'Thanks for the ego-boost, Eve. Audience was great, but my hunch is they were mostly buddies of the cast. Maybe I'll take you more seriously when I read the reviews.'

'Better stoke up with a few hundred calories before then, my dear. Aren't I right, Dolly?'

Dolores Finchley, who had changed into a traditional Filipino tunic-dress in embroidered coral silk, was carrying a trayful of savouries wrapped in lettuce leaves. As she joined the group, Paul muttered an excuse and withdrew, with Emma in tow.

'Let's sit down for a bit.' A low table was found for Dolores's tray. Eve subsided thankfully on to a rusty metal chair, and the younger women sat on the parched grass at her feet. Relax, Eve urged herself. The party, like the show, had been a success. She'd been right, absolutely right, to go ahead.

'Haven't had a chance to thank you two angels properly

for all you've done. I'm not one to panic, Lord knows, but when I got that call from the caterers—'

'It's Dolly we should both be thanking. This yummy finger food!' Stacey helped herself to a second leafy package.

'Absolutely delish!' Eve followed suit. 'But the decorations were your doing, Stacey.' She looked round with real pleasure. The patchy light from the several dozen coloured paper lanterns was suitably festive, whilst concealing the scars inflicted on the Victorian house and gardens by her recently departed lodgers.

'No big deal.' Stacey retrieved a blob of spiced spinach from her flowery pants. 'Actually I found it therapeutic, having something to fiddle with during rehearsals. Great show, great party, Eve. And you're the one who's making it fizz. Only thing that bugged me was not seeing Rupert around tonight.'

'He just can't cope with parties. Never could,' Eve said firmly. Or with the sight of Plumtrees in its current rundown condition.

'So he told me. But I'd counted on seeing him at the show. He more or less promised he'd make the first performance, when he turned down the invite to the dress rehearsal. Thought I'd let him know how things had gone.'

'But you didn't?' Eve was struck by the sharpness in Dolores's tone.

'No—not when I saw the notice on his door. Thought maybe he'd taken something to help him sleep. He's had some low spells recently, hasn't he, Eve?'

She nodded. 'He told me the only good thing about being away from work this last fortnight would be dodging goodbyes from his clients. But they've been calling in shoals, so he tells me.'

'Yes,' Dolores confirmed. 'When I'm at my kitchen sink

I can't help noticing the comings and goings. Phil Beresford called around lunch-time today.'

Eve nodded. 'Official presentation, I expect. Di told me some weeks ago her father wanted Rupert to have an old engraving of Princes' gardens.'

'He'd like that,' Dolores said.

The tone was authoritative, proprietary even. Eve stifled a rare pang of jealousy.

'The presentation may have felt like the point of no return, all the same,' Dolores went on. 'Anyhow, Rupert must have stuck up the DO NOT DISTURB notice soon after Phil had gone. It was there half an hour later—stopped me in my tracks on my way to see him.'

'Leavetakings can be hell,' Stacey volunteered between nibbles. '

'Don't brood, dear,' Eve said more sharply than she'd intended. 'Rupert wouldn't want to blight your big night. Up you get, now, and meet someone who's absolutely dying to meet you!'

Eve semaphored energetically to a slim, blonde woman in pale blue. The type who had been wearing chambray for twenty summers and making anything else look overstated. 'Zoë Grayling, drama critic for the *Sentinel*. Stacey Caldwell, our clever scriptwriter.'

Zoë nodded graciously. Stacey pulled a face.

'Excuse the possessive,' Eve went on. 'But as a founder Friend of the Fringe and Stacey's landlady—'

'I'd say you're entitled.' The journalist flashed shapely eyebrows above her wineglass.

'Zoë tells me the show's really enlightened her about our Town-Gown scandals,' Eve went on. 'Never even heard of the Vice-Chancellor's Court, had you, my dear? Not to mention our Victorian poverty statistics.'

'Nor had I until six months ago,' Stacey protested.

'Rabbiting, aren't I?' Talking had always come easier to

Eve than listening. 'You'll want to slip off somewhere quiet for your natter. Conservatory, I suggest. And, Zoë, you absolutely must persuade Stacey to write a sequel!'

Stacey made small protesting noises, but departed in the journalist's company. Something accomplished, something done, Eve told herself. She would sleep well tonight. It came as a shock to see that Dolores was sober-faced, sad even.

'I was really sorry to see Rupert's DO NOT DISTURB notice this afternoon.'

Not that again. 'Why? He's put it up before—when the children's noise got on his nerves, for instance.'

'I know, and I've always respected his privacy—this time too, of course. It's just . . .' Dolores hesitated, biting her lip. 'Just that something cropped up since I saw him this morning. I'll be taking an early train to King's Cross tomorrow—too early to disturb Rupert—and I hate not being able to say goodbye to him.'

'Goodbye?' Eve was stunned. 'I don't understand.'

'I've had bad news from London. A young woman I've come to know quite well has tried to commit suicide. She's going to need a lot of help these next few weeks.'

'A Filipina? A domestic worker?'

Dolores nodded.

Eve knew better than to press for details. Dolores was well aware of her scorn for the immigration laws that had for so long bound immigrant servants to their employers on pain of deportation. Even so, she had been resolutely tight-lipped about the Kensington-based support groups she had been visiting weekly throughout her stay in Cambridge.

'I'm sure you've done all you could, Dolly.'

Dolores shook her dark head. 'No. Once I might have kidded myself you were right, but not any longer. Not now I've more time on my hands.'

More time? Eve didn't understand. But there was so much about Dolores she didn't understand.

'Chita will need to see someone on a daily basis for several weeks—someone to be within reach round the clock in a crisis. My grandparents live in the village she grew up in—I can speak her dialect. I'm the obvious person to help, but I can't do it from Cambridge.'

The truth but not the whole truth, Eve guessed, and mocked herself for playing detective.

'You'll be away for several weeks, then? Keep in touch, won't you? I'll miss you. Especially if Stacey takes wing. She's talking of heading back to the States after the Edinburgh Festival.'

'Really? I'd no idea.' Dolores laid a hand on the older woman's arm. 'I'd be sad to think of you here all alone.'

'Not for long, I'm sure.' Eve already regretted her brief display of vulnerability. 'Rose and Jean-Pierre sent a card from Burgundy promising to come back after the grape-harvest, and Steve and Ruth are booked in for the Cherry Hinton Folk Festival next weekend. Haven't heard from the others recently, but they're not all good communicators. Anyhow, the place isn't fit for children until we get the roof repairs finished and the rewiring done.'

'About those roof repairs—' Dolores began.

'Not tonight, please. Slating's a marginally more cheerful subject than damp-rot, I grant you, but it doesn't make good party-talk all the same.'

'Forgive me, Eve. But autumn's just round the corner. I'd hate to think of you shivering under a sheet of plastic with frost on the ground. And considering your young houseguests left you in the lurch with the job half done—'

'They'd their reasons. The tourist season's when most of them earn their living.'

'Are you sure laziness didn't come into it, Eve? What happens if they cop out again?'

Eve's anger flared. 'I shall have a word with my bank

manager. Listen, Dolly, I don't want to squabble. But my domestic arrangements are really none of your business.'

'That's true.' Dolores's black eyes filled. 'I don't like interference myself, Eve, and I hate to sound interfering. But you've been a kind neighbour and I just couldn't leave without speaking out. I really feel you should get the job done professionally. Eric feels the same. I'm not sure if he's approached you himself, but if there are insurance problems—financial problems of any kind—I know he'd be delighted to help. He's not a man to show emotion, Eve, but I know he's genuinely concerned about you and Rupert—'

'Concerned? About us?' Eve laughed shortly. 'Sorry, my dear. I don't doubt your own motives. Tell me honestly, now. This London trip of yours—there's more involved than helping Chita, isn't there?'

Dolores nodded, fiddling with her silver bracelets. 'There are so many other Chitas. And changes in the immigration law won't solve all their problems.'

'Could the weeks stretch into months, years even? Are you thinking of leaving your husband?'

Dolores got to her feet, visibly distressed. 'No comment. Sorry, Eve. But you do understand that if it came to that, Eric would be the first to be told.'

'Not Rupert? And you've always been so close!' Eve heard herself saying.

Dolores stared down, angrier than her neighbour had ever seen her. But she spoke very quietly. 'Go on, Eve. You're not usually one for innuendoes. Ask me what you want about my relationship with your brother.'

But Eve didn't. She daren't. The younger woman walked away.

'Stacey about?' a man's voice asked.

Eve swivelled to confront the gaunt figure of Julian Otley, stooping even more than usual under the weight of a rucksack and bedroll. A welcome distraction. 'Come to shack up with us? Good-oh!'

Julian turned pink. 'If it's all right—if you don't mind, that is.'

'Open invitation. Glad you've taken it up at last.'

'Thanks—but I should have warned . . . forgot about the party. Came straight from the lab, you see. Meant to ch-check things out with Stacey.' Julian's pink deepened to crimson.

Eve flashed him a quick diagnostic stare. 'Last seen with a critic in the conservatory. Do investigate. And come back later for a nightcap, both of you.'

Emma and Paul had helped themselves to ices labelled *makupuno*, which turned out to be a delectable species of coconut, and had taken possession of two deckchairs in a small summerhouse.

'Cast an eye over this lot!' Paul exclaimed after a long period of companionable silence. He toed a pile of battered toys, tricycles and dismantled swings. 'Where you have kids you have clobber.'

'*Some* kids,' Emma corrected. 'I was obsessional about tidying up my messes when I was little. D'you know, I actually begged my dad to buy me a miniature chest-of-drawers when I was seven.'

'And did he?'

'Not the one I'd fallen in love with. Hadn't occurred to me before that police sergeants' pay didn't stretch to antique mahogany. But it registered that he was really upset about palming me off with plywood. Would you believe, I've never been able to tell him what I'd like for a birthday from that day to this.' Emma's throat tightened. It mattered. Silly that it should matter.

'I'd believe you. Dads . . .' Paul's voice trailed off.

'You haven't forgiven yours for opting out of this shindig,

have you? That's bugging you more than a wobbly bit of scenery that a nail will put right in the morning.'

Paul shrugged. 'Maybe. He should've made the effort. It's nothing personal, mind. One thing this exercise has told me is that I'm not cut out for stage-management. And I know *Spin City* won't make or break your reputation, Em. But it might be important for Stacey. Dad could've done her good here by mingling with the critics—persuading those who haven't seen the show yet that it's worth their attention.'

'Mm. Give him credit for turning up at the performance, which is more than my Ma or Pa managed. Quite honestly, from the way he looked when I spotted him in the Signal Box, I was amazed to see him in the audience. I'm not surprised he didn't feel. up to theatrical chit-chat afterwards.'

'My guess is, the name of Parsingham may have put him off as much as anything.'

'Really? Some personal grudge?'

'Shouldn't think so. But he worked here as a mason and scaffolder, don't forget. He's always been scathing about Camford élitism—including the cult of the famous academic families.'

Emma laughed. 'Quite right too. But it's hard to think of Eve or Rupert as members of a University mafia.'

'She doesn't look the part, I admit. Do you know her well?'

'Only by reputation. Which, according to my mother, was curate's-eggy. I gather a great sigh of relief went up throughout the peace movement when Eve's enthusiasms switched channels. She was super in headline-catching stunts, it seems—wire-cutting and paintspraying *doubles-entendres* on F-111s. But apt to tread on her sister's ideological corns in the long night watches at Greenham.'

'Speaking of which—' Paul yawned, a mite unconvincingly, and leant across to kiss her. 'This chair's doing terrible things to my vertebrae. What say we shove off, now we've done our social duty?'

'Nice.' And it would be. Emma allowed herself to be pulled to her feet. She'd been wary of reviving the short, sweet affair, interrupted two years before when both had graduated from Lancaster. Throughout rehearsals for *Spin City*, she'd commuted from her parents' home in Kings Covert.

But this morning her ten-year-old van had broken down two miles outside Cambridge, and was still under repair. With both her parents on duty and unable to fetch her, she could think of no good reason to refuse Paul's offer of overnight hospitality. And as he hugged her tight in the summerhouse and asked her to sleep with him, she could think of no good reason to refuse that offer either.

The party-goers had thinned out considerably as Emma and Paul headed downhill towards the front gates. Someone hailed them from the shadows. It was Stacey, her round face uncharacteristically grim. She was wheeling a tricycle. *The* tricycle—so Emma deduced from the slogans plastered on its every available surface. Eve's battle chariot in many a nominally non-violent action.

'Seen Eve?' Stacey asked.

They pleaded ignorance. 'Something wrong?' Paul inquired—redundantly, to judge by Stacey's glare.

'Found the trike outside the kitchen door—that's what's wrong. And Eve promised me faithfully she'd put it under lock and key every evening before sunset.'

'Spate of cycle thefts?'

But Paul's last question remained unanswered. For Stacey's gaze, horrified now, was fixed on someone else. Someone coming up the drive behind them.

Emma turned to see a boy of perhaps eighteen in black leathers, carrying a tote bag. His blue-green hair was stiffly lacquered and his face and hands were tattooed. But the face beneath the tattoos had an amiable expression.

'"Lo, Stace,' the newcomer said. 'Whose thrash? Any nosh going?'

Stacey let go of the tricycle and ran forward to grab his arm. 'Not for you, kid. Not any more. Think all you have to do is to walk back here and give Eve the old babyface crap, do you? No way, you filthy little murderer. No way.'

The boy swore, spat and tugged himself free. Then he turned on his heels and ran down the drive.

CHAPTER 6

'My professional instincts tell me . . .' The Chief Constable of the Mid-Anglian Constabulary tapped his newly cultivated moustache as if acknowledging the message. 'My instincts tell me this will turn out to be suicide—a common-or-garden coroner's case.'

Another time the all-too-apt metaphor might have reduced DCI Richard Baxter, the most junior recipient of this early morning briefing, to silent giggles. But he and more especially his wife Sarah had heard the news of Rupert Parsingham's death with real sadness. Besides, his daughter had said something about a first-night party at Plumtrees. With her first musical production on her hands Emma needed involvement in a murder case like she needed a hole in the head.

Not that poor Rupert had died from a hole in the head. Reports from Bill Armstrong, the duty DI at the scene of crime and from the police surgeon, pointed clearly to carbon monoxide suffocation. Hose plus exhaust pipe— common enough suicide method. Ironic that the old station-wagon whose loss Parsingham had so dreaded should have done him this final service.

'The break-in at the cottage complicates matters, of

course, but we've no present reason to believe it was any more than a coincidence.' Francis Montgomery's hairy hands bore down on the afrormosia conference table which dominated his room at Holtchester Police Headquarters. 'The ACC concurs. Right, Littleton?'

The Assistant Chief Constable (Criminal Investigation) made the strangled noise that Baxter had learnt to interpret as agreement.

'But DI Armstrong has doubts.' Montgomery's Norman nose wrinkled, as if he had named a disease transmitted by policemen of the lower sort. 'And Victor Highcroft has convinced me that it would be prudent to be seen to take his doubts seriously.'

Detective-Superintendent Highcroft's fishy face quivered pinkly.

Baxter found the Chief Constable's polysyllabic prose heavy going at 7.30 a.m. on top of a hurried breakfast. As far as he could make out, the essentials were (a) the dead man was a Parsingham and therefore only a little lower in the Cambridge University Pantheon than a Newton or a Darwin, and (b) his sister was an unpredictable trouble-maker. Montgomery laboured both themes emotionally and at length. Had he cancelled his scheduled attendance at the week-long pow-wow of European Chief Police Officers where Victor Highcroft was to accompany him as a technical adviser? Was he planning—God forbid—to take personal charge of the case?

No on both counts, it transpired.

'ACC Crime and I are agreed that territorial considerations must be waived in a case of unusual sensitivity. Our first requirements for the Acting Senior Investigating Officer are relevant CID experience and knowledge of the academic scene. An Oxbridge graduate of suitable seniority would be ideal—but lacking any such candidate, you're the obvious choice, Richard.'

Baxter, toughened by an eight-year sojourn in Cambridgeshire to insults to his redbrick Alma Mater, grunted acquiescence.

'You'll report direct to the ACC during Superintendent Highcroft's absence. Been cleared with Cambridge City, of course. Any objections?'

As if they'd count. 'What about the jewel thefts investigation, sir?'

'Back burner until our return, pending unforeseen developments. Victor has a new strategic proposal in the pipeline, which I'll cast an eye over between other commitments in Geneva.'

Highcroft smirked, obviously revelling in his honorary elevation to the ranks of the CPOs.

'Look forward to hearing more, sir,' Baxter murmured. Now that he no longer expected the Superintendent's computerized brain-children to yield useful results, he rather welcomed them as diversions from the daily grind.

'That's that, then.' The CC collected his papers. 'We'd better hit the road for Heathrow, Victor. No rest for the wicked, eh?' A standard Montgomery joke, a standard ripple of sycophantic laughter.

Baxter was surprised, then, when the old man paused for a private word on his way out. 'Extraordinary bloke, Parsingham. Finicky, too. Used to get down on his hands and knees, the wife told me, to pick up every scrap of foliage after he'd shown her one of his fancy pruning techniques. Damned embarrassing for Georgie. With him being who he was, don't you know?'

'Maundy Thursday-ish, sir?'

'What? Oh, hardly . . .' If Montgomery suspected irony he wasn't letting on. 'We've been clients of his for years, you know. Georgie's taken his death badly. She'd like to think the Force was doing its best for him.'

'So'd Sarah, sir.'

'Miss him myself, come to that. One of the few men in the county who really understood alpines.'

As Baxter drove the ten miles from Holtchester to Cambridge he reflected that his Chief might metamorphose into someone altogether more honest and likeable if he were to take early retirement and devote himself exclusively to his rockery. As to the task in hand, the Chief Inspector felt none of Montgomery's qualms about disturbing the peace of Academe. Especially not since his dealings with the sometime Warden of Gaunt College.

He'd always had qualms about working off patch, however. Official clearance with Cambridge City Division was one thing, the hurt feelings of locals were quite another. At least he'd have no problems of that sort with DI Bill Armstrong, his second string at Holtchester for the last eight years, and already on temporary assignment to Cambridge City. Or with DS Wendy Powers, whose services he had secured before leaving Headquarters.

Besides, Montgomery might just be right. Maybe this would turn out to be a coroner's case.

The garage adjoining Rupert's cottage was Daimler-size, most probably a former stable. Which was just as well. When Baxter arrived it already housed Dr Stallburn, the pathologist, Bill Armstrong and three Scenes of Crime specialists as well as the vehicle which contained the mortal remains of Rupert Parsingham.

'Like to move him as soon as poss, Baxter.' Stallburn, a tall, heavy man, backed away from the open door of the station-wagon.

Baxter peered briefly at the figure slumped in the driving seat, a garden hose still lying across his lap. 'No doubts as to cause of death?'

'Immediate cause, no.' Stallburn peeled off his plastic

gloves. 'For the rest, we'll have to wait until we get him on the slab, won't we?'

Baxter, whose absence from autopsies on several previous occasions had made him the butt of the pathologist's unsubtle sarcasm, knew there'd be no escaping this one.

'Time of death?' he asked, peering at the corpse.

'Twelve to sixteen hours ago, at a guess. He's quite stiff. Stomach contents might narrow the range.'

Baxter's own insides were protesting against the effects of his hurried breakfast. He helped himself to a sodamint as he moved away from the van.

'Your lot done their stuff on the corpse?' he asked Trevor Bly, Senior Scenes of Crime Officer.

Bly nodded.

'Best get him away, then. Any sign of a suicide note?'

It was Bill Armstrong who answered. 'In an inside pocket. Here, guv.' He handed over a pencil-written page, already sheathed in plastic, which had obviously been torn from a pocket diary. No address—only the previous day's date near the top of the page in the same small, neat script as the message that followed.

Baxter squinted and read:

My dear Pudding,

Rotten of me, I admit, to cop out, but the time was ripe. You know how I felt about packing the job in. That was why. No cut flowers at the funeral, please, but if you want to make my ghost happy ask one of your motley crew to water my geraniums.

Bear

'Shown this to Mrs Parsingham Wells, Bill?'

Armstrong nodded. 'She's sure it's authentic. Handwriting's definitely his, and Pudding was his name for her when they were kids. Eve's Pudding, you know.'

'Yes—yes.' Baxter suppressed sick-making memories.

'Besides, she says it wasn't altogether a surprise. Her brother'd been very low since he knew he'd have to give up his job. Yesterday was the official retirement date, but he'd been on sick leave for a fortnight.'

'So what's your problem?'

'This place, for starters. When'd you last hear of a suicide mopping up the ruddy garage before doing the deed?'

Baxter shrugged. 'He was a finicky type—you've that on the authority of your Chief Constable, no less. Besides, look around you.'

The garage had evidently doubled as a storage shed. A fairly standard range of household maintenance and gardening equipment was stowed in an orderly fashion on its walls and shallow shelves. The paint tins were firmly lidded, the half-used sacks of fertilizer and compost tightly tied.

'Take your point.' The DI flushed, as if recalling the cheerful chaos of his own outbuildings. 'Not just that, though.' Baxter's Ulster-born junior could be as mulish as any of his compatriots when he got going. 'What about the method? This bloke had arthritic wrists—gave him a fair bit of pain, his sister said. So why'd he mess around fitting a garden hose to his exhaust pipe—even supposing he had the wrist power to make the connection.'

'Prints around the join?'

'Oh, his. Both hands—nice and clear. Ditto on the inner door handle. But who knows what was wiped off before he made them? Who knows that he didn't make them under duress or to oblige an accomplice?'

Baxter laughed. 'Going all round Will's mother's, aren't you, as they say in these parts?'

'Parsingham was—my next point. All he had to do was
start up the engine. With the garage door shut, the fumes
would've done for him sure enough anyway.'

'But not soon enough, perhaps. In twenty minutes, say,
as opposed to five. Maybe he wanted to get it over fast in
case he'd second thoughts or in case he was interrupted. If
Stallburn's anywhere near the mark in his estimate, this
was a daylight job.'

'Which raises another question.' Armstrong's square face
had the eager-beaver expression that cut twenty years off
his forty. 'Why not wait until after dark if his time was his
own? Then there's the break-in.'

'Nothing taken here in the garage?'

'Doesn't look that way. We might get Mrs PW to check
later on, mightn't we, once she's got over the shock of finding him. But I don't suppose she'd much occasion to use
the place.'

'Anything else in his pockets?'

'Nothing out of the way. Wallet with nearly £40 in crisp
notes and coins, cheque-book, Natwest Switch card, Access
card, driving licence, keys to his house and garage.'

'Both locked where his sister found him?'

'So she says. Want to give the cottage the once-over? Mrs
PW made such a song and dance that I asked the SOC
team to confine their activities to the window and living-
room. OK?'

'OK for the present. And Trev'll request some tests on
the muscle power needed to fit that hose exhaust connection, won't you, Trev?'

Bly made a note.

Smiling his 'just-you-wait' smile, Armstrong led the way
towards the adjacent cottage. Its style was that of Plumtrees—late Victorian in red brick patterned with blue, with
a fancy wood trim under the eaves. All the curtains were
drawn. The PLEASE DO NOT DISTURB notice was still stuck

on the open, blue-painted front door. To its left a prints man was at work on the frame of the ground-floor sash window through which the intruder had evidently entered.

'Any joy?' Baxter asked him.

'Not a lot, sir. Marks have been wiped inside and out. Given all the living-room surfaces the once-over, so feel free to reccy, but please steer clear of the soiled rug under the window. Garden compost or something. Inspector Bly's sending a bloke across later to take scrapings.'

'No sign of a forced entry?'

'Uh-uh. Window must have been unlocked, if not open. Might be something itsy-bitsy stuck to the curtain, I dare say. You can see the fibre caught on the catch for yourself.'

Sludge-green, Baxter would have called that colour. No doubt it was known as something prettier in the current rag trade. A lot of it about.

'Could be something for you down there, as well.' The prints man jerked his head towards some trampled foliage in the herbaceous border to the left of his ladder.

Inside, a photographer was packing his gear. The original kitchen and parlour had been merged, Baxter guessed, into the living-room whose shabby charm showed through its present disorder. The plain repp curtains had faded to the older blue of the Oriental rugs. Time had assimilated the yellowish-browns of the pine and yew and fruitwood furniture. There was a bowl of sweet peas among the old willow-ware on the table laid for one, and pots of geraniums on the window-sills. A few pieces of jade and coral among English fairings in a corner cupboard were the sole tokens of the family's tropical connections.

It wouldn't take much time or effort to put the room to rights, Baxter thought. The traces of the intrusion—if such they were—were curiously random. One of several book-shelves had been emptied of its neatly labelled contents, a table lamp had been overturned, a box of slides spilt, a desk drawer pulled out. But the Staffordshire dogs on the mantelpiece stared unscathed at the framed engravings of garden plans on the wall opposite. Eighteenth-century draughtsmanship, possibly French, probably pricey. A more recent engraving of a garden with college buildings in the distance lay in half-opened wrappings beside the ancient typewriter on the big oak desk.

'Amateur job, would you reckon, Bill?' Baxter asked, as the photographer took his departure.

'An amateur in a hurry or a flap.'

'You'd be in both if you'd left a dying man in the garage.'

'Looks to me like our friend was after something specific,' Armstrong suggested.

'Which usually means cash. Let's follow his trail.' Baxter removed the top desk drawer which had been left open and placed it gently on the floor. Using his fingertips, he removed and inspected its contents.

Here he found a mixed collection of stationery and writing materials, neatly arranged. As well as paper, pencil sharpeners, ball points, whitener and other items evidently in current use, there were a few oddities. A faded box of sealing-wax, half used, a folder full of blotting-paper, an ancient tobacco tin containing an assortment of rusting pen-knibs, holders and fountain-pens. Parsinghams had been hoarders, it seemed, long before conservation became fashionable.

Baxter held one nib to the light and squinted. 'Waverley . . . that takes me back. *They come as a boon and a blessing to men—the Pickwick, the Owl and the Waverley pen.* There was this rummy old enamel sign in a corner shop I used to visit when I was a kid in Birmingham. Edwardian, shouldn't wonder. Ads were made to last in the old days.'

Armstrong cleared his throat. A sudden thought struck his senior. 'Had breakfast yet?'

'No, but I'm not bothered, sir.'

Knowing Bill for a good trencherman, Baxter was disbelieving. With the help of a ruler, he worked his way quickly through the remaining contents of the drawer. Right at the bottom there was a cardboard box that had once contained Mars bars. And now double foolscap, he guessed, having already found samples of most other writing papers, ancient and modern.

Instead, he found banknotes.

Shifting the box from the floor to the desktop, he checked the amount. Nine packs of £50 notes, neatly banded, ten notes to a pack, were stacked two on two. And there was a tenth pack on its own, containing four £50 notes. 'Four thousand six hundred quid.'

Armstrong peered over his shoulder and whistled. 'Parsingham wasn't the sort, was he?'

'Sort for what?'

'For stashing money in the house. OK, he was a hoarder. But nearly five grand that could have been earning interest?'

'Tax-dodging's a possibility.'

'I suppose,' Armstrong conceded. 'But it doesn't fit with the old boy's background and reputation, does it? See the piece about him in yesterday's *News*?'

'No, but I knew him slightly.' Very slightly, Baxter was beginning to suspect. 'Agreed, it wasn't in character. So why'd he stow it? And why £4,600? Looks like £400 was nicked. If so, why so little?'

Armstrong, who was parting the notes with a pencil tip and noting their serial numbers, didn't answer directly. 'Mixed lot—impossible to trace their life-history, I'd guess.'

'Most obvious conclusion would be that he acquired the loot gradually. And if not through saving . . .' Baxter hesitated.

'Blackmail, do you reckon?'

The DCI sighed. 'I don't want to believe that of him, but what else . . . ?'

'Maybe we should take a squint inside the drawers our trespasser didn't bother to unlock?' Armstrong suggested.

'Didn't or couldn't.'

'Look.' His junior pointed to something glinting under the old Underwood manual typewriter on the desktop, and retrieved a set of desk keys. 'One of the commonest hidey-holes. So our friend didn't make the effort to look. Shall I do the needful?'

'Later.' Baxter wrapped the keys in polythene and stowed them in an inside pocket. 'Time I paid my respects to Rupert's Pudding.'

CHAPTER 7

'Sarah Baxter's husband!' Eve Parsingham Wells erupted from the back door of Plumtrees and intercepted the detectives on their way to the main entrance. 'Front doorbell's out of commission—this way, if you please.'

She turned on the threshold to inspect Baxter's identity card and subject his face to close scrutiny. Her own was blunt-featured like her brother's, and just as weather-beaten. The pepper-and-salt mop might well have been cut by her own hand. There were no obvious traces of weeping. Her denim jeans and cheesecloth shirt had seen better days.

'Well, well.' Eve pursed her small mouth. 'Frank Montgomery could have sent worse, I suppose, though I'll never understand why a nice woman like your wife should get spliced to a copper.'

'Don't see Sarah as much as I used to,' she went on and she led the way through a dim back passage to a large kitchen. 'Still on the anti-nuke warpath, I suppose? Tell

her from me, will you, that the Bomb isn't the number one
enemy any more. Tell her that as a medic her place is in
the front ranks of the war against poison!'

'Perhaps you'll give her the message in person some
time?' Baxter murmured, as he took stock of his sur-
roundings.

The walls and cupboards were covered with bogus tourist
posters bearing slogans such as 'Come to sunny Stinkport'
and depicting the sewage and other nasties that awaited the
incautious bather. Eve's propaganda might have carried
weight with Baxter in a more salubrious setting. But the
sink gave off a whiff of rancid dishcloth, burnt-in spillages
disfigured the Aga cooker and mouldering crumbs were
scattered underfoot.

'Coffee?' Their hostess gestured towards a chipped
enamel pot. Both detectives declined.

'I will if you won't, then.' Eve poured herself a murky
mugful and laced it with brandy. 'Do me a sight more good
than the sedatives that twit of a doctor tried to ram down
my throat. Sit down, both of you. Can't do with hoverers.'

Eve climbed on to the highest available seat, a stool that
doubled as a stepladder. She watched and waited until
the detectives had disposed themselves on Windsor chairs
facing her.

'Well then, Chief Inspector. I trust you've been able to
open your colleague's eyes to the truth that's staring us all
in the face.'

'Truth, Mrs Parsingham Wells?'

Her face reddened and contracted. For a brief moment
she pressed a tissue to her mouth. When she spoke, it was
more softly. 'No word games, please. My brother killed
himself. I knew the minute I saw him this morning. I'd
seen it coming, ever since he knew he couldn't drive any
longer. That's what I told the Inspector. How many times
do I have to say it? How long are your people going to be

trampling over the garage and the cottage? He'd have hated that, Rupert. *Please do not disturb*. Not much to ask, is it? But you did disturb him—you bloody well did.' Eve's voice almost failed her.

'I'm sorry,' Baxter said after a brief pause. 'And that's not just a form of words. I only met your brother once or twice, but I know how much my wife learned from him, how much pleasure his visits gave her. Perhaps he did take his own life unassisted. If we were sure of that beyond reasonable doubt his death would be a matter for the coroner. But Inspector Armstrong has raised questions which in my judgement deserved to be aired. For instance, had your brother the strength to fit the hose to the exhaust pipe?'

'Strength can come from despair.'

'Perhaps. If we're lucky, the forensic scientists may give reassuring answers to this and related problems within days if not hours. In that event, we shall trouble you no further.'

'And if not? Weeks and months and years of irrelevant questions? Sorry to be blunt, but I for one have better things to do than sit here answering them. Once Rupert's death becomes public knowledge, I'll be deluged with letters and phone calls.'

'Are you alone in the house? Shouldn't you have someone—'

'Not that again, please! First the WPC, then Eric Finchley, then my doctor whom Eric rang without my knowledge or consent. No, no, no. I'm alone, and for the present I prefer it that way. If and when I feel the need of company, I'll make my own selection. Understood, Chief Inspector?'

'Certainly.' What he also understood from the heightened pitch of her voice and her laced fingers was that she was fighting off a fit of weeping. 'Who, by the way, is Eric Finchley?'

'Director of the Parsingham Institute and my next-door

neighbour. He spotted the police at the cottage. Called on me on his way to work. Eric's always very *attentive*.' A half-smile, a tightening of the lips. Why? Baxter wondered.

'I trust DI Armstrong will agree that I answered his questions fully and frankly earlier,' she went on. 'No doubt my answers are on record, but in any event I've absolutely no intention of being put through all that rigmarole twice in one morning for your benefit, Chief Inspector.'

'Of course not,' Baxter soothed, conscious of his junior's mutterings. 'A very few questions, then. It could save us all time and trouble if you'd be good enough to answer.'

She sighed. 'Cut the cackle.'

'Was your brother right- or left-handed?'

'Left, like me.'

'For all purposes?'

'Yes. Why should that matter?' There was a hint of anxiety in her tone which Baxter couldn't account for.

'It may help in interpreting his fingerprints. I noticed the fork was to the right of the knife on the table he'd laid for supper.'

'Breakfast.'

'Really? You didn't say—'

'The Inspector didn't ask. Rupert was a creature of habit. Breakfasted at six-thirty, the only meal he ate at the table by the east-facing window. Same time every day, even on Sundays, when he wasn't leaving for work at a quarter to eight. Snack lunch at twelve if he was home. High tea—his big meal of the day—at five. Nursery tea, I used to call it. But he ate that from a trolley-table by the west window in summer or near the fireplace in winter.'

Which he or someone else must have cleared before he died. A check of Rupert's kitchen waste-bin was an urgent priority.

'I see. It would seem from our preliminary inspection that theft may have been a motive for the cottage trespass.

That cash may have been taken. Please regard this as confidential—there are puzzling features. I emphasize the *mays*. Any comments?'

Eve had relaxed visibly, as though eager to accept the suggestion. Too eager? 'Theft seems the obvious motive for the break-in,' she said. 'An alcoholic in search of drink, poor devil, though he wouldn't have found much of that in Rupert's place. There've been other incidents in this neighbourhood. We're close to Alexandra Gardens and Jesus Green, where some of the winos congregate. The DO NOT DISTURB notice would have attracted attention, and with the window open . . .'

'Perhaps.' Most winos of Baxter's acquaintance would have left messier visiting cards. 'Did your brother normally keep substantial sums of cash at home?'

'No, no. I'm sure he didn't.' She frowned. 'Sort of thing he was always lecturing me about. What little capital he had was in his building society account. A few hundreds, I imagine.' But the question had clearly unsettled her.

Armstrong raised an eyebrow, but Baxter frowned discouragement.

'I can only suppose,' Eve went on, 'that he made a withdrawal when he decided to kill . . . end his life. As an intended gift for a charity or a friend, perhaps.'

'Any friend in particular?'

'No idea.' Eve shook her head firmly. 'Our circles hardly overlapped, Rupert's and mine. He was a popular man in his quiet way—made many friends through the Garden Centre. There've been plenty of callers this last fortnight that he's been on sick leave, or so he told me. But I can't give you details. I'm out a great deal in the daytime. Besides, Rupert's front door is out of sight from Plumtrees. Our great-grandfather was quite advanced for his time. Thought his coachman deserved a little privacy. Appletrees wasn't thought of when the cottage was built, of course.'

Eve seemed more relaxed now. All the same, Baxter felt he'd better not push his luck. Besides, poor Armstrong looked in need of nourishment.

'One last question, then. Who, to your knowledge, visited your brother on the day of his death?'

'I did. Just after breakfast.'

'Who else?'

'I saw no one enter or leave the cottage.'

'That's not a straight answer.'

'I'm sorry, Chief Inspector, but it's the only answer you're getting from me this morning. It's absurd to suppose that the cottage was broken into in broad daylight, and I refuse to believe that any of his daytime visitors was responsible for a later break-in.'

More bluster, but the distress behind it was obvious. Eve's voice was strained now and high.

'There's more than the trespass to be considered,' Baxter reminded her.

Eve sighed. 'I firmly believe that my brother did away with himself, and that any properly conducted forensic tests will back me up. But I'm not God. We were at one on some issues, Rupert and I. We both felt free to kill ourselves if life became unbearable. And agreed that each of us must judge our own time. We'd no dependants, you see. Rupert is a childless widower. My daughter Ginnie and I have never been close. The young people who share my house and my resources come and go. I'm fond of them, of course, but I avoid over-involvement. Also, Rupert and I agreed to help each other commit suicide if so requested.'

'A serious offence in the eyes of English law.'

'Even if the suicide is terminally ill and the helper a qualified medic. Don't I know it! And in that respect, as in many others, the law's an ass. It hurts me to think that Rupert might have turned elsewhere than to me for help, and I've no reason to suspect it. But if I should be mistaken, the last thing in the world I'd want is for his helper to stand trial. For which reason, I refuse to amplify my answer to your question about visitors.' Her hands were fisted now, bearing down on her plump thighs.

'I don't have to tell you, Mrs Parsingham Wells, that it's an offence to hinder the police in the course of their duties.'

'That's right, you don't.' She jumped down from her perch, smiling defiance. 'Do you really suppose, Chief Inspector, that I can be browbeaten with threats of prison? I've been to Holloway three times, remember, for deliberate violations of laws I didn't respect. If the need arises, I shan't shrink from a fourth visit. In fact, it would be a comfort to use Rupert's death to advance the cause of voluntary assisted euthanasia. I like to think he would have approved.'

Baxter, disinclined to bang his head against this particular brick wall, brought the interview to a close. He was surprised, but considerably relieved, that Eve made no difficulties about a visit to the path. lab. later in the morning to identify the body.

'Euthanasia!' Armstrong repeated as soon as they were out of earshot. 'Strange that she didn't for one minute entertain the nastier possibilities.'

'Oh, but I think she did.' Once or twice, very briefly, before pushing them back under the surface. The first time—for reasons Baxter couldn't begin to fathom—had been right at the beginning of the interview when she had told him her brother was left-handed.

CHAPTER 8

'Tea and toast, please.'

'Make that two.'

Baxter couldn't remember seeing Bill Armstrong walk

past sausages, bacon and tomatoes without so much as a sniff. 'Stomach trouble?'

'Fadge trouble.'

'Come again?'

As they took their seats in the half-empty canteen of Cambridge City District HQ, the Inspector obliged. 'Last night's fadge—Ulster potato bread. We've Maureen's grandmother staying while Ma-in-law spends a few days with her sister in Slough. Old doll takes the line that no woman's fit to be a wife and mother unless she produces a batch of home-baked bread every other day. Maureen, like a fool, plays up to her. Everything was fine until Gran discovered Maureen couldn't do fadge. So she set about teaching her. And Maureen, to Gran's mind, is a slow learner. So it's try, bloody try again. Also waste not, want not. Irishwomen of Gran's generation have a folk memory of the famine, I reckon. Anyhow, there's been fadge on the supper-table four nights in a row, and I'm stuffed to the gills with it.'

'Talking of food . . .'

'If you must.'

'The PM should give us a lead on the time of Parsingham's death, if nothing else. Assuming he had high tea at five, as per usual.'

'About the only lead we're likely to get from what we've collected to date.' Armstrong did battle with a miniature milk carton.

'Something I want to check on downstairs when they've sorted things out a bit.' A large office on the floor below was to serve as an incident room, and Baxter, as Acting Investigating Officer, would have the use of a smaller office next door.

When they poked their heads round the door ten minutes later, the incident room looked if anything more chaotic than on their first visit.

'High tech, they call it!' The fiftyish Office Manager gestured helplessly at a man in British Telecom overalls on hands and knees before a floor socket and a uniformed PC who was disembowelling a computer terminal.

Baxter's eyes roved over the telephones, modems, fax machine and other assorted hardware. 'Look good when it's finished, Terry. Superintendent Highcroft's going to love it. That media release . . .'

'Got it out OK, sir. Used the 'phone next door. Here's your copy of the transcript.'

'Good man.' Baxter had kept it as low-key as possible. *Mr Rupert Parsingham was found dead early this morning at his home at Chesterton Lane, Cambridge. A police investigation of the circumstances of his death is in progress. A fuller statement will be made today or tomorrow.* 'Great. Word for word. And no comment, mind, when the newshounds come baying. Everyone clear on that?'

'Of course, sir.' The Office Manager's lower lip protruded in a wastn't-born-yesterday pout.

'Fine. Be out of your hair in a minute, Terry. At the path. lab., if anyone's asking. Let's have a shufti at this lot first, though. Over here, Bill.'

He led the way to a corner desk where a young WPC was numbering packaged exhibits. 'Mind if we have a quick riffle, Officer?'

He could sense her resentment as his clumsy fingers muddled her neatly sorted piles, but he persevered until he found the packaged suicide note.

'Look there, Bill.' He pointed at a dirty mark to the left of the page, two-thirds of the way from the bottom. 'Half-registered it when Bly showed me this in the garage, but I couldn't be sure. Not sure enough to mention it to his sister.'

'So what's so special? Fingermarks—where he'd steadied the paper. Oily and dusty, which'd fit if he'd written the note after fitting the hose connection.'

'Or trying to fit it and failing? Go on, Bill . . .'

'Afraid I'm not with you.'

Baxter smiled at the unwillingly immobilized WPC. 'Be glad of a peek at the prints that were lifted from this note, Officer, plus all the others from the garage. Assuming you can locate them quickly, that is, things being as they are in the office.'

'No problem. Filed them myself. Shall I bring them next door, sir? You'd be more comfortable.'

An eviction order. Baxter, mindful of the territorial struggles of his own years at a corner desk, went quietly. Within a couple of minutes he had the prints in front of him.

'OK, Bill. The suicide note, first.' Armstrong peered obediently over his shoulder. 'See what was bugging me?' The oily print had been joined by a host of others undetectable to the naked eye.

'Wrote the note with his right hand, that's for sure. And his sister swore he was left-handed.'

'So?' Baxter prompted.

'So—I dunno.' Armstrong's eyes roved to the other prints. 'Could've hurt his left wrist twisting the hose, d'you reckon?'

'In which case, why'd he use it on the mop and the driver's door of the van?'

'Mm . . . Hey, something wrong here as well!' Armstrong was squinting at the prints from the hose and exhaust pipe.

'Wrong how?'

'If you twist something tight, you go like this, don't you?' Armstrong clenched air, fingers bent and bunched, thumbs extended. 'Look at those prints—they're nowhere near right. Fingers splayed, thumb balls hardly making contact. Whether or no Parsingham could've fixed that hose, he wasn't doing it when he left this lot. That's holding, for Pete's sake, not squeezing.'

'After someone else's prints had been wiped off, d'you reckon?'

'Why else?'

'But if that someone had been there at Parsingham's request, helping him on his way and risking imprisonment, you'd think the old boy would have done a decent cover-up. He wasn't stupid—must have guessed prints might be taken. So maybe he wasn't trying.'

'And the suicide note? Reckon he could've used his right hand there to arouse suspicion?'

'Let's take it up with his sister, shall we? After the post-mortem, and after we've given that cottage a proper going-over with Wendy's assistance.'

'Wendy—DS Powers?' Armstrong brightened visibly.

'Pizza dough, wouldn't you say, Baxter?' Dr Stallburn, the forensic pathologist, held up something half-digested between a long pair of tweezers.

'Take your word for it, if you don't mind.' The Chief Inspector was concentrating on his deep-breathing, anti-nausea routines.

'Olives, Parma ham, tomatoes, mozzarella—and, yes, a sprig of dried basil. Nice, light pastry. Green salad—lettuce, fresh chives and basil, if I'm not mistaken. Raspberries with yoghurt dressing. Coffee? Harder to be sure of the liquids till we've tested. But yes, I'd say coffee.' Armstrong, po-faced, made detailed notes, keeping his eyes on his notebook.

'Makes me feel lunchish myself, actually.' The pathologist's bleak face softened. 'Nice to think the old boy had such a tasty meal before the end.'

'How long before the end?' Baxter managed.

'From his meal-time, do you mean? An hour—an hour-and-a-half. The Parma, you see—'

'OK. We understand he normally ate at five. Would a six to six-thirty death fit your other data?'

'Very well.' Stallburn nodded approvingly at the corpse as if at a cooperative patient. 'Tissue analysis suggested a time between five and seven.'

'And he died where he was found?'

'No marks to suggest otherwise. No sign that anyone else laid hands on him. Carbon monoxide suffocation pure and simple, so to speak.'

'Arthritis in both wrists, you said earlier. Bad enough to affect his grip?'

'Bad enough to prevent him fixing that hose, you mean. I'd say so, but without taking specialist advice I couldn't be sure. Major systems were in fair shape for his age and if the adrenalin was flowing . . .'

'Not to worry—it probably doesn't matter.'

Over sherry in the more congenial atmosphere of the pathologist's office, Baxter elaborated on the prints evidence.

'Suspected murder, then? You'd wonder why. Poor old bugger—a maverick, but well liked. We don't have much time for gardens, Polly and I, but to judge by the buzz when the word got round half my fellow-consultants seem to have taken his advice on matters horticultural and personal. Guide, philosopher and friend type, they'd have me believe. But the *Nil nisi bonum* syndrome may have been at work. Ready for a fill-up?'

They refused. Baxter stood up and Armstrong followed suit.

Stallburn extended a well-scrubbed hand to each in turn. 'Got your colour back, both of you. Couldn't send you out the way you were—bad advertisement. Poor old Parsingham. As I say, you'd wonder why. Your job to winkle that one out, I suppose!'

As if truth were a gallstone. Probably was, in some modern poem or other, Baxter reflected as he passed the Festival posters in the hospital foyer. The Parsingham case had put paid to his chances of seeing *Don Giovanni* and *Spin City*. The Mozart opera would be an undiluted loss, but he'd have gone to the fringe show purely for love of Emma. Musicals, in his opinion, had gone steadily downhill since *My Fair Lady*, Sondheim always excepted.

'Keep wondering about that blackmail theory,' Armstrong said as he, Baxter and DS Wendy Powers foregathered outside Parsingham's cottage. 'Doesn't fit with anything we've dug up on the old guy to date.'

'So let's keep digging.' Baxter used the keys under the typewriter to unlock the two remaining drawers and the dead man's desk. 'These and the waste-bin for starters—take your pick.'

Wendy inspected the confettied contents of the bin. 'Bags this, if nobody minds—I'm not bad at jigsaws.'

The drawers were considerably less challenging. Baxter's drawer yielded a Cambridge Building Society savings book, which recorded transactions for the previous five years. Rupert had put away monthly sums increasing over this period from five to twenty pounds, making small annual withdrawals at Christmastime. The account stood at £387.

There were also manilla folders with date labels containing correspondence. Baxter flicked through three of the most recent. They held letters on gardening topics, mostly, some apparently arising from talks Parsingham had given on local radio. Reply dates had been noted on all, but there were no copies of the replies. The horticultural correspondence was interspersed with a few letters and Christmas cards from friends and relatives, but none suggested emotional intimacy. Two of the folders in Armstrong's drawer contained the typed texts of talks delivered on radio or to local horticultural societies. A third held cuttings of gardening articles by Parsingham and others.

Here and there, both detectives found items which had
apparently been filed at random, and perhaps in haste.
These were mainly discount vouchers for petrol and other
consumables, but there were also a few betting-slips and
race cards.

'Guilty conscience, do you reckon?' Armstrong asked.
'Don't suppose his sister's a lover of the Turf.'

'Hardly. How are you doing, Wendy?'

She looked up, flushed, from the side table on which she
had spread the scraps of paper. 'Give me a few more
minutes, will you, sir? This could be important—it really
could.'

The others made a superficial study of the contents of the
bookshelves. Popular biographies, thrillers, travel books—
secondhand or paperback for the most part. More gardening manuals for the common reader than heavyweight
texts on horticulture. The collection of a man of modest
means and modest scholarship. But a houseproud man.
The books and shelves had been dusted within the last
few days.

The two men went into the kitchen which had evidently
been made out of a Victorian larder and pantry. In
one corner they found the folded tea-trolley, a few tiny
crumbs still adhering to its surface. There was a milk
carton and an empty pizza packet in the waste-bin. The
uneaten half of Parsingham's last meal had been stowed in
the table-top fridge and a scent of coffee hung around the
sink.

They went upstairs. The smaller of the two bedrooms
had evidently doubled as an office. Its contents included a
typist's chair and desk, on which stood a projector and
word-processor. Boxes of slides were ranged on one shelf,
ring-bound folders on another.

A camel dressing-gown hung behind the door of the
larger bedroom, and the bed was made up. There were

several dozen family photographs dating from the dead man's childhood and much earlier. That recurring whiskery figure, often in tropical kit, must be Sir Rupert. The silver-backed brushes on the dressing-table bore Edwardian hallmarks.

The most recent wedding photograph had been taken in the nineteen-fifties, to judge by the tight-bodiced dress with its long, swirling skirt. The bride, who looked far younger than her groom, was holding out her left, ringed hand to the photographer. Her right tugged at Parsingham's sleeve, as though urging him into the future. For reasons that he couldn't analyse, that image moved Baxter more than anything he had seen in the garage. He wondered when and why she had let go.

'Look here!' Armstrong's nasal rasp recalled him to the present. The Inspector was kneeling on the haircord carpet in the landing, sniffing at a minute brown mark. 'Peat, like they found downstairs. There's another spot just inside Parsingham's bedroom, and in the bathroom.'

Where the hand towel hung askew on the rail and a sheet of tissue floated in the loo bowl. Hardly Parsingham's style.

'Time for Bly's boys and girls to extend their activities.' Baxter rang HQ Control on his handset and left a message for the Senior Scenes of Crime Officer. 'And for us to have another go at poor old Eve.' The prospect gave him little pleasure, as he led the way back to the living-room.

'SOCOs should be back within half an hour, Wendy. Will you please make a thorough search of the bookshelves down here, when you've finished with the waste-paper basket? Could be some private papers tucked away. Then the upstairs shelves and cupboards, once they've been fingerprinted. Any luck with that litter?'

She straightened, shaking her black hair out of her eyes. 'Nearly done, sir. Bit hard to read, because the scraps of

paper won't lie flat, and I've one or two gaps to fill. But all
the same . . . Look.'

It was a photocopied letter. Baxter took in at a glance
the preprinted heading of the Parsingham Institute for the
Scientific Study of the Tropics, a March date and a STRICT-
EST CONFIDENCE directive. The addressee was a Professor
G. T. Warleybridge, Head of the Department of Microbiology in the University of the North Pennines, to whom
a Dr Julian Otley had evidently made a job application.
The writer was Dr Eric Finchley, Director of the Parsingham Institute, where Otley was employed—or had been
at the time of writing. The tone of the reference was more-
in-sorrow-than-in-anger, its content damning. Baxter
re-read the salient phrases: *long history of psychiatric illness
. . . at least two serious recurrences since graduation . . . undoubted
brilliance . . . unpredictability . . . aggressive outbursts . . . lapses
of concentration . . . failure to verify data.*

'A hatchet job, wouldn't you say, sir?'

Baxter nodded. And there was something else. In the
lower left portion of the reconstituted page, there was
the photocopied print of a man's left hand. He looked
again at the spatulate fingers, the swollen thumb-joint,
and matched the image against others they had seen that
morning.

'Well, Bill?'

'Parsingham's—bet you what you like.'

Wendy looked into each of the men's faces in turn. 'He
copied this, do you mean? He kept it? But why?'

Armstrong reminded her of the assorted £50 notes.

'Blackmail? You mean the old man blackmailed Otley?
But that's horrible. Enough to push the poor chap over the
edge, if there's any truth in Finchley's assessment of his
mental state.'

'Horrible and possibly untrue. So we'll keep it under tabs
for the present, shall we? Get the photographer to snap this

when he comes, Wendy. God knows how long they'll take with the professional reconstruction. Now for Eve.'

Mrs Parsingham Wells was in the kitchen as before, but no longer alone. Another elderly woman, like enough to have been her sister, but more conventionally dressed and coiffed, was helping her wash up lunch dishes at the sink. As the detectives entered the house, a wall phone rang.

'Don't worry about a thing, dear! I'll cope!' The visitor sprang into action. Eve made a face as she led the way from the kitchen to a larger room at the front of the house. 'Thank God for a diversion! Cousin Esther loves coping. Misses her lost status on the Bench, I suspect. Sit!'

They were all at eye-level this time, in 'forties-style tub-chairs of patched imitation leather. Baxter spotted chewing-gum on the arm of Armstrong's and hoped the seat of his own pants was unscathed.

'Your cousin is a magistrate?' Baxter flicked in vain through his mental register of the local judiciary.

'Was—not is. Retired. And she sat in Surrey, alas. I rather relished the thought of being brought up before her for a breach of the peace, but no such luck. Ever since she's moved back to Cambridge, she's been abominably interfering. I rang through Rupert's obit notices to the papers just now with heavy emphasis on *House Private*. Did Esther take the hint? Did she heck! Kindly meant, but one longs to be alone. You are here, I take it, with a purpose?'

'You may remember I asked you which hand your brother used,' Baxter began very quietly. 'The left, you said.'

She nodded, stiffening as she had at the formal identification.

'The evidence we've collected so far supports your statement—with one exception. The note that was found in his pocket was written with his right hand.'

'You're sure?' It was almost a whisper.

'Quite sure. Why should he have done that, do you suppose?'

Eve fisted her stubby hands and pressed them together. Tears filled her faded brown eyes. 'To tell me he wasn't ready to go. To tell me he was being murdered.'

CHAPTER 9

'I half expected it,' Eve said after a long silence. 'The geraniums, you see.'

'The geraniums your brother wanted you to water?' Baxter prompted.

'Yes. What Rupert grew were pelargoniums. Same family, but he was a stickler for the general name. Old schoolmastering habit, I suppose. Told myself at first he'd been teasing, but he wouldn't have . . . not at a time like that.'

'But why use his right hand?'

'We'd this game when we were children. We were both left-dominant, but somewhat ambidextrous—Rupert especially. We taught ourselves to write with our right hands as a means of sending coded messages. Statements written with the right hand were untrue—so you had to guess which hand had been used in each sentence before you could decode a letter. We became fairly adept. There were giveaway signs if you looked closely, but the grown-ups were unaware.' A quick smile, as quickly clouded.

'Do you want us to find your brother's killer, Mrs Parsingham Wells?' Baxter asked.

The question seemed to take Eve by surprise. Then: 'Yes—yes, of course! He wanted to go soon, I'm sure. But if he wasn't quite ready . . .' There could be no doubt that this hypothesis caused her deep distress.

Baxter nodded. 'Then we'll need your cooperation. Did your brother make a will?'

'Shouldn't think so. As I told you before, he'd nothing worth . . .' Again, her voice trailed away.

'Could you give us the name of his solicitor?'

'Garbutt, Garbutt and Castle. Mind you, Harrison Garbutt's the only one of the bunch I'd trust, and he's on holiday. Anyhow, I don't suppose Rupert had dealings with them since his business folded.'

'I must ask you again the question I asked earlier. Who, besides yourself, saw your brother on the day of his death?'

'No one who could conceivably have killed him.'

Baxter counted five under his breath. 'At this stage we're looking for pointers, not criminals. If Mr Parsingham let something drop to a visitor . . .'

She sighed. 'You won't let this go, will you? All right. One was Dolores Finchley—Eric Finchley's wife and a very good neighbour to Rupert and myself.' Eve paused as if to let the encomium sink in. 'Dolly told me she'd looked in yesterday morning to see if Rupert wanted any shopping done. He didn't. You won't find her at home, by the way. She'll be in London for some weeks. Voluntary social work in Kensington.'

'I see. Who else?'

'According to Dolly, Phil Beresford called at the cottage around lunch-time. He's Rupert's ex-employer. Owner of the Middlefields Garden Centre, Trumpington.'

'Any others?'

'Only Stacey Caldwell, to my knowledge. She popped over about twelve—before Beresford, I imagine—to collect some cutlery Rupert had promised to lend me for my party. First-night party for *Spin City*. Emma will have told you?'

Baxter nodded curtly.

'Caldwell with a "d"?' Armstrong checked. 'And her address?'

'Stacey sleeps here and she spent most of yesterday here too, making decorations for the garden-party. Normally she spends her days at Julian Otley's flat. Quiet for her work, she says. Green Street—not sure of the number, but it's over a shoe-shop.'

The detectives exchanged glances.

'Julian slept here too last night, as a matter of fact. Both of them left early this morning before . . . before I found Rupert. Julian works at the Parsingham. Stacey's American—historian turned playwright. But you must know this, Chief Inspector. She's a friend of Emma's. Wrote the book and lyrics for *Spin City*.'

'*That* Stacey? Sorry. Didn't make the connection.' Irrational anger swamped Baxter's pity. What right had this garrulous old woman to drag his daughter's name into a murder investigation?

'No more questions?' Eve's bluster had failed her. She looked shrunken, exhausted.

Baxter tried to speak gently. 'Not now. The Scenes of Crime team will be back, I'm afraid, to complete the search of your brother's home. You'll appreciate why?'

She nodded dumbly.

'Good. We shan't trouble you further today.'

Eve reached for his sleeve. 'There's something else.'

Obedient to her gesture, Baxter resumed his seat beneath a poster of Nelson Mandela.

'Last thing I wanted to come out, but I must put in my oar before Stacey does. Wonderful young woman, clever too, but not the world's best judge of character. English character, anyhow.'

'No?' Baxter belched discreetly.

'Fact is, someone cut the brakes of my trike a couple of months ago.'

'Good God!'

'Camouflaged the damage with insulating tape—not a

brilliant job, but good enough to deceive me without the benefit of my reading specs. First thing I knew I'd lost control half way down the drive. Zoomed straight out on to Chesterton Lane and into the path of a lorry. That would have been that in the morning rush hour, my usual time for leaving the house. But it was only seven-thirty—I'd decided late the night before to attend a Deep Green meeting in London. The road was quiet and the lorry-driver managed to take evasive action. Welsh chap—frightfully shaken up. Found myself recommending hot, sweet tea. Real WRVS stuff.'

Baxter caught Armstrong's eye and raised interrogative eyebrows. The Inspector shook his head. 'You failed to report the incident?' Baxter checked.

'*Decided* not to. Lorry-driver didn't argue the point for long—he was already behind schedule.'

'Didn't the chap who repaired the tricycle ask awkward questions?' Armstrong put in.

'Chap, Inspector! I was stripping down car engines long before you were thought of. Bertie, my late husband, was a qualified mechanic. No, I bought replacement brakes— did the job myself. My bad luck that Stacey caught me at it and insisted that the police must be told.'

'But you silenced her?' Baxter asked, amused in spite of himself. 'How and why?'

'Emotional blackmail, I'm afraid. Not a weapon for a feminist to be proud of. Why? Who'd want police and reporters swarming all over their place?' Especially not if there were druggies among their houseguests, Baxter reflected.

'But we're talking about criminal damage with intent to endanger life,' Armstrong put in. 'Surely, as a responsible citizen—'

'I'd been irresponsible to leave the trike out at night. A temptation to some unfortunate psychopath.'

'Who might do more damage to the next victim?' Armstrong's Belfast brand of moral indignation had a cutting edge.

'That occurred to me afterwards. At the time, I was concerned to protect Damien Ronson. Former member of our collective with a petty juvenile record. Stacey suspected him, and I guessed she wouldn't be alone, but I *know* he wasn't responsible.' Eve's left hand decapitated an invisible objector.

'No? So why did Stacey disagree?' Baxter asked.

'There'd been a row among four members of our community who were working on the roof repair. According to the other three, Damien wasn't pulling his weight. He was hauled over the coals at House Meeting—not for the first time. I'd pleaded for special consideration in the past— he's just eighteen and he's spent half his childhood in care. This time I felt the censure was justified, so I let the "Conform or get out" ultimatum go through without comment. Next morning poor Damien and his van had departed.'

'Was that when you found your brakes cut?'

'No. Twenty-four hours later. I'd left the trike under cover in one of the outhouses on the evening of the House Meeting. Rain had been forecast. Stacey's line is that Damien couldn't find it straight away when he left, and was in a hurry to get off the premises. Came back the next night, according to Stacey, to administer my personal punishment.'

'Which makes some sense if he'd anticipated your support at the House Meeting,' Baxter suggested.

'He'd want to hit back—of course he would. I can see him slashing the brakes, but not applying the sticky tape. Lacked the guile, for one thing. Besides, you'll never persuade me he was a murderer. Never!'

'But you expect Stacey to finger him? Break her word to you after two months' silence?'

'Because of Rupert's murder . . .' Her mouth twisted. 'You'll soon be issuing a new media release?'

'Yes.'

She sighed. 'When Stacey hears the news, she'll be on to you straight away. It's absurd, of course, to make that connection. Damien had nothing against Rupert. And, besides, if he'd . . . done either of us any harm, he'd have been daft to show up last night.'

'He was here? At your party?'

'Would have been, but for Stacey. She met him on the drive, she told me. Sent him packing.'

Once back in the police car, Baxter radioed a request for an all-stations alert, and massaged his stomach. Life, his insides were telling him, was becoming altogether too complicated.

The plump receptionist at the Parsingham Institute marked her place in *Seventy Summer Suppers*. 'I'll try Dr Otley for you.' But not too hard, Baxter suspected. 'What name shall I say?' Her fingers hovered over an intercom keypad.

If the Chief Inspector's rank and occupation sparked a flicker of curiosity, she wasn't letting on. 'Down in a tick, he *says*,' she reported in a tone that might have been cynical or plain bored. As she resumed her study of Macaroni Magic, Baxter pottered about the spacious entrance hall with Detective-Constable Gary Browning in his wake. In his present weary state, he was guiltily glad of a companion too junior to draw attention to weaknesses in his conduct of an interview.

The interior of the Institute was superficially more attractive than the Downing Street frontage in its present state of grime. But there was nothing inside to match the mélange of palms and serpents and elephants' heads on the area railings, or the exuberantly carved foundation date, 1887, which was also the year of royal jubilee.

Perhaps, Baxter mused, the stuffed crocodiles and alle-
gorical marble maidens for which he had hoped were tucked
away behind the door labelled DIRECTOR/DIRECTOR'S SEC-
RETARY. This waiting area, with its models in well-lit
showcases, blown-up colour photographs and TV monitors
offering on-demand video presentations of the Institute's
recent achievements, might have been part of any modern
museum.

With a sense of having seen all that too often before,
Baxter turned his attention to the leafy banisters of the
staircase. He was kneeling on a low step lecturing Browning
on the finer points of the wrought-iron foliage when he was
interrupted by throat-clearings. He got up hastily, brushing
dust off his knees. Damn sneakers. The thin young man
was wearing them—who wasn't, nowadays?

'Dr Otley?'

The newcomer grunted, frowned. 'What can I do for you,
Chief Inspector . . . Black, is it?'

'Baxter. Be grateful for a few minutes of your time, in
connection with the death of Mr Rupert Parsingham.'

'Parsingham?' The tone was chilly. 'Don't want to sound
disobliging, but I'm hellishly busy, and I hardly knew the
old chap.'

Nor liked him, Baxter surmised. 'But you knew he was
dead?'

'Well, yes. Stace—a friend—mentioned it on the phone
at lunch-time. Did himself in, she reckons.'

'I fear not.'

'You mean someone . . . God! That's incredible.' Julian
clapped a hand to his mouth, as if to adjust its expression,
'Poor bastard. All the same . . . don't see where I fit in.'

'You spent last night at Plumtrees, I understand?'

'Yes, but I didn't see the old boy. That's when it was
done, was it?'

Baxter avoided the question. An elderly couple in shorts

and sunhats had come in by the front door and were bearing
down on the receptionist. 'We'll be interviewing everyone
who was in the vicinity of his cottage yesterday, Dr Otley.
Routine. Now is there anywhere we can have some privacy?
Your office?'

'Shared.'

'Come out for a cuppa, then? Thirsty weather. Where'd
you suggest?' Baxter, who had lunched late off cheese sand-
wiches in the police canteen, spoke from the heart.

Julian, still clearly reluctant, conceded that Tattie's, if
approached through the grounds of Downing College, could
be reached within five minutes and might, at this off-peak
hour, provide a quiet table. This they found on the balcony
screened by a sycamore. Baxter gazed through its branches
at the pinky-gold collegiate buildings in the classical style
which he found most congenial.

'Fire away, then!' Julian blew on his black coffee. Not
his first that day, to judge from the smudges under his
reddened eyes.

Browning took a clean page in his notebook.

'Care to give us a run-down of your activities yesterday
afternoon and evening, Dr Otley.'

'Worked in the Institute lab and my office till around
seven-thirty. Biked home for a snack. Back to the Parsingham until eleven or so. Home again to pick up some gear
before biking to Plumtrees.'

'Any witnesses?'

Julian frowned. A handsome face, half way between
Michael Ignatieff and an emaciated Keats. The look that
appealed to maternal women of Baxter's acquaintance.
'Bloke who shares my office left for the day around five.
Guess the other staff on my corridor had gone before I did,
too. Didn't see anyone as I let myself out and in again. I've
a key to one of the back doors. Next time I saw anyone I
know was at the Plumtrees party. Remember speaking to

Mrs Parsingham Wells and Paul Sinton and Emma Baxter. No relation, I suppose?'

'My daughter,' Baxter replied tersely. 'There's something else, I'm afraid. We found the torn-up copy of a letter which concerned you in Mr Parsingham's cottage. Any comment?'

'I'm bloody astonished, that's all!' But also embarrassed, to judge by the sudden flush.

'Can you suggest how it came to be there?'

'Not a clue. What kind of letter?'

'A reference written by your Director.'

'Good God!' Surprise, but relief as well. 'Can I have an eyeful? Brought it with you?'

'No, and if I had I wouldn't be prepared to let you read it at this juncture. It was written in strictest confidence.'

'But surely you can give some indication of the contents?' Julian's angry colour had faded. He took his first sip of coffee.

'Only to say I could understand your concern about the letter falling into the wrong hands.'

'A bad reference, then.' Julian chuckled. 'But you drew the wrong conclusion. Six more weeks and I shake the dust of the Parsingham off my feet. Couldn't give a toss what lies my present employer cooked up about me. Said I was mad, shouldn't wonder?'

'Are you?'

Julian sipped more coffee and smiled. 'Why should I answer that?'

Baxter drank tea and smiled back. 'You don't have to. On the other hand, I'm conducting a murder inquiry and I need to evaluate the trustworthiness of the evidence I collect. You might save me some time and yourself some embarrassment if you came clean.'

'OK, just testing. Only too ready to come out of the psychiatric closet, so to speak. Condition goes by the name of post-traumatic incident syndrome. May sound a mouth-ful, but I can tell you I was bloody glad when they came up with a correct diagnosis and effective treatment pro-gramme. Just six months ago, that was. Problem goes back to when I was nine. Car accident. Schoolfriend's father was driving, his mum was in the passenger seat. She went through the windscreen—died instantaneously, so they said. The father took longer. Hell of a lot longer.'

'Before your eyes?'

'Yep. My friend and I were trapped in the back. Tim banged his head—no compulsory seat-belts then—and passed out.'

'You remained conscious?'

'Uh-huh. Broke a few ribs—medics patched those up OK. They didn't do such a good job on the nightmares and daymares. All sorts of stimuli would set them off—a wooded hill like the crash site, a flowery design like the pattern on Tim's mother's dress. My parents didn't always notice. When they did I couldn't find words to explain. Sounds daft.'

'No.' Baxter recalled his own childhood horror of a tiger skin rug and his fear of naming the fear.

'Symptoms eased off gradually during my grammar school years. Next instalment came my second October in Cambridge—one of those blue-and-gold Michaelmas days.'

'Another car crash?'

'I was sitting in the front seat of a bus in a traffic jam on Castle Hill when a cyclist twenty yards ahead tried to overtake the jam and swerved into the path of a lorry. Girl with buck teeth and red hair and a Newnham scarf. Nobody I knew. Red hair and redder blood. They held up the bus to make way for the ambulance. They'd have let me out, I suppose, but I couldn't budge. It felt as if I was trapped in the back of Tim's father's car again. Waiting and watching. They carried me out in the end.'

'To hospital?'

'Uh-huh. More shrinks. More hospitalizations. More drugs. Nobody seemed to get to the nub of the problem. Having gone off the rails rather flamboyantly at one of my Tutor's sherry parties and again in Chapel, I guessed some mention would be made of my medical history when I sought a post-doctoral post at the Parsingham. Dr Finchley's weapon was sent gift-wrapped, as it were.' Julian laughed.

'What gave him cause to use it?'

'Fear of the brain-drain, I guess. When an academic outfit loses too many research staff in a short space of time it begins to lose credibility.'

'There've been other recent defections?'

'No more than from other British university institutions, perhaps. But Dr Finchley takes these things very personally. I guess anyone who's been fundraising and publicizing day in day out for twelve years is bound to be ego-involved.' A guarded note had crept into Julian Otley's replies.

'Why are people leaving?'

'The usual reasons, mostly. Pay, conditions, promotion.'

'You hope to better yourself in these areas?'

Julian smiled. 'In Karachi? Not financially, anyhow. Other factors have influenced some of us. Ethics, if you like.'

'Oh?'

'Nothing dramatic. Just the feeling that PISST—bloody apt acronym—is an anachronistic relic of Empire. That a tropical research institute should be sited in the tropics. I've met undergrads who wouldn't dream of taking a post there. For some of us, conversion to their point of view came later. On a fieldwork assignment two years ago, in my case.'

'That's when you started trying to make a move?'

'Oh no. I'd the psychiatric problem, remember. Also, although I'd ceased to believe in the legitimacy of the

organization, I'd no doubts—still haven't—about the legitimacy of the project I was heading.'

'Can you fill me in on that?'

'Only roughly. It's strategic research. Our detailed
findings are confidential to our clients, an ASEAN
pharmaceutical consortium with United Nations backing.'

'ASEAN?'

'Sorry. Association of South-East Asian Nations. We're
analysing the self-cleansing systems of certain marine
micro-organisms found in the Pacific. The aim is to provide
scientists in our clients' Singapore-based biotechnical lab-
oratories with the blueprints they need to create improved
versions of these organisms for use in local marine cleansing
programmes and hopefully for export.'

'Thus pipping the established multinationals to the
post?'

'Right!' Otley's enthusiasm was obvious. 'Speed was of
the essence, you see. If I'd backed out early it mightn't
have been possible to find a suitably qualified substitute
straight away.'

'But you did back out in the end. How was that?'

'Personality clash is the standard phrase, I suppose. Dr
Finchley breathed down my neck rather. Requested fort-
nightly progress reports. Got his secretary to make copies of
my data sheets with and at least once without my consent.
Caught her at it.'

'Do you believe you were singled out for special
treatment?'

'Sure I was, from what my friends told me. Hard to
prove, though. When I tackled Finchley, he just hinted that
I was being paranoid—part of my general instability. That
shut me up for a bit. I was afraid he was right. Until my
friend Stacey—Stacey Caldwell—came along.'

'Was she staying at Plumtrees then?'

'Yes. And researching in the History Department. Eve

Parsingham Wells found her a temporary job in the Institute to help her through a financial crisis when she chucked in her research and her grant. That's where we met. Stacey bossed me into getting myself properly diagnosed and treated. Made me see that Finchley's behaviour was paranoiac, my reactions normal. Persuaded me that I'd work better in an environment where I was treated as a sane responsible adult. That's when I started applying for other jobs.'

'Risking the success of your project?'

'Not at all. The bulk of the work's done. The deadline's nine months away, and we're ahead of schedule. Cambridge is bursting with young microbiologists who could wrap the thing up on time, with the prospect of a follow-up contract to motivate them.'

'No regrets, then?'

'Yes, but my work in Pakistan will be equally important. And there with luck I'll be treated as a mature scientist, not a neurotic schoolboy. Besides, I'm grateful to the Karachi appointments board for disregarding what must have been another bad reference from Finchley. First time I've even made the short list.'

'To get back to the letter. Would it surprise you to know that Rupert Parsingham himself photocopied it?'

'Amaze me. I've only spoken to him once or twice at the Director's parties. Grim occasions, but I went with the rest in my first year.'

To curry favour? Surely not. Why, then, did Julian look embarrassed? 'I get the impression that you didn't much like the deceased.'

A grimace. 'No, to be frank. I was disgusted by the way he kept looking at Mrs Finchley those evenings at Appletrees—must have been twice her age. Not that she would have let him lay a finger . . .'

'Did you ever see Parsingham at the Institute?'

'In passing, yes. He and his sister often rendezvoused there. He'd pick her up in his van—wait for her in Valerie's—Mrs Gates's office. She's the Director's secretary.'

'And in charge of personnel files.'

He nodded, biting his lip. 'Filing cabinet—same office. Look, I haven't a clue what's behind this, and I don't care. But if Finchley found out Mrs G. had left that cabinet open, he'd go bananas. Give her the sack, perhaps. And she's not a bad stick . . .'

Baxter smiled. 'I've no immediate intention of raising the matter with the Director.' He sipped tea. Tepid—his preferred temperature. 'You'll want to be on your way, Dr Otley. Thanks for being so frank.'

A blackbird in the sycamore contributed a timely coda. Baxter's pocket radio joined in.

CHAPTER 10

'So friend Julian's an unlikely blackmail victim—always supposing there was a blackmail victim. Agreed?' Baxter checked.

Bill Armstrong and Wendy Powers, now conferring over a second round of tea in the Chief Inspector's Cambridge cubby-hole, made affirmative noises.

'Which is not to say he mightn't have killed for some other reason,' Armstrong added. 'Jealousy, for instance. He's no proper alibi as yet, and who's to say he's one hundred per cent sane?'

'Which of us is?' Powers murmured.

Baxter nodded. '*Nobbut thee and me, and even thee's a bit daft* . . . True, Wendy. Let's keep Bill's point in mind, though. Meanwhile, what joy at the cottage?'

'Thought I'd check up on the peat, sir.'

'Peat?' Baxter asked stupidly. Information overload was setting in. Time to switch off for the day, his central nervous system was telling him. But he daren't. Not yet.

'They found traces,' Powers reminded him. 'On the rug below the window and upstairs.'

'From Parsingham's garden?'

'Seemingly not. All the bags of compost on his premises were peat-free. I didn't trouble Mrs PW, but her cousin was positive that Rupert hadn't used the stuff for twelve months or more. He was involved in a Fenland conservation campaign.'

'Lord, yes. Remember Sarah telling me, but I didn't make the connection. Any other ideas?'

'The Beresfords—Rupert's Trumpington employers, assuming they weren't campaigners. Suppose Phil made a return visit?'

'Sounds like our best bet. Anything else, Wendy?'

'Don't know if it matters, but I found a TMA instruction sheet tucked inside a book.'

'Come again?'

'Tutor-marked assessment, Open University.' Bill Armstrong, whose wife was a spare-time student of long standing, provided the translation.

'Really? What subject, Wendy?'

'Third-level honours course in economics, dated July of last year. Also there were some recent texts on economics and politics stashed away behind horticultural books in the spare room. No reason why Parsingham shouldn't have taken OU courses. Plenty of old folk do. But why hush it up?'

'If you'd seen and heard as much of his sis as we have, you'd understand,' Armstrong assured her. 'Mature students need morale-boosting and Eve's hardly one to be tactful about bad grades.'

'OU enrolment may well be a cardinal sin among the

Cambridge mafiosi,' Baxter added. 'Any other finds, Wendy?'

She shook her glossy dark head. 'Sorry, sir.'

'Don't be. My fact-crunching plant is feeling the strain. What's new with you, Bill?'

'Nothing that could explain the £4,600. According to the transactions in his Natwest account, Parsingham's sole sources of income were his state pension and his salary from the Garden Centre.'

'Which was—?'

'Meagre. £7,000 or thereabouts.'

'No occupational pension from teaching?'

'I queried that. Bank manager reckons that if he'd taught outside the state sector he'd have been insured through a private scheme and could have cashed in when he set up in business.'

'Withdrawals?'

'Nothing exciting. Largest recurrent item was a monthly standing order for £150 to his sister. Token rent, presumably. Otherwise, irregular small cheque payments—to local shops, mostly. Small withdrawals from cashpoints.'

'And his will?'

'Everything to the sister, but Goronway Garbutt confirmed that he'd little to leave.'

'So Eve owns Plumtrees?'

'Not outright. In view of the trike development I raised the issue of her resources. My informants switched off—confidentiality, much as my job's worth, the usual. But when I pointed out that her daddy's will is in the public domain, Garbutt unbent a millimetre.' Armstrong paused to dunk his second ginger nut—a slow process in the cooling beverage.

Baxter chewed his Rich Tea with the thoroughness recommended by his gastro-enterological consultant and counted ten.

'Old Ralph Parsingham made a pile as a stockbroker,

but Garbutt reckons he'd a conscience about his deviation from family tradition,' Armstrong volunteered at last. 'Anyhow, he left the bulk of his estate to the University.' Armstrong consulted his notepad. 'To be used to further the scientific study of the tropics.'

'At the Parsingham Institute?'

'There was no formal stipulation, but that's where the money went. Appletrees had been leased to the University rent free for the use of directors of the Institute ever since Ralph's father's retirement. Ralph said this arrangement was to continue through his children's lifetimes, perhaps to prevent redevelopment.'

'And the family legacies?'

'Ralph's wife had predeceased him. Son Rupert got £25,000—a sum worth having twenty-three years ago—which he blued on the market-gardening venture. Eve got the contents of Plumtrees, some of which had belonged to her mother. Plus a life interest in the house, grounds and cottage. Plus the income from trust holdings valued for probate at around £50,000.'

'And subsequently multiplied by six or sevenfold under competent trusteeship?'

'The lawman clammed up on that one, and on the current value of the property. Eve's life interest, whatever it was, would have been transferred to Rupert if she'd died first. So maybe Ralph didn't trust his son's financial competence a hundred per cent either.'

'What about the grandchild . . . Eve's daughter?' Baxter checked.

'A nun—doesn't fit, does it? Grandfather Ralph left £10,000 to her convent.'

'So who gets the properties and trust capital when Eve and Rupert are dead?'

'The University. Same earmark as before. To further the scientific study of the tropics.'

'Interesting—very interesting. If Julian Otley's to be believed—'

'Big if,' Armstrong cautioned.

'Eric Finchley's got a motive for eliminating the brother and sister, hasn't he? Plumtrees is on a prime site—sale of the house and grounds should yield a handsome sum, even allowing for planning restrictions on redevelopment. Sum that could be more than doubled if Appletrees were thrown in. If Finchley's as devoted to the Institute as Julian would have us believe, the prospect of a massive injection of capital must have been very appealing.'

'True. Fund-raising must be an uphill struggle these days. And with only a couple of septuagenarian mavericks standing in his way . . .'

Baxter shivered a little.

'One of whom, according to Julian Otley, has been making passes at his wife,' Armstrong continued.

'OK, OK. We'll talk to Finchley. But not yet—I need to do some homework.'

'What next, then?'

'I want someone to mind the shop in case young Damien is located. Also, the Office Manager may need guidance on the finer points of the Super's ew computer system. And seeing as Wendy was his s tudent on the advanced induction course . . .'

The softest of sighs brushed crumbs off her dark green dress. She ter well enough to be sure she'd get her share of t ction sooner or later, so no time-wasting gripe.

Which was one of the characteristics he appreciated in his favourite detective-sergeant. That and her sharpness and trimness and humour. And how much did the Welsh lilt in her voice and her shiny black hair count for in the assessment? He worried about these things when he was making out reports. But not for too long today.

She stood up. 'Where'll you be, sir?'

'Green Street—Julian Otley's flat. With luck, he'll still be at the Institute, and we'll catch Stacey Caldwell on her own before curtain-up.'

'What would a scriptwriter be doing at a second night anyhow?' Armstrong wondered aloud.

'Ushering, prompting ... who knows? From what Emma's told me of shoestring productions, everyone's expected to do everything.'

Five minutes later Stacey greeted them through a mouthful of pins at the door of the top-floor flat.

'OK, OK.' She cut into Baxter's introduction. 'Eve told me to expect you. But I'd appreciate it if we could get through quickly. I'm helping out with costume repairs, and you see how it is back there.' She gestured across her shoulder to the scene in the living-room behind her. One young man was at work at an ironing-board in one corner. A second stood, arms outstretched, whilst a third pinned up the sleeves of his academic gown. A girl was feeding something tartan and voluminous through a sewing machine.

Baxter nodded. 'We'll be as quick as we can. Somewhere else we can talk?'

'The bedroom. Go on through.' Stacey indicated a door, lingering a few moments to confer with her co-workers.

The seating options comprised a mattress laid on the floor, and two canvas director's chairs. The detectives chose the latter. A mistake, Baxter realized, when Stacey flung herself on the mattress a few seconds later, and stared up at them, hands clasped behind her curly fair head.

'You don't mind, do you? When I'm screwed up like I've been this last couple of days I think better lying down.'

'No problem,' Baxter muttered. It was, though. *Screwed*

up hadn't helped. She wasn't to know that he'd had this thing about curly-haired blondes ever since . . . oh hell.

'Funny, a woman like Emma having a fuzz for a father.' Stacey eyed him with interest, as though visited by literary inspiration.

They were all at it, dragging Emma into the case. The child with Sarah's eyes and his cheekbones who had grown up one year in London when he was too busy to notice. The woman of whom he knew almost nothing that mattered. Not even what she would like as a birthday present.

'You saw Mr Parsingham yesterday, we understand,' he began.

She nodded. 'At lunch-time. But only for a few minutes.'

'Tell us about that meeting.'

'Not much to tell. I was in and out within five minutes. Eve had asked me to collect some cutlery she was borrowing for her party.'

'What did you do after that?'

'Made paper lanterns until four-thirty, as I'd been doing for most of the morning.'

'In Mrs Parsingham Wells's company?'

'Our paths crossed now and then, yes. But I worked mostly in my room. I was edgy about the show and other things. Personal things. Didn't want company. Four-thirty, I shoved off to Eastside Community College, where *Spin City* is playing, to help with various last-minute chores. OK? Ask Emma if you want.'

Baxter addressed the air above her head. 'Let's get back to your meeting with Mr Parsingham. What was his state of mind, would you say?'

'Low. But no worse than at other times over the previous fortnight.'

'You'd been a frequent visitor?'

'Over that period, yes. To help Eve out—she was really

concerned about him. He'd had a virus infection, which pulled him down, I guess. That and the prospect of quitting his job.'

'Did he ever talk about taking his life?'

'No, but he wouldn't to me. We weren't tight.'

'Oh?'

'Look, don't get me wrong.' Stacey sat up, ran her fingers through her curls.

Baxter's gaze dropped. She was Mary Martin, damn her, washing that man right out of her hair, and he a nine-year-old in the Upper Circle at Drury Lane.

'Rupert was a nice old guy,' she was saying. 'Kind, sympathetic. A good listener—up to a point. But when I went on too long about serious issues, he'd blank off. Make a joke or dish out some Pollyanna-brand reassurance. This I couldn't relate to. And people like that can't cope when Fate plays the joker. So it crossed my mind more than once that Rupert might kill himself. Can you be sure he didn't?'

'Quite, I'm afraid.' Baxter forced himself back into his middle-aged and professional present.

Stacey's open face puckered. 'Oh hell. What could anyone get out of killing him?'

'Money?'

'Didn't have a dime. At least . . .' She frowned.

'Well?'

'Look, I don't know . . . I could be wrong.'

'Tell us all the same.'

'One Sunday—five weeks or so ago, it would be, I called to see Rupert. Left my purse behind. Guess he didn't hear my knock when I came back. Tried the handle, and the door wasn't locked. I was late for a date with Julian so I sang out and barged in. Not for the first time. Rupert had never minded before, but that day he looked quite put out. He stashed something into a drawer double quick and I could've sworn it was banknotes.'

'He offered no explanation?'

'Nope—and in the best English tradition I let on I hadn't noticed. But it bugged me. Rupert never came across as a miser. Generous to a fault, I'd have said.'

'And obliging?'

She stiffened. 'What's that supposed to mean, Chief Inspector?'

'In photocopying that reference, for instance. If he did so on request, that is. I take it Dr Otley's been in touch.'

She nodded. 'Julian knew nothing about that bloody reference—need never have known. Why'd you have to tell him?'

'He's clearly an interested party.'

'If Julian had wanted to copy the stuff in his file, he'd have done the job himself, wouldn't he?'

The sewing-machine buzzed in her long silence.

'That all you propose to say on the subject, Ms Caldwell?'

'I'm not clued up on British law. Do I take it that un-authorized copying would be an offence?'

'That's right.'

'And the case would go to court if I admitted to com-plicity?'

'I doubt it, but it'd be up to the Crown Prosecution Service. You have, of course, the right to remain silent on the matter.'

'And if I do?'

'We'd probably raise the issue with Dr Finchley. Dr Otley thought that might make trouble for his secretary.'

'Yeah, he's a soft spot for old Valerie. Can't say she showed me much sisterly solidarity during my three months with that outfit, but twelve years' exposure to Finchley has probably eaten into her soul.'

'You found him uncongenial?'

'Our paths hardly ever crossed—if he could tell one

junior secretary from another he sure as hell didn't let on. But I saw enough of the way he harried Julian to hate him. Finchley's an ecologist, two-bit ecologist—what I hear. Modern microbiology's way outside his range. And Julian's work is world class, according to his colleagues. OK, he'd a temporary psychological problem—told you, he said.'

Baxter nodded.

'But that's history. He'd really got his head together before I left the Parsingham to write full-time. About six months ago, that would be. Julian had started to believe in himself—in his ability to find a better working environment. Then Finchley applied the double-bind. Stepped up the petty interference and blocked his efforts of escape.'

'How could you be sure of that?' Armstrong asked.

'Not just from Julian. I nosed around, sounded out his contemporaries. Everyone gave me the same story. The jobs he was being turned down for in Cambridge and elsewhere were going to his inferiors. Which could only mean Finchley was badmouthing him.'

'Did Dr Otley share your view?'

'Not at first. And by the time he did he was feeling too boxed-in and depressed to take any action. When I suggested he should have a peek at his file, he was horrified. Shot me the school prefect line about sneaking. Nor was he prepared to confront Finchley and demand to see what he'd written. But I couldn't just sit on my hands and watch him cracking up. Which is why I turned to Rupert.'

'You asked him to filch Dr Otley's personnel file?' Baxter checked.

'Yeah. Last May, I asked him. Sounds crazy, I know. I'd have done the job myself, but Valerie knew I'd been glad to quit the place, and it would've looked kind of sussy if I'd started hanging around. Whereas Rupert was there at least once a week to pick up Eve and her shopping, and most often she'd be late.'

'Did he agree right away?'

'Not right away.'

'Did money change hands?'

'You just have to be joking. OK, I've a little capital from my grandmother's estate, which is why I could afford to give up the Institute job. But just enough to launch myself as a playwright, and most of it's tied up in the States. Besides which, Rupert would have been mortally offended . . .'

Baxter didn't think she was lying. 'Go on, please.'

'At first he flatly denied that a Director of the Parsingham could do the dirty on a fellow-scientist. Guess I hadn't registered up to that point how much the Institute meant to him, how proud he was of the family connection. But once I presented my evidence, he crumbled. He didn't say, but I got the impression that he'd other grounds for disliking Finchley.'

'Something to do with Mrs Finchley?' Baxter asked softly.

Stacey leapt to her feet. 'Eve dropped hints, did she? Just because Dolly's a Filipina and she was so goddamn possessive of her little brother! Emma's dad or not, you're as bad as the rest. Scratch a fuzz and uncover a frigging stereotype.' She retreated to the window.

Baxter rose rather wearily. 'Mrs Parsingham Wells dropped no hints that I was aware of, but Dr Otley seemed to think her brother was attracted—'

Stacey swung round to face him. 'As was Julian, before I came on the scene. Dolly's a very attractive person. Which doesn't mean that she has it off with every guy who propositions her.'

Wherever that speech had come from, it wasn't from the script of *South Pacific*. 'Look, Ms Caldwell, no one's saying—'

'But I bet they will, you know.'

Baxter held his peace.

Stacey slipped gear, spread apologetic hands. 'Guess I'm not helping Dolly any by going all defensive. She visited with Rupert quite often—out of kindness, I'm sure. Helped him catalogue his slides and stuff like that. My guess was, she'd let slip that her marriage was less than fulfilling, and that Rupert would have given his all for a suit of shining armour.

'Anyway, he shed his scruples pretty fast, and agreed to my plan. With the proviso that if the file contents were as libellous as I suspected, there'd be a showdown with Finchley in which Rupert would do the talking. I think he meant to force Finchley to resign.'

'When was the file copied?'

'Second and third weeks of June. Don't remember the exact dates. Rupert needed two bites of the cherry—Eve nearly caught him at it the first day.'

'And when was the showdown?'

'It wasn't.' She returned to the mattress and sat down, knees drawn up to chin. 'My doing.'

'Why so?'

'If the references had been all of a piece, I'd have had no doubts. But the last one Finchley had sent to Karachi—its file copy, I mean—was way out of line with the others. It was favourable. Glowing, even. No hint of a psychiatric history.'

'Remember the date?'

'May, but further than that, no. Julian was really keen on the Karachi post—he'd just been shortlisted. Last thing I wanted was to spoil his chances. So I begged Rupert to hold off until the appointment was made.'

'And afterwards?'

'We both sort of backed down. We began to doubt whether the evidence was strong enough to pressure Finchley into resigning. Also, I was still concerned about the impact on Julian. He wasn't finding it easy to accept the fact that I wouldn't be coming to Karachi with him.

'But mainly, I guess, other priorities took over. I'd begun to work round the clock on *Spin City*, and I got the distinct impression that Rupert was involved in some new project of his own.'

'What sort of project?'

'That I don't know. It was little things. Like, he began to take more interest in the evening paper I'd bring over next morning from Plumtrees. He'd chuckle over some item or other, and clam up when I asked him what the joke was. Then there was the episode of the banknotes. Private business venture, I guessed. It annoyed me somewhat that he didn't confide in me, but I was glad he'd something to take his mind off his retirement.' She glanced at her wristwatch. 'Oh my God! I need to eat before the show, and there's nothing more I can tell you about Rupert.'

'Mrs Parsingham Wells was sure you'd want to tell us about Damien Ronson.'

'Oh-oh.' Stacey bit her lip. 'Twenty-four hours ago I'd have shot my mouth off on the subject.'

'So what's new?'

'Your daughter, would you believe, Chief Inspector?' A giggle. 'Thought you mightn't appreciate that.'

Stay out of this, Emma! But she'd always gone her own way.

'She and Paul Sinton saw me turf Damien out of Plumtrees last night. I was so mad about him showing up again, I told them about the damage to Eve's trike. Has Emma put you in the picture?'

'Mrs Parsingham Wells.'

'No kidding? Well, your daughter reacted by accusing me of class prejudice, which didn't sit well with me at the time. But since what happened to Rupert, I've revised my position somewhat. I was wrong to badmouth Damien. He'd motive to kill Eve, sure, but I've nothing else to go on. And as far as I'm aware, he'd no grudge whatsoever against poor old Rupert. Guess somehow it'll be a long, long time before I call anyone else a murderer!'

'Glad to hear it.' All the same, Baxter hadn't the slightest intention of letting up on the hunt for Ronson.

CHAPTER 11

On his way downstairs on Thursday morning Baxter caught sight of his daughter's minivan.

'Emma back?' he asked Sarah as he joined her at the breakfast-table.

'Mm.' She licked marmaladey fingers. 'Told you last night she'd rung, didn't I, to say they'd fixed her van?'

'You did. Slipped my mind.' He helped himself to muesli. No need for Sarah to know he'd taken the van trouble as an excuse. She'd remind him fast enough that Emma had never felt the need to lie about her sleeping arrangements. That she wasn't likely to start now.

'How's the neck?' Sarah asked.

He rotated it cautiously. 'On the mend. So you noticed?' She nodded.

'Then why the hell—'

'You know why, Richard.' He caught her quizzical eye. They'd been through this many times before, especially in their last fraught year in London. Emotional withdrawal was a weapon of last resort. Silent martyrdom would be silently ignored.

'Sorry, love.'

All in all, Wednesday evening had been less than satisfactory. Jaded after the interview with Stacey, Richard had returned to his temporary office and forced himself through two hours of tedious but necessary paperwork.

Things had improved temporarily on the drive home. His late start had delivered him from the rush hour traffic out of the city and the later incoming streams of Festival patrons. His spirits had risen at the prospect of Sarah's cooking and cosseting. A little drink perhaps, an early night . . .

Then he had read her note on the fridge. He had quite forgotten about the monthly meeting of the Holtchester Horticultural Society. No point in sulking. The contents of the casserole were fragrant if mushy. He had dined off a tray in the living-room, munching slowly and drinking moderately. Balking at the prospect of the early but empty bed, he had dozed off on the settee to the accompaniment of Mozart's C Minor piano concerto.

But Wolfgang Amadeus had let him down. Disturbed by Sarah's headlights around eleven, he had jerked into consciousness and pain. Piqued by his wife's failure to pick up his non-verbal signals, he had fended off her inquiries about his day's work and faked absorption in ground cover, the horticultural topic of the month in Holtchester.

He must, he supposed, have been dozing when his daughter came home. But he'd spent most of the night awake and rigid, ill-prepared for a 7.30 call from Police Headquarters.

'ACC Crime wants you to report to him at eight-fifteen, sir, before you leave for Cambridge. Says the jewel thefts investigation has come off the back burner . . . No, nothing else, sir.'

One murder, one aggravated criminal damage. Now this. He'd replaced the receiver, appalled.

Fifteen minutes later, crunching muesli in the sunny kitchen, he chuckled. When life becomes impossibly complicated, it becomes farcical.

'What's the joke?' Sarah asked.

He explained. They both laughed, the last barriers between them dissolving. His neck hurt again, but less sharply.

Seated now in an HQ office enlivened only by a huge map of the county, several dozen silver cups, group photographs of policemen and three fleshy-leaved pot plants, Baxter waited for the Assistant Chief Constable to clear his throat. For this was the preliminary to Littleton's every significant utterance. A nervous habit, Baxter assumed. Substitute for a pipe-tamping ritual, perhaps. The man seemed healthy enough.

'Hm-hm. I sent for you, Baxter, because I had a disturbing phone call at home at five-thirty this morning. From Mrs Thurstone.'

'Mrs Alma Thurstone?'

'Hm-hm. The same.'

Baxter braced himself. Phone calls from Alma Thurstone inevitably meant trouble.

'Hm-hm. Of the Police Committee,' the ACC added unnecessarily. 'At her urgent request I made her a personal visit.'

'I see, sir.' As stand-in, no doubt. It was no secret that Alma had wiped the Shire Hall tiles with Francis Montgomery on more than one occasion. She wouldn't have thought twice about dragging him out of bed in the wee small hours.' Anything serious?'

'Hm-hm. Theft of a brooch to which she was much attached. Emeralds and rubies. Bird design.'

Baxter's spirits sank. 'That scraggy stork thing?' Alma had worn it every time he had seen her in the ample flesh, and in the photograph the local newspaper printed above her periodic fulminations.

'Hm-hm. Liver bird, actually. Liverpool emblem, y'know. Wedding present to her mother from the family shipping firm. Insured for eight thou, great sentimental value. Mrs Thurstone is naturally most anxious for its recovery.'

'Safe broken into, sir?' The likeliest hypothesis, given the hour of the phone call.

'Hm-hm, no.'

'You mean she was wearing it at the time?'

'Not that either, hm-hm.'

Baxter brightened. 'Embarrassing for her, isn't it? I mean, when she's not lambasting the Force, she's laying into members of the public who fail to keep tabs on their goods and chattels. If she's left a valuable brooch lying around . . .'

'Hm-hm. Mrs Thurstone didn't. The brooch was stolen from her youngest daugher, who had borrowed it. Mrs T. only became aware of the incident this morning. My impression is, Angela had been afraid to break the news—'

'That figures.'

'The theft occurred on Tuesday night at a Jazz Concert in the Cambridge Corn Exchange. Angela left her jacket with the brooch in it on her seat during the interval.'

'Tuesday night! In a town overflowing with Festival visitors and other assorted tourists. My God, sir, we haven't a hope at this stage.'

'Hm-hm. Probably not, Baxter. But we must be seen to make our best efforts. I feel sure the Chief Constable would wish it.'

'No doubt, sir.' The Chief Inspector was thankful that Montgomery's wishes impinged only rarely on his decision-making processes.

Baxter's visit to the Old Rectory, Fen Holton, home of the Thurstones, yielded little of substance. In demanding the early recovery of the brooch, Alma was clearly asking the impossible. The all-stations alert initiated by the ACC

had been thirty hours too late. The Liver bird had almostly
certainly fled the region, if not the country. Baxter made the
point politely, out of sympathy for Angela, a tear-blotched
nineteen-year-old who would probably have liked to follow
its example.

It was ten before Baxter reached his office in Cambridge.
DI Armstrong, as requested, was sorting the contents of his
in-tray.

'Wendy not back from the Parsingham?' He had asked
her to obtain Dolores Finchley's London address from her
husband.

'On her way.'

'Coffee, Bill?'

An affirmative grunt. It had already been brewed. Armstrong helped himself to a generous segment of shortbread,
not his first to judge by the scatterings of sugar.

'Dog get your fadge this morning?'

'Maureen's passed the test, so Gran's moved on to
champ.'

'Sounds revolting.' Baxter unwrapped his second sodamint of the day.

Armstrong's square face took on a dreamy look. 'Spuds,
milk, chopped shallots, all mashed up with a well for the
butter. Great stuff, but filling. So I'm lucky it's not a breakfast dish. How'd it go with the Thurstones?'

Baxter gave him the gist. 'What's new that I need to
know about?'

'Couple of leads on Damien Ronson. Traffic cop cautioned him for speeding Monday last. He was driving a candy-striped Ford transit—eye-catching number,
wouldn't you say?'

'Which he'll have flogged pretty quick if he's anything to
hide.' Baxter rubbed his stomach.

'We've also got three addresses supplied by his former

probation officer, and we know he works off and on in the roofing trade—'

'Where cowboy contractors are two a penny. Oh, great! Sorry to wet-blanket, but it's obvious that we'll get nowhere fast with the trike business unless we go public. And the ACC—pressurized by Eve—has vetoed an early media release. What else, Bill?'

'DI Mercier of the Met wants a personal word. Be in conference, he said. He'll ring you back.'

With an invitation to some Met shindig, no doubt, which like many another would have to be turned down. Baxter wouldn't miss the wining and dining bit too much—there'd be few familiar faces from his London days. But he relished the after-dinner gossips on police and antiques matters with his old friends Lou and Jo Mercier.

DS Powers arrived as Baxter was scanning the printouts in Armstrong's top priority pile. He gestured an invitation to coffee.

'How'd it go, Wendy?'

'I'm not sure, sir.' She smoothed the skirt of her pink cotton two-piece.

Nervous gesture. Not like Wendy to be nervous.

'Slight problem with Dr Finchley's secretary, to begin with.'

'Valerie whatsername?'

'Gates. She knew me by sight, unfortunately. Lives next-door but one to Keith's mother.' Keith—the estate agent and house-sharing boyfriend. Time was, a house-sharing boyfriend would have been grounds for dismissal from the Force.

'Does she know your job?'

Powers wrinkled her nose. ''Fraid so. And worse still, she twigged I was on the Parsingham case.'

'Hell.' The whole point of sending Wendy was to keep the thing discreet, low-key. To avoid embarassing Finchley.

'I didn't confirm or deny—but I'm sure she suspected. Also, I've a strong feeling she's something she wants to unburden. She followed me out into the entrance hall when I was leaving—actually grabbed my arm. Then the receptionist came after her with some query or other and I scarpered.'

'Could've been hoping to pick up some gossip,' Armstrong suggested.

'Could have, but Val struck me as a sharp lady. I'm sure she'd know better.'

'How'd you get on with Finchley?'

'Stuffy bloke—like his office. I played it as per instructions. Explained that we wanted to question everyone who had seen Rupert on Tuesday—that his wife's name was just one of three Eve had given us. That Mrs Finchley—or perhaps he himself—might be able to add other names to that list.'

'And?'

'He said he couldn't come up with any names. Volunteered a rundown on his own programme for Tuesday, by way of demonstrating how few opportunities he had to observe Rupert's cottage. But it came over as a little defensive.'

'Where was he at the times that mattered?'

'Parkside swimming-pool, he says. Five forty-five to six forty-five.'

'Mention meeting anyone he knew?'

'No. Didn't think you'd want me to ask at this juncture.'

'Quite right.'

'All the same—and, mind you, sir, this is just a hunch . . .'

'Fire away.' Wendy was canny with her hunches.

'I believe he's a fair idea of the approximate time of death, which he certainly didn't get from me.'

'Mm. Talked to Eve on Wednesday morning, didn't he?

She might have said something about the state of the body when she found it.' But that wasn't enough. 'Get a contact number for Mrs Finchley?'

'Not sure. He gave me the number of a migrants' welfare organization she'd worked for at one time, but he claimed not to know her current whereabouts.'

'Odd. Could be he's shielding her,' Baxter said. 'If she's involved with domestic workers at risk of deportation.'

'Could be, but he was really edgy. My guess is he's scared she's walked out on him.'

If so, why? Baxter asked himself. Also, why now?

'So when do I get my gold medal?' Clive Sinton emerged unhurriedly from his son's bathroom and lowered himself into the only comfortable armchair in the small Victorian flat.

'Silver.' Emma played his game for Paul's sake, and despised herself for it. 'This morning's effort was your penance for skipping the Plumtrees party.'

'Which will incidentally get you out of a visit from the cops,' Stacey put in. 'Eve's been asked to supply them with a guest-list.'

'Furthermore,' Emma continued, 'Eve was the one who softened up the Eastwave TV team and I was the one who spent yesterday morning on their producer's doorstep.'

'And finally,' said Stacey, now embarked on a stretch-relax routine on the hearthrug. 'Finally, Clive, you just loved belting out those gags about the Camford higher education system. Bet they transmit every last one, and scrap the *Spin City* footage.

'Let me guess.' Paul abandoned all pretence of studying an 1851 Census Report. 'He gave them the one about Cambridge being the only place in the world where wet feet are a status symbol. Am I right? Also the one about the light blues of the—'

'Stuff it!' Clive fired a cushion. 'I'll settle for a bronze gong. Anything is better than hearing my finely honed one-liners being done to death. God knows how I sired a son with a cloth ear for the rhythms of his native tongue. No fault of his mother's.'

'Mum rang me when you were out, Dad.' Paul addressed the space above his father's head. Oh God, Emma thought. Why did I bother? This is going to spoil everything. He's making a terrible hash of sounding casual.

'She's managed to wangle Saturday off work,' Paul went on. 'So she'll be coming to the final performance and shacking up here tonight. And I thought, if you can hang around that long, Dad, why don't we all eat together somewhere cheap and cheerful after the show? You, Emma, Mum and me. Stacey and Julian too, if they'd like to.'

'Yes, why not, Clive?' Stacey urged. 'I just love family reunions. You get a whole new slant on your friends when you see them interacting with Mom and Pop.'

Paul flinched, but Clive seemed unruffled. 'Can't think the Sinton generation games will make scintillating spectator sport. But you can chalk me up for tomorrow's team, Paul, if I can talk my way out of dinner with my agent. Where d'you keep your phone?'

'Hall. Oh—just remembered. A bloke left a message for you, Dad.' He dug in his hip pocket and handed his father a crumpled piece of paper. 'Rang about an hour ago. Didn't leave his name, just the number. Said it was rather urgent.'

Clive read the digits, wrinkling his elegant nose. 'Cambridge number, too. Chair of Drama going begging, perhaps? Honorary D.Litt.? How d'you say no in Latin?' He got up, stretched and unhurriedly left the room.

Stacey departed to the kitchen to make coffee. Emma perched on the arm of Paul's chair, and began to play with his hair. 'Pleased your dad's accepted the invite?'

'Mm. And surprised he agreed to meet Mum in Cambridge. I get the impression he holds the place responsible for their divorce. God knows why.'

'When was it they split?' Emma searched her memory for the few scraps of family history Paul had vouchsafed in their Lancaster student days.

'Seven years ago. But it was a bumpy ride for as long as I can remember . . . They stuck it because of me, I guess, but I often wished they'd get it over with. It was rough hearing him shout one minute, plead the next, seeing her try not to cry in front of me.'

'And neither remarried?'

'No. They've had other relationships—quite a few in my father's case—but nothing seems to work out. They can't live with each other or without each other, it would appear. Corny old cliché.'

'Sad old cliché.' Emma kissed the crown of his head. 'For them—and you.'

'Yeah—well.' He caught her right hand and kissed its palm. 'I wonder sometimes if I've inherited the jinx, if any marriage I make will founder. Daft, eh?'

'Utterly daft.' But Emma, who had her own reasons for giving matrimony a wide berth, disregarded the mute appeal for a reassuring cuddle.

Clive reappeared when they were drinking coffee, but refused to join them, saying he must be on his way.

'To stake your claim to the Chair or the D.Litt.?' Stacey prompted.

An instant's blankness before he switched back into facetious mode. 'Both, of course. Besides which, there's this rumour that HRH will shortly chuck in the Chancellorship.'

Stacey giggled appreciation, but Emma, sensing a new anger beneath the bonhomie, was puzzled and a little frightened.

'Spare us an hour of your precious time for lunch or

supper, sir?' Paul's heavy-handed humour didn't help.

'Not today. Sorry, folks—truly.' And perhaps he was, Emma thought. 'Something's cropped up, as they say. But I'll keep the Saturday dinner-date, so help me, and I'd like to foot the bill. Ring my hotel when you've made a booking. OK, Paul? I'll let myself out.'

'OK,' Paul said in a bleak voice and reached for his census report.

'Better shift my ass too.' Stacey drained her coffee mug. 'With any luck the sewing-party will have quit Julian's place by now, and I can get down to some work.'

She made tracks for the kitchen. 'Did I tell you, Em?' she called over her shoulder. 'I've been rerunning some tapes my grandma made for me when she was dying? About Brooklyn the way she remembers it from the 'thirties. And they've given me this fantastic idea for a new musical—'

Paul raised his eyes to the plaster ceiling-ornament.

'Tell me in the van,' Emma called back. 'I'll run you over to Green Street on my way to Brixton. Had an offer of a house-share there, which I want to reccy. See you at the show, Paul. Oops! Sorry, Stace.' The two women had collided at the door between hall and kitchen. Stacey's hand sent the telephone receiver flying and with it a scrap of paper.

As her friend bent to retrieve both, Emma saw that the paper bore the message 'Dad, please ring' and a six digit number which meant nothing to her but something, apparently, to the American.

'About this dinner-party on Saturday—I'm gonna take a raincheck,' Stacey said on the way downstairs. 'Tell Paul it's not personal.'

'OK—but why the flip-flop?'

They had reached the front door of the house before Stacey answered. 'Truth to tell, Em, I'm going off Sinton

Senior fast—on account of the company he keeps. Know whose call he was returning just now?'

Emma shook her head. None of anyone else's business, she tried to say but couldn't.

'Dr Eric Finchley's. That's the number of his direct line at the Parsingham.'

Emma followed her friend across Mawson Road in puzzled silence.

CHAPTER 12

Lou Mercier rang Baxter just after lunch.

'Drinkwater—You're sure it was Drinkwater?'

'Listen with Uncle, boy. It's all on your desk at Holtchester District, but I gather you're on the hoof. Simon Drinkwater, as ever was. Ex-Eton, ex-Balliol, ex-Pentonville. Heavier, browner, but the same eyebrows. For Chrissake, Dick, which of us could forget those eyebrows? Nine-thirty this morning I'm seeing off these customers of Jo's at King's Cross, when I rumble our old pal behind a ticket barrier.'

'Heading where?'

'Heading for the Smoke. Having stepped off a train from Cambridge, sleepyhead. So, bearing in mind your little local difficulties—'

'You brought him in? I appreciate this, Lou, I really do. If there was one brain behind those jewel thefts, it had to be a good one. And quirky. Which fits old Simon.'

'Aka Sam Dunnett nowadays. Been breeding racehorses in Argentina for over a decade now, according to our info. Squeaky clean as far as Interpol can tell us. Which is why my bosses won't bring him in without good cause.'

'For crying out loud! One session with our Alma bloody

Thurstone is good cause in anyone's book. If you'd any idea of the grief that woman's caused us . . . I've half a mind to pass her the word, Lou.'

'You wouldn't.'

'Why wouldn't I?'

'Apart from the job's worth angle, there's the old pal's worth angle. Remember the runaround friend Drinkwater gave me last time, only to stumble into Wee Willie Brougham's arms? Which happy event put our Willie into orbit. It's Commander Brougham now, would you believe?'

'Courtesy of Simon D? Come off it, Lou. You over-simplify.'

'Maybe so. All the same, Drinkwater owes me, and he's not going to make a monkey of me again. Which is why I'm backing Them Upstairs. Stands to reason he's not car-rying a load of rocks on his person. So it's obbo and nothing but obbo until he leads us somewhere interesting. And if you jump in with two flat feet, Dick, we're through. I mean that.'

Lou probably did. The memory of the Lakes Bank affair hung awkwardly between them.* Not Baxter's fault that Mercier had been transferred back from the City Force to the Met without the promotion he had hoped for, but all the same . . .

'Message understood, but keep in touch, won't you?'

'Trust Uncle. By the by, Jo tells me you've never been up to see this new shop of hers.'

'Soon, Lou, so help me.' He had a sudden thought. Jo did Victorian jewellery, which fitted with a Victorian musical. Emma might fancy a piece for her birthday—or would she? Like as not, he'd end up giving her money again.

Plastic. You couldn't get away from the sight of it. Worse

* *Murder in Good Measure.*

still, the stink. In the Middlefields Garden Centre shop, the detectives' first port of call, it had mingled with flowery, earthy and fertilizer smells. Here in the store of plastic garden furniture, containers and ornaments, there was no competition apart from body odours. And Phil Beresford, who had been helping unload a lorryload of fencing, was sweating freely. At Baxter's request he opened a skylight. They sat down on three plastic chairs.

'This won't take too long, I hope? Busy time for us.' Beresford scratched his left temple. A habit born of past skin trouble? His strong brown face was faintly pock-marked.

'That will depend on you as much as us, Mr Beresford.'

A shrug. 'Tell you what I can—won't be much.'

'Let's talk about the last time you saw Rupert Parsingham.'

'Tuesday that was—day he died, poor old bugger. Two o'clock—five to, something like that.'

'You're quite sure—' Armstrong began.

Baxter frowned. 'What the Inspector means, it was an unusual time of day for a busy man like yourself to go visiting.'

'Special occasion—Rupert's retirement day. We wanted to give him a little something. My wife had intended to pop over—'

'Was Mrs Beresford close to Mr Parsingham?'

'Close? What exactly are you getting at?' Beresford's big hands fisted on his bare thighs.

'I just wondered if she was friendly with him. Friendlier than you, for example?'

Beresford opened, then laced his fingers as if to prevent a second betrayal. 'Di was softer-hearted, being a woman. Besides, her granddad was head gardener at Princes', Rupert's old college. It was different for me. Can't afford to be too palsy-walsy when you're boss, can you?'

'So why did you take your wife's place on Tuesday?'

'We'd hoped to fill a staff vacancy Monday, but things didn't work out. I decided to go head-hunting in and around Cambridge next day.'

'You can let us have names . . . addresses?'

'Sure. The wife and I can't both be off base in working hours, so it made sense for me to hand over Rupert's retirement presents.' Beresford's thumbs were playing footsies.

'Presents?'

'Yeah. Your blokes'll have turned them up, I reckon, unless the burglar got there first. Poor old Eve is really chewed up about the break-in, Di tells me. Worried that one of her pet punks might have done the job, shouldn't wonder.'

'Please describe the presents,' Baxter said coldly.

'Old print of Princes' College gardens—belonged to Di's father. Di might be able to fill you in about the artist. Plus a cheque for half a grand.'

'A print has turned up, but not a cheque.'

'Yeah, well, I suppose that figures.' Beresford's black eyes caught Baxter's and sheered away. 'Some druggy kid after cash for a quick fix. We stopped the cheque, natch, once we heard about the break-in.'

'Take us back to that visit. Notice anything special about the cottage when you arrived?'

'Special—what sort of special?' Beresford's finger-lock tightened.

'The front door, for instance?'

'A DON'T DISTURB notice, you mean? Eve told Di he'd stuck one up.'

Baxter nodded. Damn and blast Eve.

'Wasn't there when I arrived. Shouldn't have knocked if it had been.'

'Remember what Mr Parsingham was doing when you got there?'

'Let's see.' The uncertainty seemed genuine. 'Oh yes. He'd been washing dishes—lunch things, I guess. Came to the door with his hands all soapy.'

'How'd he seem?'

'Bit paler than usual—thinner. He'd been off work for a fortnight with some virus thing.'

'Did he look or sound depressed?'

'No more than usual. Di reckoned he'd been low ever since he realized he'd have to pack the job in. If so, he put a brave face on things when I was around.'

'What did you say to each other on Tuesday?'

'Word for word? Oh, come on!' Beresford's fingers were back at his hairline. 'Wasn't listening too hard. I'd plenty else on my mind—business worries. We didn't say much, come to think of it. Hardly more than hello, thank you, goodbye. He seemed embarrassed—know I was. He asked me in, but I got the impression he didn't mean it, so I made some excuse and stopped on the doorstep. Told him Di would visit at the weekend, which seemed to please him. Then I left.'

'See anyone near the cottage as you were entering or leaving?'

'Nope. Not a soul. So that's that, Chief Inspector.' Beresford got up. 'All I can do you for, I'm afraid.'

Baxter stood to confront him. 'I think not. Suppose you do what I asked you at the beginning of this interview.' Beresford's head jerked backwards. 'Tell us about the last time you saw Mr Parsingham.'

'You saying I've just given you a load of garbage?'

'We've no reason at present to doubt your account of the afternoon visit. That's not the point.'

'That was the last time I saw old Rupert, swear to God. If anyone's told you different he needs his head examining!'

Beresford looked wildly round, as if for a weapon. As

Armstrong slipped behind to block his exit, Baxter gave wry thanks for the ubiquitous plastic.

'Yes?' Baxter said softly. '£500's a generous handout from a man like yourself. Man with business worries—cashflow worries, shouldn't wonder. The little lot you've stowed here isn't earning its keep, I'd guess.'

'It will. Just what are you driving at, Chief Inspector?'

'Whoever entered Plumtrees Cottage on Tuesday night left traces of peat behind him.'

'Peat! What's that prove? Could've picked it up anywhere.'

'Not from Rupert's garden, or his sister's. And there was more—green fibre and footprints. Shoeprints, to be precise. From trainers—not sandals like those you've on you. You'd be surprised what the boffins can do with sole-marks these days. Factory of manufacture, date of manufacture, wear and tear distribution, especially if the wearer leads an active life.' Beresford made a strangled noise in his throat.

'Message received? Good, Mr Beresford. You're a busy man, we're all busy men. So if you don't feel like talking just now, suppose you just show us the shoes you were wearing on Tuesday? If you can't remember which ones, your wife may.'

'No!' Beresford staggered, then let Armstrong help him to a chair. 'Keep Di out of it. She loved the old guy. She'd never forgive me.'

'Forgive?' Armstrong echoed nasally.

The detectives sat down. Beresford stared at them dully, his eyes drifting from one face to the other.

'I didn't kill him, you know. As God's my witness, I'd nothing to do with his death.'

'No?' Armstrong challenged. 'Because whoever drove him to it made him mop the garage to cover their tracks. Which might mean they'd something mucky on their feet.'

'Swear I'd nothing to do—'

'All right, then,' Baxter cut in. 'Tell us what you did do.'

Beresford scratched his hairline, viciously this time. 'Promise me this won't get back to Di.'

Baxter shook his head. 'We can't—you know we can't. But it'll go harder with you and her and the business if you hold out on us. Think of it. Interview after interview. Police cars at your door day after day. Round-the-clock surveillance. I'm not a quitter, Mr Beresford.'

A long silence. 'All right,' he said at last. 'I went back to the bloody cottage. But not to kill, not even to steal. Oh, maybe it would count as stealing in the law books. But I went to retrieve what was mine by rights, mine and Di's. The £500 cheque she'd talked me into parting with to a man who'd no need of it.'

'No need?' Baxter's eye caught Armstrong's. 'Why'd you say that?'

'Rupert had his state pension, hadn't he? I'm prepared to bet his sister didn't charge him rent. Besides, he'd plenty of well-heeled friends. Nipped off abroad most winters for a cheapo fortnight in the villa of one old pal or another. People like that don't need handouts from the likes of me.'

'You didn't take to him?'

'Truth to tell, no. Fair do's, he taught me a lot. But there was something. I dunno . . . Partly it was the Cambridge University connection, I guess. I'm a Cockney by birth, myself. When Rupert and Di and Di's people got talking about the college gardens and college fellows, I felt pushed out, know what I mean?'

Baxter nodded. 'When did you decide to make a return visit?'

'Before the first. Early hours of Tuesday morning, when I was trying to get some shuteye.'

'And what time did you get there?'

'Twenty after midnight or thereabouts. Later than I'd intended. I'd rung Di to say I'd met a friend in a pub, which was true. Meant to do the job soon as I split with him at eleven—knew Rupert was an early-to-bedder. Hadn't reckoned with Eve's party. Heard the racket from the service road. So I beat a retreat, walked the streets for an hour or more.

'Nobody in sight when I got back. It was nearly dark, bit of a moon but cloudy. Could just about read the notice on Rupert's door when I came close. Shook me up a bit, might have put me off in my right mind. But I was woosy. Not drunk, but not reacting too fast.

'I'd no problem getting in. Sash window squeaked, but not badly. Rupert's hearing wasn't a hundred per cent. I went for the cheque first thing. Tore it into scraps, shoved the scraps in my hip wallet. That cheque was flaming well asking to be pinched, the way he'd left it on the desk beside the print.'

'Anything else out of order?'

'Not so's I noticed, but, mind, I wasn't noticing too well. Plus I'm not sure how Rupert usually kept his place. You could count the number of times I'd been there on one hand. Table in the window was laid for a meal, that I do remember. I messed things up a bit, quietly, so's not to wake him. Oh Christ. If I'd known, if I'd had any idea . . . I wasn't too keen on the old boy, but I'm not a vulture, so help me. I couldn't bear for Di to think I'd been robbing the dead.' His strong face puckered.

'You messed things up,' Baxter repeated coldly. 'How exactly?'

Beresford shook his head. 'Sorry. Can't remember any details. I was muzzy, like I said. Plus I was beginning to be scared. Plus I'd the runs. Nerves, I guess. All in all, I wasn't concentrating any too well. Scattered some books and papers on the floor, as I recall. Upended a standard lamp.'

'And then?'

'Went upstairs. Last thing I intended, but I was desperate for a loo. No sound from either of the bedrooms as I went past. It was only afterwards, when I was coming out of the bathroom, that I registered there should have been breathing.

'Then I remembered the DON'T DISTURB notice and I really got the wind up, convinced myself that the old guy had overdosed or something. The door of one of the bedrooms—the spare room, I guess—was ajar. I wriggled inside. Bed wasn't even made up.'

Beresford paused to scratch fiercely, drawing blood from his temple.

'The other bedroom door was shut. I listened again, just to make sure. I'm not a religious man, but I kept praying I wasn't going to find his body, not after what I'd done downstairs. And when I didn't, I couldn't get out of the place fast enough. The garage never entered my head until I was half way home. Too late, I reckoned. Besides, I didn't want to get involved, you see.'

'No? Who saw you leave?' Baxter asked sharply.

Beresford flared up again. 'Bastard that put you on to me, of course. All this peat business was so much crap, wasn't it?'

'On the contrary, Mr Beresford,' Baxter said wearily. '*You* put me onto *him*. "If anyone's told you different, he needs his head examining." I somehow don't think you're in the habit of hypothesizing. But if I were in your position, I'd be bloody glad of any witness I could find, sane or potty.'

'Witness? The more I think about it, the more I'm convinced that drunken sod had a hand in Rupert's death. Murderers return to the scene of crime, don't they?'

'Not if they read crime fiction,' Baxter said drily.

'No? Well, you'll not believe me, but I had it in mind to tip you off, anonymously of course.'

'Where was it you ran into this guy?' Armstrong sounded disbelieving.

'In Rupert's garden—took a header over his legs. Sticking out from behind some lavender bushes, they were. For a sec I thought he was Rupert. Hadn't been there when I entered the cottage, that's for sure.'

'What'd he look like?' Armstrong persisted.

'Oh, I don't know. Light wasn't good, remember, and I didn't see him standing. He just sat up after he'd sent me sprawling, gave me the once-over. Fiftyish, broad, around six feet tall, I'd guess. Not bad-looking for his age, but nothing special that I can remember, except for the scar on his forehead. V-shaped, it was. About here.' Beresford's forefinger hovered an inch above his right eyebrow.

'Clothes?' Armstrong prompted.

'Greenish safari suit. Shabby, but clean. Too clean for a wino.'

'Speaking voice?'

'Wouldn't know. Didn't stop for a chat. He came out with something incoherent when I made contact. When he saw me, he just laughed. And when I made off he started singing.'

'Singing what?'

'God knows. Nothing from Top of the Pops, that's for sure. Trad folk, you might class it. Bloke's voice was slurry. Only words I caught were "Stourbridge Fair".'

'Give us the tune?'

Beresford, still sweating, made an unmelodious effort to comply.

'Stou-erbridge Fai-ai-air, Stou-erbridge—'

'Like a hand with the new bumf?' Armstrong offered.

Baxter interrupted his search for a half-remembered song to contemplate the latest additions to his in-tray.

'Let's have the life and times of Drinkwater aka Dunnett.
Assuming the national network did its stuff.'

Armstrong abstracted the printout, which was easily the
bulkiest item in the in-tray.

Baxter skimmed its pages rapidly, then returned to the
beginning. 'Want you and Wendy to read, mark and
inwardly digest our Simon's criminal record, before I tackle
the ACC on the subject. What I'm after more immediately
is any legitimate link with the county.'

'Right.' Armstrong, mug in hand, came behind the desk
to squint over his shoulder.

Baxter read aloud: 'Mm. Born 'forty-three, Bourne-
mouth. Only kid. Father in the Parachute Regiment, killed
at Arnhem. Educated Stonecrop House, Keswick, then
Eton and Balliol College, Oxford. Unmarried. Not doing
too well, are we?'

'Stonecrop House . . . Pure coincidence, I dare say. But,
according to the piece about Rupert Parsingham's retirement in the local paper, that's the prep school he used to
teach in.'

'My God. Might mean nothing as you say, Bill. But all
the same, if their dates should overlap . . . Ring the school,
will you, Wendy?' Whatever the outcome, Baxter felt sure
that Drinkwater hadn't been the drunk in Rupert's garden.
Beresford couldn't have failed to register those pointed
eyebrows.

Armstrong left the office and Baxter began to read the
statements so far collected from guests at Eve Parsingham
Wells's party, his daughter's among them. *Stou-erbridge Fai-
air, Stou-erbridge Fai-air.* The jack o'lantern phrase danced
enticingly between the lines of print.

CHAPTER 13

'Stou-ourbridge Fai-air.' Baxter tried it on Sarah. As she was going on to *Spin City* they had met for an early supper in Cambridge, in a basement restaurant off King's Parade.

'Pity you can't sing in tune, love. Does it go on like this?' She hummed a slightly extended version between mouthfuls of asparagus crêpe.

'Yes, yes. What is it?'

'Something Emma's got on tape, that's all I know. Could even be in the show. Pop round with me and ask her before curtain-up if it's important.'

Emma again. Now her mother was dragging her into the case. 'Not that important. Tell me about your day.'

'Par for the course this morning. Two barneys with stroppy patients, three with hospital administrators. Odd sort of phone call this afternoon, though. From Sylvia Straker.'

'Have I met Sylvia Straker?'

'Probably not. Hon. Sec. to the Horticultural Society. She missed last night's talk and rang to check the agenda for tomorrow's committee meeting. Level-headed type, I'd have said. But she told me the oddest thing . . .' Sarah fortified herself with Liebfraumilch.

'Apparently Sylvia and her husband arrived home from holiday about three weeks ago in the early hours of the morning. Twenty-four hours early—weather had been lousy. They'd just turned into their side road—they're way out in the Fens and there are no other houses for miles—when they saw Rupert Parsingham's brown station-wagon coming towards them. At least, Sylvia was sure it was Rupert, and hooted. No reply, so she thought she might have been mistaken.

'But next morning, when she was catching up on her garden chores, she noticed that someone had fixed the windshield round their daphne bush. Neighbour's puppy had trampled it before they went on holiday. Rather sweet, don't you think?'

'Habits of immature canines?'

'Not funny. Sweet of poor Rupert to say a quiet goodbye to a garden he'd done so much for.'

'Can we be sure he did?'

'Sylvia never tackled him on the subject—so as not to embarrass him, she says. But how else would you explain it?'

Baxter shook his head. 'Sorry, love. Not up to explaining much this evening—maybe a strawberry ice will help.'

It didn't, and he was only half way through when Sarah checked her watch, shook crumbs off her swirly yellow dress and kissed him goodbye.

Ten minutes later he was back at his office desk, when his phone rang.

'Chief Inspector Baxter? Dolores Finchley.' Her voice was light and lilting, the accent faintly North American.

'Ah, good. Did you get my message?'

'Message?'

He quoted the number that her husband had provided and Wendy had rung. 'Oh no. Haven't been in touch with that Centre for weeks. They wouldn't have known where to contact me. I rang because of Rupert—when I got over the first shock. Not that I can be of much help, but I saw him the day he died. His sister will have told you?'

'Yes.'

'Poor Eve—I'd hate her to think I'd held back anything that might help you track the killer.'

'Can you come to Cambridge tonight—tomorrow?'

'I thought . . . can't we just talk on the phone?'

'I really need to see you, Mrs Finchley, and I'd like a colleague to be there. Make it London, if you prefer.'

'And if I refuse?'

'We should make every effort to find you—with the help of the Met.'

'I see. Very well.' She sounded tired. 'As Eve might say, there are better ways of spending public money.'

She gave him the address of a delicatessen near Lancaster Gate, and promised to be there between ten forty-five and eleven next morning. 'Someone's told you I'm a Filipina, I expect?'

'Yes.'

She laughed. A little bitterly, but only a little.

He pushed papers for another hour-and-a-half, breaking off every so often to breathe down the necks of the skeleton staff in the incident room. His spirits lifted as an audio-typist's screen filled with a report of a Damien Ronson sighting in the city. Then he realized it had occurred forty-eight hours before. Time to go home. He was half way there when he was radioed.

'Mr Philip Beresford—had to be you, he said, sir.' The duty sergeant sounded nervous.

'OK, OK.' Baxter turned down Mozart's Coronation Mass.

'Look, I hope you don't mind . . .' Beresford began.

Baxter heard or thought he heard accompanying scratch-ings. 'I'm off duty, actually. So if you want to change your statement—' More bloody paperwork?

'No, it's not that. I've just seen that bloke I told you about. Drunk I fell over in Rupert's garden.'

'Yeah? Where?' Baxter braked, eased on to the verge and prepared for a U-turn.

'On the box. Local programme called Eastwave that our girl watches. Arty-farty stuff—not my line.'

'Go on!'

'When I woke up from a kip, there was this bloke plugging some show—*Sin City*—that his son's connected with. Then he got in a few cracks about Cambridge nobs and snobs. My bread and butter, but I had to laugh. Anyway, it was the same fella. Thin lips, scar on the forehead. Same sort of voice, though he wasn't singing on the box—'

'Name? Did you get his name?' Baxter asked wearily.

'Sinton, Clive Sinton. That's S-i-n-t-o-n, I guess.'

'Sounds plausible. Keep this to yourself for the time being, will you? Thanks, Mr Beresford, and good night.' He passed back the word to the incident room and reactivated Mozart.

Clive Sinton. Clive chip-on-the-shoulder Sinton by the sound of him. Paul's father, Emma's Paul's father. And later, when Sarah and Emma came home, Baxter learnt that the song he'd been singing was indeed from the show that he thought of as his daughter's. Bloody cheek.

Not that he'd disclosed the reason for the question. Try as they might, Sinton and his like weren't going to involve Emma in a murder case.

He slept better than the night before, courtesy of Mogadon. He dreamt, as he often did in the early stages of an investigation, of eel-like creatures tangling in a murky pool. One of them was trying to swallow Alma Thurstone's Liver bird.

'DCI Baxter?' Dolores Finchley had materialized in the doorway of the Kensington delicatessen. He and Wendy Powers showed their IDs.

Dolores nodded. 'I thought we might talk in the Gardens—or a restaurant if you prefer. My friends here are pushed for space, I'm afraid.'

His brief survey of the thousand-and-one types of foodstuff crammed on to the narrow shelves inclined Baxter to believe her. 'The Gardens would be nice,' he said.

He had taken Emma to sail her toy boats on the Round Pond on occasional long-ago Sundays, but he couldn't think when he had last used this Lancaster Gate entrance.

'There's a seat down this way I often use when I'm talking to people,' Dolores said, as they skirted the fountains of Long Water. 'It's usually quiet.'

'People—clients, do you mean?' Baxter prompted.

'Just people—we're a mutual befriending network, there's no them and us. But you're here to ask about Rupert, aren't you?' Physically, she looked completely at ease in her black-and-brown cotton shift, with her black hair tied up in a hot-weather style. And mentally? She might well be a tough customer. Baxter decided to postpone serious questioning until Powers had her notebook at the ready.

They walked three abreast. As they drew level with the bronze figure of Peter Pan, Dolores halted. 'First time I saw that statue was when Rupert brought me. He'd loved it since childhood.' She spoke gently.

'And you?'

She pulled a face. 'Can't say I'm enamoured of its base. Look! All those grovelling little women and animals. Not a male rival to Peter among them. A little boy's fantasy. Rupert empathized with little boys. Not that he approved of them running wild. Eve's lodgers' kids brought out the schoolmaster in him.'

The detectives exchanged glances.

'Did Mr Parsingham ever talk of his teaching days? Mention any of his pupils by name?' Baxter asked, when they had laid claim to a bench overlooking the water.

Dolores frowned. 'Occasionally, but I doubt if I'd remember.'

'Drinkwater ring a bell—Simon Drinkwater?'

'No—oh, wait. That might have been the name of the boy he taught to conjure. Who turned to crime later on. Rupert felt responsible, I think.'

'Sounds like the one.' Baxter tried to make it casual. 'Did they have any contact after Drinkwater left school?'

Dolores shook her head. 'Not that I heard of. But Rupert could be reticent about some things—as I can. It didn't stop us being friends. I'll miss him, I'll miss him dreadfully.' She stared unseeing at the waterfowl.

'Tell us about the day he died.'

'What do you want to know?'

'What you talked about—his mood?'

'It was a short visit. Only ten minutes or so. If only . . . but that's foolish. I'd shopping to do, so I asked Rupert if he needed any errands done. He said not. I asked him how he felt—he'd had this virus. He insisted he was OK. He was rather dreading an official retirement visit from Di Beresford of the Garden Centre, he told me. Her husband came instead, I noticed later, when I was in my kitchen. We talked very briefly about me—about my work here and what else I might do. And when he said goodbye he said—' Her voice broke.

'Take your time.' Baxter touched her arm.

'He said . . . one day soon it would be our last goodbye. I said "Not yet, Rupert. Promise." And he promised. So I'm sure, you see, that he didn't kill himself. Not of his own free will.'

'But he had it in mind?'

'Oh yes. Since early May—since he realized he'd have to retire. Though I often wondered, if he hadn't known I was going away . . .'

'Going away?'

'Leaving Cambridge, leaving my husband.'

'How long had Mr Parsingham known that?'

'For nearly five years—since I started my Open University course.'

'In Political Sciences?'

'Yes. Who told you? Eve? Eric?' There was fear in her voice.

'We found an OU document among Mr Parsingham's books.'

'I see. Not that it matters now. I told my husband when I rang him last night. The graduation lists will soon be in the papers. It was just . . . if Rupert had gossiped about that, he might have gossiped about other things.'

'Your relationship, do you mean?'

'My work here, my friends,' she said in a small, cold voice.

'Did Mr Parsingham give you tuition?'

'Goodness, no. Politics were a closed book to Rupert. Didn't pay my fees either, though he offered. I raised the cash by selling patchwork, would you believe? Suitable pastime for a home-based Varsity wife, don't you think? Poor Eric had no idea I was paid for it. I registered from a London address, so that's where the correspondence went. But Rupert encouraged me, provided study cover. He'd a massive collection of botanical slides, partly his, partly inherited, which I catalogued several times over.'

'Why so much secrecy?'

'My husband was totally opposed to the idea. He'd have been quite happy for me to top up my Mod. Langs. degree from Quezon with a Master's at Lucy Cavendish. But a politically minded wife would do him no good in the University, or so he claimed. And, as far as Eric is concerned, his job comes first, second and third. You must think me dishonourable.'

'I didn't say so.'

Dolores smiled wryly. 'You don't have to. I can sympathize with that viewpoint. There should be verbal loyalty between partners even in a marriage of convenience honestly made.'

'Which yours wasn't?'

'Not quite. I met Eric when he came to Manila for a conference. I was a schoolteacher, earning just enough to keep body and soul together if I stayed healthy. There was nothing romantic about his proposal, but that didn't bother me. All I had to show for romance was a bundle of airmail letters from the States and the memory of a botched abortion.'

Wendy Powers made sympathetic noises.

'What interested me was money. My youngest sister wanted to be a doctor. My parents were also teachers, also poor. Eric promised to finance Carmel's medical education. It wasn't a great financial sacrifice. He's a private income in addition to his salary. Nevertheless, I was grateful. He said he wanted desperately to marry, he was heterosexual with no major hang-ups, but he was shy. I promised—I'm a Catholic of sorts—to make him a good wife as long as I lived.'

'But you changed your mind?'

'Yes. Nothing to do with Rupert, whatever Eve may think.'

'No?'

She sighed. 'Five years ago I found out that my husband had a pastime he hadn't told me about. Nothing illegal, nothing offensive to some women, perhaps. But to me, seeing what I've seen on the streets of Olongapo—' Her voice cracked. 'Let's just say I took my future back into my own hands.'

'And enrolled with the Open University?'

'As a means to an end. I'd met many other Filipino immigrants by then, who'd had a far rougher deal than I had, who'd been forced into emigration by poverty. And it wasn't enough for me any longer to dole out the emotional sticking-plaster. I wanted desperately to go back home, to help fight the debt problem, the social injustices, all the causes of that poverty.

'I couldn't go straight away—couldn't cut off Carmel's income while she was still training. She didn't complete her internship until last January. Besides which, I couldn't afford the fare—still can't. So I decided to study while I was waiting.'

'The BA course?'

'Yes. I'd have left Eric and moved up to Town the minute Carmel became independent, but for Rupert. I could see retirement on the horizon months before he did—his eye trouble and arthritis were so much worse. I thought if I hung on for a bit, he'd come to terms with his situation, but it didn't work out that way. I lost patience with him in the end. Started telling him to pull his socks up, count his blessings. All the usual futile platitudes. When a crisis call came for me on Tuesday, I was half glad of the excuse to go.'

'And now you don't intend to go back?'

'Only to collect some clothes some time. I've told Eric, but I don't think it's fully registered. There's a teaching job going begging in Docklands which will see me through my Master's course at Birkbeck, and leave something over for an air fare. I've friends who'll put me up free in exchange for babysitting.'

She bit her lip. 'Odd I should be offloading all this on you. Perhaps it's because my friends here have so much else to cope with. It doesn't seem fair to burden them.'

'Did Mr Parsingham tell you he was planning to kill himself?' Baxter checked.

'Oh yes. Soon after he'd told the Beresfords he was retir-ing. But he promised he'd work out his notice first, and say goodbye to me beforehand. I tried to raise the subject two or three times—tried to talk him out of the idea—but he was quite determined.'

'Was he often depressed these last three months?'

'Often, but not always. Sometimes he seemed rather pleased with himself, almost as though he was up to some schoolboy prank. Also, he'd taken to going out in the van at night.'

'Every night?'

'No. Two or three times some weeks—then not at all for a fortnight or more. But always in the early hours of the morning. My husband never mentioned it, probably wasn't aware. We didn't sleep together in summer. He's allergic to bee-stings, so he has nylon screens on his bedroom windows which make me claustrophobic. From the room I was using at the back of the house I could hear Rupert's comings and goings quite distinctly.'

Baxter made a hasty reappraisal of Sylvia Straker. 'Did you raise the subject with him?'

'No. I half hoped that he'd found himself a lover, someone who'd fill the emotional void when I'd gone. But it seemed a weird schedule for septuagenarian love-making.'

'Indeed. Did he ever say anything to you about a will?'

'Not as such. But he told me there was money he wanted me to have—a nest-egg to fall back on during my MA course or to pay my fare home afterwards. His savings, I suppose.' Dolores looked and sounded as though she meant what she said. 'I was embarrassed—kept telling him I didn't want it, that I'd rather he gave it to Eve to help with her roof repairs.'

'Let's go back to last Tuesday. Did Mr Parsingham have visitors other than Mr Beresford and yourself?'

Dolores frowned. 'He said Eve had been in early that morning, but I didn't actually see her. I did notice Valerie Gates, Eric's secretary at the Institute, coming out of his

garden gate late in the afternoon. Four-thirty or thereabouts.'

'After the DON'T DISTURB notice went up?'

'Yes, it must have been.'

'Was she a frequent visitor?'

'No, but Eve, for all her Radical leanings, is inclined to
regard the Institute staff as her personal servants. I wondered if she'd asked Valerie to run an errand for Rupert,
collect a prescription perhaps.'

Or return a photocopy? 'Anyone else?'

Dolores hesitated. 'No.'

'Tell us how you spent Tuesday evening, if you will,
between five and seven.'

'Me? But you can't—Of course you can. Sorry.' She fixed
her eyes on the waterfowl. 'I'd been in the kitchen for at
least an hour before my husband came home shortly after
five. I went upstairs to bath and change while he was in
his study.'

'See him again when you came down?'

Another hesitation. 'No. He'd . . . he'd said he was going
for a swim before returning to the Institute.'

'I see. What next?'

'I loaded our car with the party food I'd prepared and
transported it to Plumtrees. Eve had rung me in a last-
minute flap about drink. Hadn't ordered nearly enough,
she'd decided. Asked me to buy in extra supplies from a
downtown off-licence and the Milton Tesco's.'

'*And* not *or*?' Wendy Powers checked.

'Yes. To take advantage of two special offers she'd read
about. I obeyed. Crossly, but I obeyed. Left about six, at
a guess. Back around a quarter to seven. Drove straight to
Plumtrees. Stayed there until after the party.'

'I don't think she told us the whole truth,' Wendy Powers
said when the detectives were alone. 'I reckon she was
shielding someone.'

'Her husband, most likely.'

'Whom she's leaving? Why? From fear? Or guilt?'

'Or a sense of fair play? Not a British prerogative, Sergeant.'

'No, sir.' She watched him unwrap a sodamint.

CHAPTER 14

'Allow me, Chief Inspector.' The WPC whose filing system Baxter had slighted held open the main door of Cambridge District HQ. He sidled in, his arms braced beneath a carton that he steadied with his chin.

'Mr Baxter? Mr Armstrong led us to believe you'd be back rather sooner.' His path was blocked by a short middle-aged woman in a grey pinafore dress.

'Really, Ms—'

'Sister Immaculata.' In swerving to avoid her, Baxter almost dropped his burden, but achieved an emergency landing on the reception counter. 'Mrs Parsingham Wells's daughter,' the nun elaborated. 'This is Damien Ronson,' she added with a light tap on her crucifix. 'Been in the wars, as you see. Promised I'd ferry him back to keep Mother happy, but I've other errands. When will you have finished with him?'

Damien advanced, pale in the gaps between his facial tattoos. He wore a faded Grateful Dead T-shirt and parti-coloured shorts, and his left arm and leg were in plaster. 'Like I told you, Sis, there's no call for that. Not with the rafts of fancy wheels that's parked round the back here. Shan't hold out for the Merc this time round, Mr B. Ride in a posh Porshe'd do me nicely.'

Baxter unwrapped a sodamint. 'We'll take over, Sister. Find us an interviewing room, would you, Sergeant?'

Powers and he exchanged frustrated grimaces. On the way back from Town she had argued for an early assault on Eric Finchley. But Valerie Gates took precedence in Baxter's list of priorities.

He had just transferred his package to the desk in his temporary office when Bill Armstrong chucked the second spanner of the afternoon. 'Sarah's just off the phone. Like you to ring her back at the Health Centre.'

Apocalyptic scenarios flashed in fast-forward. Sarah hardly ever called him at work.

In half a minute they put him through. Her 'hi' sounded unruffled, but she'd been trained to sound unruffled.

'Hi, love. Something wrong?'

'Nothing domestic, if that's what you had in mind. It's just—oh hell, maybe I'm wasting your time.'

'Try me.'

'One sec.' As she took a reassuring farewell of a patient, he opened the carton with his free hand. The miniature chest-of-drawers gleamed darkly in its nest. 'Right,' she went on. 'I'd a Horticultural Society committee this morning—remember?'

'Mm-hm.' He'd forgotten.

'Well, over coffee everyone was talking about Rupert— he was one of our show judges.'

'Mm.'

'Sylvia Straker went through her spiel, which caused a bit of a stir, as you can imagine.'

'Easily.' Sensations were rare and prized commodities in Holtchester horticultural circles. Baxter accepted a mug of tea from Armstrong and gestured an invitation to inspect the chest-of-drawers.

'Then Barton Yarwood got in on the act. Remember old Barton? Dog-breeder, Desert Rat as was.'

'Who won the Battle of Alamein single-handed?'

'The same. But reliable in other respects, I'd have said.

Anyhow, he's troubled by insomnia, and around three on Wednesday morning he went downstairs to raid the fridge. Spotted something moving in his garden from the kitchen window. Or someone. Too big for a dog, he reckoned, but he's shortsighted. Doubled back upstairs for his specs and stick he keeps in his bedroom just in case. Heard an engine revving on his way down. His first thought was for his prize begonias, but they were all quote present and correct unquote. Only puzzle was the mulch layer around his *Eleagnus pungens*. Been meaning to top it up for weeks, he said. Looked like someone else had done the job.'

'Wednesday morning? You're sure he said Wednesday?'

'Shouldn't have rung you otherwise. Sylvia Straker's convinced it was Rupert's ghost, but that didn't wash with Barton. Some weirdo, he reckons. He's talking of keeping a night-watch in his greenhouse.'

Baxter heard distant knockings. 'Come in, please,' he called out over his shoulder.

'That's it, love. Over to you.'

'Got Yarwood's phone number on you?'

She supplied it.

'Thanks, sweetie. Thanks for everything.'

Armstrong answered the intercom. 'Wendy's got Ronson in Room D. Ready when you are.'

'Not yet. Tell her to read his palm or something.' Baxter was trying to contact the Assistant Chief Constable.

Littleton was less than enthused by his narrative and his proposal. 'Hm-hm. I don't know, I really don't know, Baxter. Suggestion's a powerful thing. One dotty old dear comes up with a cock-and-bull story, second old dear follows suit. Yarwood sounds the type who wouldn't care to be upstaged by a woman . . . No. Hm-hm no. You can't seriously expect me to make representations to the Met on his say-so.'

'No, sir. But I should like to make a suggestion.'

Several dozen throat-clearings later, the ACC gave it his grudging agreement.

Baxter joined Wendy Powers and Damien Ronson in the interview room.

'Lost quarts of the red stuff over that little lot. On my tenth life, the doc said. Two years ago, that was.' Damien, his left sleeve rolled up to display a jagged scar, had evidently been treating Wendy to his surgical history. ''Lo, mate.' He grinned at Baxter.

'Chief Inspector, Mr Baxter. Take your pick.'

'Pardon me—lost the habit. Blame it on old Eve and the Plumtrees mob. Dead against handles, they was.'

'Was?'

'Skived, ain't they? Left the old b. in the lurch.'

'As the pot might have said to the kettle.'

'You got it wrong, Mr B. Don't class me with them effing arse-lickers. Never had no intention of staying away for good. Always had a soft spot for the old doll—take more than that argy-bargy at the House Meeting to put me off her. Why else do you think I'm here?'

'Because the good sister took you in charge?'

'Come off it—rang Eve from Addenbrooke's this morning soon as I could hobble to a phone. Guy in the next bed passed me his paper to read, which was the first I knew about Rupert. Been out of touch these last few weeks, you see. Some bastard nicked my radio.'

Possible if not probable. Better let it go for now. 'Eve got Sister Maccy to pick me up when they discharged me and run me over to Plumtrees. Then she put me wise about the trike job. News to me, as God's my witness, but she kept on till I promised to tell you so in person.'

'Thanks.'

'You know who dunnit?'

'Not yet. Any ideas?'

' 'S 'matter of fact I do. Not hard evidence, mind. What you might call an intelligent guess.'

'I might call it time-wasting, Ronson, if you don't come to the point soonish.'

'Remember Matt Vickery? Wino that drowned hisself in the Cam a few weeks back?'

'Inspector Armstrong will.'

'Funny old prat. Didn't get on with the other bums. His first summer in Cambridge—wouldn't help, I suppose. 'Sides, he acted stand-offish. Hung out with the Milton Man mostly when he was sober.'

'Milton Man?' Powers echoed. Baxter wished she hadn't. Attention was obviously meat and drink to young Ronson. Accidental-on-purpose injury was one of his chosen baits: fantasizing might well be another.

'Geezer that spouts poetry in the Market Square— dead ringer for Jimmy Savile with this great buckled hat on.'

'Let's get back to Vickery and the tricycle, shall we?' Baxter suggested wearily.

'OK, OK, guv.' Damien's one mobile arm gestured surrender. 'Lady copper asks me a question—I answer up, that's all. When old Vickery was hitting the bottle hard, the Milton Man didn't want to know, right? Bad for trade, I guess. So Matt would make off with his booze to Midsummer Common or Jesus Green or Alexandra Gardens, if he could make it up the hill. I've seen him many a time, hanging on to the railings on Chesterton Lane or sitting on the wall outside the DHSS, bracing himself for the climb.'

Damien paused briefly, staring into the middle distance.

'Matt was outside the DHSS one day when I came out after some hassle or other. Crouching on the wall, as per usual. Taking no notice of nothing except the Johnnie Walker he was clutching like an effing hot-water bottle. Then wham! Leapt to his feet like he'd been electrocuted.

Bloody near dropped the booze. Just stood there, cursing under his breath and staring.

'So I looked where he was looking, natch. It was Eve, would you believe, riding by on the old trike.'

'Oh, come on. Bloke was drunk, you say. Even if he stared at Mrs PW, who knows what he saw? Pink elephant, like as not.'

'But that wasn't all. Day or so after—around five one evening, it'd be—he showed up in the service road back of Plumtrees. Eve wasn't there but the trike was, not for the first time. Her memory's going, you know. She'll pop into the house, meaning to take a few minutes, and get stuck into something for hours on end. Anyhow, there was the trike and there was old Matt on his hands and knees working out how many Johnnie Walkers it was good for. Or so I thought.

'Couldn't have been more than a week later that the brakes was cut, if Eve's right in what she told me this morning. But I wasn't to know anything about that at the time, was I?'

Baxter grunted non-committally.

'Bawled Vickery out—wheeled the trike into the garden—gave Eve a talking-to for leaving it around. What else could I do, Chief Inspector?'

'What you can do now, Ronson, is to fill us in on your whereabouts since you left Plumtrees.'

'Every hour of every day?' Damien traced a snake tattoo on his forehead with a ringed forefinger.

'First thirty-six hours, for starters.'

A broken-toothed smile. 'You're in luck, Chief Inspector. They was special, them days. Half my life's a closed book to me. Got this blanking-out syndrome—honest. It's all there on my record. One of the Youth Custody shrinks wrote me up in a thesis.'

'Now look here—'

'OK, OK. Don't get the knickers in a twist, guv. Left Plumtrees half an hour after that effing House Meeting. Van was low on juice, I was low on bread. So I headed for the Square and Tassel in hopes of a free jar. Which is where I met Rosa and her girlfriend.'

'Rosa what?' Powers checked.

'Corelli. Eye-tye language student—New Way College if you're interested. Rolex watch, Gucci handbag, but no current nightlife. No wonder. Ninety per cent of those language school kids is birds. Someone somewhere gets their sums wrong, wouldn't you say, Mr B.'

Baxter growled.

'OK, OK. Gist is, I spent the next couple of nights at Rosa's pad. Scruffy dump off Milton Road, not her style, but the landlady was away for a week . . .'

'Address?'

'Slipped my mind, but I could take you there easy. Better still, take the Sarge.' Tattoos twitched as he waggled his eyebrows in Wendy's direction.

'Go on,' Baxter said.

'High-class cook, that kid. Didn't need much tuition in the other thing, either. Don't suppose I'm the type Mamma Mia would go for—maybe that was an added attraction. Then Rosa's Eye-Tye boyfriend phoned to say he was flying over. Kid panicked. Gave me my petrol money and a stack of pizzas. I upped sticks for Fenport.'

'To work in the brickyard?'

'Which I did for a week. Then they started laying people off. So after a while I headed back for Cambridge.'

'The day Rupert Parsingham died?'

'Day before, actually. Ran into a bunch of folk singers I'd met at Plumtrees. They'd come early for the Cherry Hinton Folk Festival—was milking the tourist mobs downtown in the meantime. Hung out with them that day and the next—food was OK if you don't mind vegetarian.'

'You were with them all that time?'

'All the time you'll be interested in, guv. Tuesday afternoon, Tuesday evening we was stuck like limpets. Ran them over to the Fen Skaters, far side of Midsummer Common, for a Folk Club night. By eleven I'd had it up to here with *Dirty Old Town* and the rest. So I thought, why not get a breath of fresh air, why not see how old Eve is getting on?'

'Not old Rupert?'

'' 'Course not. Never had anything against the poor bugger, but never had much to do with him, either. Headed straight for Plumtrees. Was a bit fazed by the fancy lights— Eve didn't go much for entertaining. But I thought maybe if she was in the party mood she'd be ready to let bygones be bygones.

'Which she might, if her Yankee lodger, that Stacey, hadn't muscled in. Wheeling Eve's trike, she was. All of a sudden she let it go, grabbed hold of me, called me a filthy little murderer.'

'And you ran?'

'OK, I ran. Daft, you're thinking, but I'd a few pints inside me. When I heard "murderer" and saw the trike I remembered the way Matt Vickery had looked when Eve was riding it. And I thought, Oh Christ, she's dead. Some other old soak has done for her. And they'll blame me, Stacey and the rest. Comes second nature to their sort to blame me. So I scarpered.

'Drove the van out the Holtchester Road, blew what remained of my last Social handout on a bottle of vodka at a service station, parked on some waste land I knew about. Conservation area, the notice says, but nobody does any conserving outside weekends far as I can see. Ideal location for a spot of off-the-record nookey, Sarge—'

'Ronson!' Baxter heard himself shout. Powers raised an amused eyebrow. Amused by Ronson? By him?

'That's about it, guv. Stay off the vodka as a rule, so it

works a treat when I need it. Spun it out until yesterday
evening. My head hurt, of course, but I was thinking positive. Ever find a headache does that for you, guv? Focuses
you, sort of?'

Baxter growled.

'I mapped it all out. First I'd line my stomach, then I'd
find out what happened to Eve, then I'd go to the fuzz and
tell them I hadn't done it, whatever that crazed chick
Stacey had tried to put across. Veggie food's OK, but I
really fancied Rosa's Bolognese and a little TLC, so, just
on the offchance, I tried the Square and Tassel. There she
was—on her tod, as I thought, in this grey-and-white mini
dress. Nothing fancy, but it brought up her tan—'

Baxter tried counting ten backwards. Forwards wasn't
working any longer.

'Sight of me shook her up too. I could tell. She mumbled
something I couldn't make out. Next thing, she was staring
over my shoulder and someone was grabbing me. Then she
started talking Italian to this bloke—he'd been in the
Gents, I guess. Started crying.

'Talk about community spirit, guv! That Eye-Tye bastard—six six with muscles to match—strong-armed me out
of that bar, bloody near strangling me in the process, and
nobody took a blind bit of notice. Finished off by kicking
me down the steps outside, which did for my shoulder. Be
there now, I dare say, if some crumblies hadn't come out
of a Bingo session opposite.'

Baxter despatched Damien five minutes later by standard issue Vauxhall, not before checking Armstrong's
recollections of the late Matt Vickery. It had been an acci-
dental drowning. The coroner had had no doubts, nor had
the multinational clutch of passive onlookers or the two
Swedes who had attempted a rescue. Archibald Shanks, aka
the Milton Man, had identified the body. Leaving Wendy
Powers to extract anything else of interest from the Vickery

file, and Armstrong to track down Shanks, Baxter turned his attention to his in-tray.

He couldn't settle, his resentment of time wasted on and by Damien remaining to distract him. Tea might help. No harm in a quick shuteye while the kettle was coming to the boil. It boiled. It switched itself off. Next thing he knew, Armstrong was at his elbow.

> 'From morn
> To noon he fell, from noon to dewy eve,
> A summer's day.

Old boy knew how to write, didn't he?'

'What the hell!'

'Milton. *Paradise Lost*. Didn't they make you learn hunks of it at your school? Came back to me the minute I heard Shanks. Not that he put it over the way our English teacher did—touch of the Cockney. But all the same. With an Oliver Cromwell hat and a cloak and a Jimmy Savile wig, he could make it quite creepy. Tourists were lapping it up. No wonder he wouldn't take much time out for me.'

'Enough?'

'I reckon. You're going to like this. Old Eve's going to like it.'

'Well?'

'Vickery was ex-civil service, like Shanks. Which is why Archie felt sorry for him, he says. Been on his uppers himself before he hit on the Milton thing. Father played the Northern clubs—memory man act. Taught Archie the tricks of the trade, so he knew memorizing wouldn't be a problem. Then he saw that little Irish chap who used to spout Shakespeare—'

'Vickery,' Baxter interrupted. 'For God's sake, Bill, concentrate on Vickery.'

'Getting there,' Armstrong said coldly. 'Archie nagged

him to build on his skills the way he had. Go in for wood-carving or something else in the craft line. Matt could do anything with his hands, apparently.'

'Ah!'

'Thought you'd like that one. Matt had a skill, but he also had a gripe. Variation on a popular theme. A stretch twenty-odd years ago that had sent him on the downward spiral, or so he wanted to believe. And the old lady who had dished the gravy—in Guildford. Guildford, Surrey, please note.'

'Pass.'

'Three weeks before he drowned, Matt butted in on one of Archie's performances to announce that he'd just seen the magistrate who'd done him down. Archie didn't attend to the details. He wasn't best pleased about the loss of trade. Besides, Matt was sloshed. But he's sure Archie said the old girl was riding a trike. On Chesterton Lane. Geddit?'

'Eve?'

'Supposing her to be Cousin Esther.'

'Of course. Fancy a cuppa, Bill?'

'Any chocolate digestives?'

'For those we go through channels.' Baxter rang the incident room.

CHAPTER 15

'There you are, sir. And there.' Wendy Powers's forefinger stabbed twice at the inventory of items found in the drowned man's pockets. Stashed among his box of matches, six dog-ends, sixty-seven pence, Social Security payments book, St Christopher medal, nylon pak-a-mak and *Playboy* centrefold, Vickery had carried a penknife and a length of insulating tape. 'Pretty strong evidence, wouldn't you say? Pity it's only circumstantial.'

'Thanks to Eve,' Armstrong lamented. 'If she hadn't been so damn quick to chuck the cut brakes.'

'What does it matter?' Baxter soothed. 'The late lamented can't stand trial. We've confirmation that Esther Parsingham sent him down at Guildford in 'sixty-eight. There's enough in my estimation to put our live suspects in the clear. Eve's safe. Let's break the good news to her, Wendy, before we tackle Valerie Gates. Any problems about getting Valerie's home address?'

'Not really. She sounded nervous when I rang, but she was obviously relieved that we didn't want to interview her at the Institute. I don't think somehow that she'll alert Finchley.'

'Let's hope you're right. How d'you feel about a night shift, Bill?'

'Yeah, sure.' Armstrong sounded less than eager.

'But what?'

'But nothing. It's just . . . well. It's Gran-in-law's last night, and Maureen says she's moved on to colcannon. Lovely grub, that. Cabbages, spuds, lashings of butter—'

'Take your word.' Baxter's ulcer had lodged a token pro-test. 'After supper would be fine. What I had in mind was a horticultural job half a mile from your place. The item I cleared with the ACC earlier on.'

'Oh right, fine. Nice tie-in, if it works.' Armstrong agreed, native caution tempering his optimism. Baxter outlined the project and its rationale for Powers's benefit.

Her response was less inhibited. 'Cripes, guv!' Then an afterthought: 'Doesn't the Chief Constable belong to the Horticultural Association? Wouldn't it be a hoot if—'

'Three hoots,' Baxter agreed. 'But Montgomery wouldn't see the joke, I fancy.'

*

'It's the money, isn't it?' Valerie Gates paused just inside the door of her living-room. 'It's all here, you know. Never touched. Four hundred.' She went to a writing bureau by the window and retrieved a sealed, stamped foolscap envelope addressed to Rupert Parsingham.

'It was a present—whatever you may think. Just a present. Mr Parsingham wanted to show his gratitude, he said. I refused at first, but he was most insistent. In the end I took it to please him.'

Baxter nodded. 'Why don't we all sit down, Mrs Gates?'

'Yes, yes, I'm sorry.' Valerie tugged at the peplum of her tight tan two-piece. The same tan as the dralon sofa cover, perhaps, before time had faded it.

'Odd sort of sum, four hundred,' Baxter said, accepting the envelope.

'He offered me five to begin with—he'd these bundles of notes in his desk drawer, but you'll know that. He kept on and on. Hadn't much longer to live, he said. Token of appreciation, he said, for all I'd done for the Institute. In the end I gave in, just to keep him happy.

'Wouldn't take the five, but there was a suite in Eaden Lilley's sale that my fiancé and I coveted. Four hundred more than we could afford, so I took that. Didn't think how it would look. Norman—my fiancé—hit the roof Tuesday evening when I told him. Especially when he heard about the other cash in the drawer. Tax evasion or worse, Norman reckoned. He's a job at the Guildhall, so he can't afford to be mixed up in anything iffy.

'I promised to post it back first thing Wednesday, and I meant to. Truly. Told Norman I had. But somehow, I couldn't bring myself. Then the news came through about the old boy's death. And I thought, well, it's not like he's going to get any good out of it. My Norman's worked hard half a lifetime, without much to show for it. I wanted to make this place nice for us, that's all. What's wrong with that, eh? Tell me what's wrong with that!'

Valerie dabbed brimming eyes with a small embroidered handkerchief. 'How'd you find out? Did he tell his sister before he copped it?'

Baxter shook his head. 'Someone saw you leaving the cottage.'

'Oh no!' Valerie's orange-tipped fingers flew to her mouth. 'So I needn't . . . you didn't know. Oh, bloody hell.' She hugged herself, rocking. 'Yes, I'd have kept the cash, spent it on this and that. Little gadgets, fuel bills, holidays. Norman would never have guessed. Is that so terrible? What happens to it now?'

'That'll depend on how Mr Parsingham came by it. Did he throw any light on the subject?'

''Course not. Never dreamt of asking. Old people hoard money all the time, don't they? Never entered my head there could be anything fishy, not until Norman said . . . He needn't ever know, need he? He worries.'

'No promises. But it'll help if you cooperate with our inquiries. Why did you go to the cottage in the first place?'

Valerie hesitated.

'Come on, Mrs Gates. You'd something to give Mr Parsingham, hadn't you?'

'If you already know—'

'We need to hear it from you.'

'All right. The engineer was here on Tuesday to give the photocopier in my office a routine service. When I was cleaning up afterwards I found a spoilt sheet with a thumbprint copied on to it that must have slipped down between the machine and the wall. The thumb was a funny shape. Couldn't think whose it might be, till I smelt tobacco off the paper.

'Then I thought of Mr Parsingham. He used to meet his sister in the Institute—pick her up in his car. If she wasn't on time, he'd wait in my office, smoking his smelly old pipe.'

'Of which you didn't approve?'

She wrinkled her nose. 'There's a no smoking notice, and other visitors are made to toe the line. I've complained to Dr Finchley. But he wouldn't let me say boo to a Parsingham. Anyhow one day—last May or June, can't remember which—Mr Parsingham had been in my office when I went to lunch. Not for the first or last time by a long chalk. But this day, when I came back, I had to use the photocopier. It felt warm. And there was a shred of pipe tobacco on the top cover.'

'Did you raise the matter with anyone?'

'No. I naturally assumed Mr Parsingham had been copy-ing his own private papers. Dr Finchley wouldn't have turned a hair over that. Just another perk, like the coffee he expects me to lay on for his visitors.'

'Can you describe the photocopy you discovered on Tuesday.'

'It was taken from the file copy of a letter.'

'Go on.'

She licked orange lips. 'A letter written by Dr Finchley to a Professor Something—can't remember the name.'

'Sergeant Powers, if you please . . . This letter, Mrs Gates?' Wendy Powers handed over the document, sleeved in polythene.

Valerie skimmed its contents.

'A confidential letter, copied without authority, and writ-ten by your boss, Mrs Gates. Surely the first instinct of any loyal secretary would have been to take it back to him?'

She flushed. 'Maybe I'm not the one you should be lec-turing on loyalty, Chief Inspector.'

'Oh?'

Valerie took a deep breath. 'Fancy a sherry? No? Mind if I indulge?' A quick trip to the drinks cupboard, a second

tug at her peplum as she resettled on the sofa. 'If the letter
had been taken from any other file, or if the copy had been
made by anyone else—yes, I'd have gone to the Director
straight away. There'd have been a row, I'm sure. Dr
Finchley would have accused me of leaving the filing cabinet keys lying around, which I haven't. But I'd have gone
all the same. You don't believe me, do you, either of you?'
Her glance zigzagged between the detectives' faces.

'What was so special about Dr Otley's file?' Baxter's
neutrally toned question cut through Powers's reassuring
murmurs.

'I felt Julian Otley had been badly treated. OK, he's an
uptight little sod, takes himself and his work very seriously.
But to read the references Dr Otley gave him, all except
the last, you'd think he was crazy. In the four years I've
known him I've seen no sign of it.'

'You typed those references from dictation, I imagine?
Did you raise the issue with Dr Finchley at the time?'
Wendy Powers asked.

'The first time, yes. But no go. He said he'd seen sides
of Julian I hadn't, that the Institute's reputation would
suffer if he sold a goose as a swan. Then he shot the "more
in sorrow than anger" line. All lies, of course. I knew it
was just that he didn't want Julian to resign. That he was
prepared to hang on by fair means or foul.'

'So you left it at that?' Powers followed up.

'What could I do? Warn Julian? Dr Finchley might have
found out that I'd spilt the beans, might have fired me.
Different for you, Sergeant. You don't chuck in jobs when
you're forty-nine. Not without thinking twice. Hadn't
twigged then that the job wouldn't always be there to
chuck.'

'Meaning?' Baxter prompted.

'Meaning that Dr Finchley's precious Institute is for the
chopper.' Valerie poured herself a second sherry.

'How'd you know?'

'"Informed sources."' She giggled, crossing plump thighs. 'That's what they say on the box, isn't it? Don't ask me for details—Secretary to the Chairman of the Board of Management handles stuff like that. But it's an open secret that a big sponsor has backed out, leaving a hole no one else is likely to plug. Chances are, the outfit will be disbanded within two years. Doesn't worry me. Made contingency plans a couple of months ago. I'll be down that gangway before the ship founders, thank God. Only reason I could risk telling you what I've told you.'

'OK,' Baxter said. 'But I'm still unclear why you returned the photocopy to Mr Parsingham.'

'I was hopping mad that he'd been so careless. Didn't want any repetitions. When I leave the Institute, I leave of my free will. I'm not giving Dr Finchley the satisfaction of showing me the door. So I told Mr Parsingham this would be the last time I covered for him and Stacey.'

'Stacey Caldwell? What made you think she was involved?'

'Likeliest person to have told him where to look for the cabinet key. I'll swear I never let anyone outside the office staff have sight of my hidey-hole. Stacey worked at the Parsingham for a time last winter. She's Julian Otley's girlfriend. American, pushy type. Mr Parsingham wouldn't admit it, but I'll bet anything you like she put him up to it.'

'Let's get back to basics. When exactly did you arrive at the cottage?'

'Four-fifteen, near as I remember. I left my office at five past—cycled over.'

'In working hours?'

'I'd flexitime owing. Besides, I knew the Director would be at a Board meeting until five or later.'

'Was there a notice on the cottage door when you arrived?'

'Yes, PLEASE DO NOT DISTURB.'

'But you did?'

'Yes. Felt I'd a right, after what Mr P. had done. I'd have given up pretty soon, I guess, in case he was laid up. But he answered the third knock.'

'Go on.'

'Don't remember every word, but I complained that he'd put me on the spot. He was very apologetic. Gave me his word that he'd destroyed all the other copies he'd made from the file. Swore the whole thing was his responsibility. Said Julian had no idea. He begged me not to tell him— not to tell anyone.'

'Who raised the subject of money?'

'He did—honestly. Like I said, he kept on and on.'

'Then you took it and went? Was that that?'

Valerie stared for several seconds at the dregs in her sherry glass. 'No—no, it wasn't.'

'Go on.'

'Easy for you to say, isn't it? I've got to go back to work tomorrow morning. "Yes, Dr Finchley, no, Dr Finchley." And after what happened to that old man, I'm scared, you see.'

'You mean Mr Parsingham may have died because he passed on something you told him?'

Valerie nodded dumbly.

'If that were so—big "if", mind you—aren't you at risk as things stand? Assuming the murderer could guess the source of Mr Parsingham's information?'

'I don't know . . .'

'You'd do better to tell us, Mrs Gates. If the need for protection arises, we're in a better position than Mr Parsingham to provide it.'

She sighed. 'Oh, very well. I'd been worrying for a long time, but there was no one I felt I could talk to, not before I knew Mr Parsingham had read that file. That's what gave me the biggest jolt, you see.'

'I don't quite.'

'Last May Dr Finchley did a complete turnaround. The last reference he wrote for Julian Otley—the one for the Karachi post—was a hundred per cent positive. Not a word about mental illness. It didn't add up. Except that he wrote it the morning after he'd had dinner with Aubrey King, and that didn't add up either.'

'Aubrey King?'

'Makes science documentaries for TV. He and his team had just spent two days shooting at the Parsingham. He'd said goodbye to Dr Finchley—heard him myself. No word of another meeting. But they had dinner together that evening. Restaurant called the Ruffled Feathers—near Royston.'

'I know it. You're sure?'

'Absolutely. Didn't see them face to face, mind. We weren't eating in the same part of the restaurant, my fiancé and I. But Norman ran into Dr Finchley in the Gents, and I spotted his car and King's in the car park. Odd, wasn't it?'

'Perhaps, but I don't see why you should have made the connection with Otley.'

'On account of the Pacific pollution research Julian is in charge of. Dr Finchley took a special interest in it. Mind you, he kept a close eye on all the strategic projects—'

'Strategic, is that what you said?' Wendy Powers checked.

'Yes. That's what they term the studies that are commissioned and paid for by governments or international bodies. As distinct from purely academic projects and commercial projects. Not that they do any private commercial work at the Parsingham—against its constitution, or something. Anyhow, funds for straight academic stuff being in short supply, Dr F. wants more strategic contracts. He's forever telling project leaders that the standard of their

work is the Institute's best advertisement. Churning out
memos on deadlines, quality control, client confidentiality . . .'

' "Careless talk costs contracts"?'

'That sort of thing, yes. He took it further with the Pacific
pollution project. Never could understand why—don't
think Julian does either. The funding isn't brilliant. But for
whatever reason, Dr F. was forever demanding copies of
progress reports, statistics. Quality control exercise, he
called it. Filed the copies in his personal safe, he said. And
at first I believed him.' Valerie paused for dramatic effect,
her braceleted right wrist dangling from the arm of the
settee, her fears seemingly forgotten.

'What changed your mind?' Baxter prompted.

'One afternoon last March I went into Dr Finchley's
office to collect his teacup. He'd been called out to talk to
the Chairman of the Board—Sir James Ogilvie-Walnutt—
in the waiting area. Left his desk in a hurry, by the look of
things. As I reached across for the teacup, my sleeve caught
a pile of papers and scattered them. When I was putting
things to rights, my eye fell on an airmail envelope.
Addressed, filled, but not properly sealed.

'Shouldn't have peeked, should I?' Valerie leant forward,
compressing her freckled cleavage. 'But every so often I get
this funny little feeling—sixth sense, my late hubby called
it. Odd enough seeing an envelope addressed to anyone in
Dr F.'s writing. Odder still seeing Aubrey King's name
on it. Chalk and cheese, that pair. King—seen any of his
shows?'

Wendy Powers grunted affirmatively.

'Smarmy type, wouldn't you say? And Dr Finchley's a
cold fish—no wonder he used to go in for underwater photography. Be that as it may, something told me this wasn't
a personal letter.' Valerie wagged her right forefinger.

'The envelope opened ever so easy. As if it was meant,

you might say. I took one quick peek before I resealed it. There were two sheets of A4 inside, photostats of the last progress report on the Pacific pollution project that the Director had demanded from Julian Otley. I'd been sent to collect it as per usual. Dr F. had made the copies on his personal photocopier, I guess. The Institute letterhead and the names of the research team had been masked out, also one or two words in the report. Place names, mostly. But I'd no doubt what it was. None.'

'Remember the address on the envelope?'

'Yes. Made a special point of memorizing it. Some day, I thought, someone's going to ask me that. 113 Rue des Chouxfleurs, Lucerne, Switzerland. Got that, Sergeant?'

'Yes, thanks.'

'And you told this to no one—no one at all—except Rupert Parsingham?' Baxter checked.

Valerie nodded. 'I was out of my depth—scared. Didn't take it in at first. The way Dr F. carries on, you'd say his life was bound up with the Parsingham. I just couldn't believe he and King had something going on the side. Then I realized it might tie in with those awful references. If Julian was laying golden eggs for Dr F. as well as the Institute, he'd use fair means and foul to hang on to him.'

'So why should he change his mind?'

Valerie shrugged. 'My guess is that King backed out of the deal at that hush-hush dinner in May. Dr F.'s been different ever since—edgier. I noticed it first thing next morning, even before he dictated the reference for Julian's Karachi job. Other people have remarked on it.'

'You put all this to Mr Parsingham?'

'Yes. Didn't mean to at first. But, well . . . Someone had to be told. I've worked all my life for the University, you see. Just because I've had to look after Number One doesn't mean I don't know right from wrong, does it?'

Wendy Powers made soothing noises.

'Thought Mr Parsingham might appreciate being told, on account of the family connection.'

'And did he?'

'Oh yes. Came as a shock, of course. But he told me I'd done the right thing. Told me he'd take appropriate action next morning. Maybe he didn't wait, poor old sod. Maybe that was why . . .'

'It doesn't quite add up,' Baxter complained on the drive back to the police station.

'No, sir? Why not?'

'Mrs Finchley said her husband had inherited capital. Also, he comes over as a canny type. It doesn't make sense that he'd risk his academic career for the sake of a few dirty thou.'

'Expect you're right, sir. But you don't mind if I look into King, do you?'

'Feel free, Sergeant. I can think of more beautiful sights.'

'Such as—or shouldn't I ask?'

'Actually, I was thinking of gemstones by starlight.'

'Any gems in particular, sir?'

'Nope. Pearls, sapphires, diamonds . . . I'm easy.'

CHAPTER 16

It was in fact rubies and emeralds that winked up at Baxter at three o'clock on Saturday morning. In the light, not of stars, but of the flickering fluorescent strip that overhung the work-bench in Barton Yarwood's garage.

The ex-soldier donned his bifocals to make a detailed inspection. 'Rum sort of birdie! Half starved, by the look of it. Stork, crane, would you say?'

'Liver bird.' Baxter began to replace its earthy wrappings.

'Really? Hang on. Seen something like that before somewhere . . . Got it! Councillor woman who's always getting her pic in the paper. Alma . . . Throstle, is it? No, Thurstone!'

'Best if you forget about her for the time being, Mr Yarwood. You gave us an undertaking earlier on—'

'Which I'll honour to the letter, Chief Inspector. Mum's the word. You're talking to one of Monty's men, remember. This little episode puts me in mind—'

'Sorry, sir,' Baxter interrupted. Armstrong didn't look fit for a guided tour down Memory Lane. 'Duty calls. Thanks again for your cooperation.'

'Delighted. My *Eleagnus pungens* is a hardy specimen, thank God. If you'd wanted to ferret around the root system of a camellia, I'm not sure I could have seen my way . . .'

The half-hour at Yarwood's place had been a doddle compared with the subsequent interview with the Assistant Chief Constable. In Baxter's view, a case could now be made for a search of Simon Drinkwater's London accommodation, if not of his person. But the ACC flatly refused to rouse senior Met officers from their beds with a request for such action.

Baxter was surprised to find Emma as well as Sarah at breakfast when he came down after a short nap. Bill Armstrong's and Sarah's reassurances notwithstanding, he had become more and more convinced that the miniature chest-of-drawers, now stowed at the back of his wardrobe, would be out of place in his daughter's London home. A denial of her adult tastes, a conspicuously expensive embarrassment.

He listened gloomily as Emma negotiated the loan of her mother's car for the day. The repairs to her van had left it

with a tendency to stall at awkward moments. Talk turned
to *Spin City*. Sarah was enthusiastic—declaring herself more
than willing for a second visit in Richard's company. The last
Cambridge performance was impossible, he declared, but he
promised to defy Heaven, Hell and if necessary, his Chief
Constable, to make the Edinburgh Festival.

The previous night's show had, he learned, been less than
perfect in the eyes of its director. Three of the cast had
been incapacitated, and Paul Sinton had been among those
pressed into last-minute substitution.

'He did very well, considering,' Sarah insisted. 'Splendid
singing voice. Bass-baritone—ideal for a Proctor's Bulldog.
Spoken sequences weren't quite as good, perhaps, but he
didn't have much to say.'

'Just as well,' Emma muttered into her muesli. 'Timing,
pitch, stress. Poor old Paul got everything wrong he could
get wrong. Two of Stacey's best cracks went off like damp
squibs. Not his fault, I grant you. His father's the actor in
the family.'

'What makes you say that?' Baxter asked, suddenly very
wide awake.

'Oh, lots of things. Clive's TV interview yesterday. The
sober citizen image he projected at the interval on our first
night. The way he looked in the Signal Box when I passed
at six-thirty, I reckoned he'd never make it to the show, let
alone mingle at half-time.'

'Six-thirty? You're sure that's when you saw him in the
pub, Emma?'

'Sure. I was stuck in a traffic jam right outside. Remember checking my watch to find out how long Clive had to
sober up. But why should the time matter? What is this,
Dad? An interrogation? Working from home now?'

'Please, darling!' Sarah put in.

'Keep out of it, Mum.' Emma was on her feet, glaring
down at him. 'Listen, Dad. If Clive Sinton's on your list of

suspects, OK. But play by the rules. Ask me whatever you want in a police station, before a police witness. Mind you, I'm not guaranteeing I'll answer.'

'You're right, Emma. I'm sorry. Truly. It could help quite a lot, actually, if you were prepared to sign a sworn statement repeating what you've just told me. You wouldn't be doing the dirty on Sinton—quite the reverse. Think it over, will you?'

'OK, but no promises.' She didn't say another word to him before he left for Headquarters.

'Sit you down, Baxter.' The Assistant Chief Constable gestured, pen in hand, and signed the last of a batch of outgoing mail. His secretary departed.

'Any luck with the Met, sir?'

'All sewn up.' The ACC leant back in his executive chair. No throat-clearings, Baxter noted, as he returned Littleton's rare, gold-and-white smile.

'You mean, they've raided Drinkwater's London pad? Found what we're expecting?

'Not yet.' Littleton carefully replaced the top of his pen. 'Not until he goes out this morning. Things look promising, all the same. Drinkwater's phone's being tapped. He's a meeting lined up with an old acquaintance we'd all like to talk to.'

'Oh?'

'Wright Cratchitt. Name ring a bell?'

Baxter nodded, his excitement growing. The jewel fence who had gone abroad after the Norwich Museum theft. 'Thought he was in the Low Countries.'

'Crossed back to Harwich yesterday by the late ferry. Overnighted in a motel off the M11. Essex have him under obbo. Look, Baxter. I've yet to be convinced that Rupert Parsingham was involved—criminally involved—in this business. All the same, I'm happy for you to go up to Town as the Force's representative, if you've nothing more urgent to attend to.'

'Thanks, sir, but no, thanks. Couple of Cambridge interviews lined up in Cambridge I'd better not defer or delegate.'

An hour later, on the threshold of Clive Sinton's room in the University Arms hotel, Baxter half-wished he had given a different answer.

'Well, well.' The playwright returned his ID. 'I've met your daughter. Perhaps she's told you? Very good friend of my son's, as we used to say. But I hardly imagine you and your colleague are here to talk dowries?'

'Hardly.' Baxter bit back his anger, as Sinton stood aside to let the detectives enter.

'Then to what or whom do I owe the pleasure?' Sinton asked over his shoulder as he bent to log off from his word-processor.

'To a witness of your excursion into Mr Parsingham's garden on the day of his death.' Baxter had expected radical chic in the playwright's appearance, but found none. His grizzling hair was of medium length. He wore a striped Breton sweater and neatly pressed navy shorts. The scar on his forehead was too small and too old to disfigure his sallow face, which was attractive in a thin-lipped way.

'Oh Lordy. Sit down?' Sinton waved towards the rumpled bed, and commandeered the single chair. 'Beer? Whisky? No, you wouldn't, would you?'

There were no glasses or bottles on open display, and no smell of alcohol.

'If you're here to quiz me about that brief encounter, I'm afraid you're wasting your breath. As he, she or it will have told you, I was pissed at the time. When I came to God knows how many hours later I didn't recall a thing to begin with. Then I felt this bloody great bruise on my shin—' He broke off to display its multicoloured splendour. 'And I remembered this bod—male, I think, but I wouldn't swear to it—falling over me. Also, I believe I was singing.'

'Right. Let's take another tack. Why did you go to Plumtrees Cottage?'

'To see Rupert Parsingham.

'And did you see him?'

Sinton shook his head. 'There was a DON'T DISTURB notice on the door.'

'Lights inside? Noises?'

'Not that I registered. I couldn't decide whether to knock or not, and I wasn't in any great shape for deciding. Reckoned a kip might clear my brain. That was that, until this guy ran into me.'

'I see. Tell us now, what was the purpose of your visit?'

Sinton hesitated. 'To renew an old acquaintance, you might say. To set a record straight.'

'You and Mr Parsingham knew each other?'

The playwright grimaced. 'By sight only. Our last confrontation was twenty-five years ago—a somewhat traumatic occasion. I suspect he remembered my face. I certainly remembered his, although it wasn't until I saw the piece about his retirement in Tuesday's local paper that I was able to put a name to it.'

'Are you telling me you and Mr Parsingham once had a quarrel?'

Sinton shook his head. 'He saw me doing something of which he disapproved. He showed his disapproval. I resented that—I still resent it. When I saw his picture in the paper Tuesday evening, I decided to pay him a visit, have it out with him. Daft idea, but the little grey cells weren't at their sparkiest.'

'Can you fill us in on the where and why of your confrontation?'

'Can but won't. Until further notice anyhow, Chief Inspector. Not just being bloody-minded. But (a) this has nothing to do with Parsingham's death, of which I know nothing, and (b) other parties are involved, one of whom doesn't deserve to be embarrassed. OK?'

'In the short term. What I want more immediately are details of your activities last Tuesday from mid-afternoon onwards.'

'Let's see. Mooched about in the colleges for a couple of hours. King's, Princes', Trinity—the usual tourist round.'

'But you don't strike me as the usual tourist.'

A wry smile. 'Maybe not. Let's call it a sentimental journey. I was curious to see how my past labours had stood up to wind and weather.'

'Labours?'

'You disappoint me, Baxter. I assumed you came fully briefed. To save your gofers the hassle of trawling through the cuttings files, let me fill you in on my career. Started out here in Cambridge as a mason—facer mason, if you like to dot the "i's", Inspector Armstrong. Before I read *Jude the Obscure*, you understand. Chucked that for scaffolding, chucked scaffolding for playwriting. Downhill all the way, wouldn't you say, Inspector?'

'No comment,' Armstrong replied in his flattest Belfast drawl.

'How long did your sentimental journey last?' Baxter asked.

'Till fourish, at a guess. Not given to measuring out my life in coffee-spoons. One reason for my lack of progress in masonry, no doubt.'

'Where next?'

'To the pub. Hadn't done my daily stint of writing that morning, wasn't in the mood to begin. Guilt-provoking situation, also thirst-provoking. Don't pretend you understand, Baxter.'

'Which pub?'

'Signal Box, just off Mill Road. One of my nicest discoveries in Cambridge. Easy-going establishment. No students, no tourists. No Real Beer, either, but I'm not a beerdrinker.'

'Go on.'

'Not much to say. Lowered a few whiskys, chatted to the barman, watched a thriller on the box so abysmal I worked up a head of steam about overpaid scriptwriters. Lowered another whisky and asked the barman to turn down the sound so I could make up my own dialogue. Half way through the car chase I got bored with that game. Besides, it was time to sober up if I was to make the show, as promised.'

'Time—what time?' Armstrong prompted.

Sinton laughed. 'Oh, for a literal police mind. I covet it, Inspector. Kid you not. Life would be so much less disconcerting. Didn't consult my watch at that juncture because the biological early-warning system did the needful. I took head and switched to caffeine.'

'So you drank a cup of coffee?'

'Several. Also, I read the local paper, and saw the photo of the late lamented Rupert. Plus name, plus address.'

'Go on.'

'Back here to change, with a swim at Parkside Pool on the way. Don't look so sceptical, Inspector. It's a thing I do.' Quite possibly. The biceps half-exposed by the short-sleeved T-shirt were not unimpressive. 'Then straight to East-whatever school for the kiddies' show.'

'All this on foot?' Baxter checked.

'That's right. Knew the route. Someone—your daughter, come to think of it—had given me a lift to the dress rehearsal. Back here after the show for a hair of the dog. Or two. Or three. I'd time to kill, because I wanted to steer clear of the Plumtrees party. Then to Rupert's. Which is where you came in, metaphorically speaking.'

'Remember the time you arrived at Parkside?' Baxter asked.

'There you might just be in luck, would you believe?' Sinton looked and sounded amused. 'As I explained, I'm not a clock-watcher. But I'm told I was seen in Parkside at six-thirty.'

'Told? By an acquaintance?'

Sinton shook his head. 'Sorry.'

'Someone else who doesn't deserve to be embarrassed?' Baxter countered.

'On the contrary. But not just yet.'

Baxter's patience broke. 'Now, look here, Sinton. We're investigating the murder of a vulnerable old man, a man who may have wanted to die, but at a time of his own choosing. Nothing melodramatic. Nothing you could wow them in the stalls with. But we take it seriously. Last thing I want is to play damnfool games.'

'Really?' Sinton steepled his fingers. 'In that case you should seek vocational guidance, Chief Inspector. From where I sit, ninety per cent of police work is games. The power game, the intimidation game—'

'Save the rhetoric for your word-processor, Mr Sinton.' Baxter prepared to leave. 'Don't assume the matter is closed—far from it. But for the present I suggest we stop wasting each other's time.'

'Egotistical bastard! Why'd you let him off so lightly?' Armstrong demanded on the way downstairs.

'Because I take him for the type that softens if stewed in his own juice and because he's an alibi.'

'Courtesy of the anonymous friend?'

'Courtesy, I regret to say, of my daughter, who saw him in the pub at six-thirty.'

'So his anonymous friend, if he or she exists, is a liar.'

'Ten out of ten, Bill. And faintly depressing. But say not the struggle naught availeth. With luck, HQ will soon have something more from the Met.'

Instructions for Baxter to ring the ACC from his Cambridge office came through on the car radio as they were parking. Steering a swift course through the chuntering terminals and fax machines in the incident room, he hurried to comply.

'Hm-hm. First the bad news, Richard.' His heart sank. 'Essex have made a booboo.'

'WC?'

'Hm-hm. Wright Cratchitt—'fraid so. We can speak freely, by the way. I'm using the hot line.'

Which meant he was also using the Chief Constable's desk. Baxter pictured Littleton's skinny frame behind that sea of afrormosia.

'What went wrong?'

'Cratchitt spotted his tail, or one of his henchmen did. Can't be sure. Anyhow, he did a runner from the motel before daybreak. All-ports alert, but with his resources . . .'

'Point taken, sir. I can hear stable doors banging. And the good news?'

'Cratchitt didn't warn Drinkwater before he left home to meet him.'

'So they pulled him? What was he carrying?'

'What you predicted. One hand-drawn map of one garden. Crazy paving, lily-pond. Not Barton Yarwood's, by all accounts. Hm-hm. Owe you an apology, Richard. If I'd backed your hunch more strongly, made representations to Essex—'

'Oh, I don't know, sir. Cratchitt was always a slippery eel. He'd probably have scarpered however many bods were staking out that motel. Drinkwater talking?'

'Not yet.'

'Any joy with his London pad?'

'More than we'd any right to expect. Three dozen more garden maps hidden in a cistern, the linings of suitcases— all the obvious places.'

'List of addresses?'

'No, but Parsingham's ex-employers could presumably supply a list of his clients.'

'There's evidence of his involvement?'

'Botanical dictionary, with his name in the fly-leaf.'

'Careless bastards! So it's out with the metal-detectors, is it, sir? Or does X mark the spots?'

'Not quite. They found a list of numbers, you see, one to thirty-seven. And opposite thirteen of the numbers—those that were used, one assumes, were alpha-numeric codes. My thought was that the numbers in the codes might indicate distances and the letters plant names. In which case, we've a sporting chance of retrieving a substantial number of gems with or without Drinkwater's cooperation.'

'And without upsetting the local gardening fraternity.'

'My God, Baxter. It'll be like offloading an albatross. You haven't seen the confidential memos from the Home Office. You've no idea how much damage those jewel thefts were inflicting on our image—on the image of every force in the region.'

'No, sir. I'm delighted, of course.' It occurred to Baxter for the first time that Drinkwater's activities had put the ACC's job on the line.

'To be frank, Baxter, you don't sound delighted.' His senior's atypical bluster had evaporated. 'Not—hm-hm—sickening for anything, I trust?'

'Nothing like that, sir. It's just that the murder case takes priority.'

'Hm-hm, naturally. When have I ever implied otherwise? Should have thought—hm-hm—that Drinkwater deserves promotion to the top of your suspect list?'

Baxter murmured emollient nothings and rang off as soon as he decently could. The more he recalled of Drinkwater, the harder he found it to cast him in the role of killer. In the last couple of days the case against his preferred candidate had strengthened, but he felt underequipped for a confrontation none the less.

He briefed Bill Armstrong and Wendy Powers on recent developments over coffee. Then he asked his sergeant what if anything the national police network had yielded on Aubrey King.

'Just this, sir.' Reproach tinged Wendy's voice as she fished the relevant printout from his in-tray.

King's name had been referred by the Department of Inland Revenue to the Fraud Squad in connection with suspected tax offences. 'Good, but not good enough.'

'Want me to ring them, sir?'

'No, thanks.' Instead he phoned Louis Mercier.

'If this is about Drinkwater, old son, you've punched the wrong button.' His friend didn't sound like a man with a long-awaited promotion in his grasp.

'Oh? Thought you'd be dancing on your desk by now. Nothing wrong, is there? You're not telling me Drinkwater's scarpered?'

'I'm telling you our big boys have taken him over. Top brass shall speak unto top brass. Your ACC'll hear what's what a damn sight sooner than yours truly.'

'Which is not to say he'll rush the story to me,' Baxter soothed. 'Wanted something else from you, actually. Something easy. Is there anyone I know on the Fraud Squad?'

'Des Charrington, late of Star Street. Mean bastard, as you'll remember.' Lou said it with a certain sour satisfaction.

Baxter sighed. 'I remember.' No point in pursuing that line. Not yet.

Wendy Powers approached as he rang off. 'Been thinking about Finchley, sir. Mind if I make a suggestion?'

CHAPTER 17

'Go ahead,' Baxter invited.

Powers resumed her seat beside Armstrong on the far side of the Chief Inspector's desk. 'If Valerie Gates told us the truth, it's likely that King had a profitable sideline in scientific espionage. That Finchley was supplying him with data from the Pacific pollution project and who knows what else. Agreed, sir?'

Baxter nodded.

'Data which King presumably sold to a commercial client,' Powers continued.

'Cutting Finchley in on the proceeds,' Armstrong added.

Powers shook her head. 'I'm not so sure. From what his wife said, Finchley isn't on the breadline. On the other hand, he's hooked on his job. And finance for research institutions is in short supply. Suppose his price for the deal was a big donation to the Parsingham?'

'And when King backed out he turned to more desperate remedies?' Baxter put in. 'And tried, if my hunch is right, to implicate Sinton in a false alibi. But why didn't he act sooner, assuming he'd nothing to do with the tricycle business?'

'How do we know he didn't use Vickery as his agent?' Armstrong objected.

Baxter shook his head. 'That pathetic old picklebrain? Won't wear it. Ten times riskier than doing the job himself. Your ball, Wendy.'

'Suppose he explored other avenues. Tried to persuade the University to keep the Parsingham afloat until he'd tapped new private sources. Suppose it wasn't until this month's Board meeting that he got the big turndown.'

'Nice, Wendy, but too many supposes,' Baxter replied. 'Want to try for some facts? Like a list of firms making grants to the Parsingham over the last five years, plus the sums donated. Stuff like that should be in the annual reports.'

'Where do I go for those? To the Institute?'

'No—too risky. Especially if Valerie took that sick leave we suggested. Try the City Reference Library—the *University Reporter* should have what you want. Follow up every company listed in *Who Owns Whom*.'

'For an associate or subsidiary in the decontamination business?'

'That would be neat,' Baxter agreed. 'But anything pharmaceutical will do. If you strike lucky, note the directors' names. *Kompass* should provide the needful. I'll take it from there. Oh, and dig out the University address and Department of Sir James Ogilvie-Walnutt, while you're at it.'

'Ogilvie-which?' Armstrong echoed, as Powers left the office.

'Walnutt, would you believe. Chairman of the Institute Board of Management. Time for us to shuffle the backlog, Bill.' So saying, Baxter upended his overflowing in-tray.

Fifteen minutes later he received a telephone briefing from an ebullient Assistant Chief Constable, who was about to leave for a meeting on the jewel thefts to be held in Scotland Yard. A high-level Inter-Force strategy meeting, Baxter learnt with some relief, where his presence would not be required.

Drinkwater, whether from greed or fear of retribution from his former fence, had so far admitted to only thirteen of the crimes. One object of those assembled would be to discuss ways and means of persuading him to come cleaner. Baxter didn't give much for their chances.

The thefts to which Drinkwater had confessed were those for which documentary evidence had been seized. They had all been committed on and after the day of the Newmarket 2,000 Guineas, where he claimed to have met Parsingham.

The dead man, according to Drinkwater, had provided temporary hiding-places for items stolen on or after the day of their meeting. He had buried all except the last—the Liver bird brooch—in person. Drinkwater had hoped that his knowledge of his clients' habits would enable him to escape attention, or, failing that, to provide a plausible excuse for his activities.

Drinkwater had assumed that the old man's motive was financial. The sum of £5,000 had been agreed in advance for cooperation in the period before his retirement—after which he would no longer be mobile—and was paid in four instalments. Drinkwater had heard Parsingham speak of his death, but not of suicide. He had supposed he was suffering from a terminal illness.

After a brief show of amnesia, Drinkwater had revealed the alpha-numerical code in which the locations of the buried pieces of jewellery had been noted. He had parted less reluctantly with his alibi for the estimated time of the murder. A drinks party at Henley. Some names and a couple of addresses were available and would be faxed through to the incident room. Baxter might wish to liaise with Thames Valley.

Armstrong, who had been sweating in the stuffy office, agreed to give the matter his personal attention. Baxter returned to his paper-pushing.

Fifteen tedious minutes later he was buzzed by the desk officer. Sister Immaculata would appreciate a few words. She was rather concerned about her mother.

It was a nuisance, as he had by this time used all available surfaces, including the two spare chairs, for separate subspecies of paperwork. All the same, recent events had revived his own anxieties about Eve Parsingham Wells. And he was concerned that her daughter should be concerned.

'Are you any nearer to finding Uncle Rupert's murderer, Chief Inspector?' she asked, as she perched on a hastily cleared chair, clasping sunburnt hands over her plump pinafored stomach. She looked much as she had looked yesterday in the crowded lobby, Baxter supposed. Same pinny, same crucifix, same sensible sandals, same-different shirt. But here in tête-à-tête she was far more intimidating. A reincarnation of the only other nuns who had asked him frank questions at close quarters. About his bowels mostly, and in hospital.

'We live in hope, Sister.' He realized too late that the reply might strike her as blasphemous.

'I want to get Mother away for a while. Partly because of Uncle Rupert. She's bearing up, but his death's been a sad blow, all the same.'

'Of course . . .'

'She's always had a short fuse, but I've never found her so irritable. Every little thing seems to upset her. At first, I thought it was just me. I remind her of Daddy, always have.'

'Oh?' Baxter tried in vain to visualize Eva's husband.

'Poor Daddy—her political gesture, you know. It's hard on a man being someone's political gesture. She hustled him off to fight in the Spanish Civil War, before her conversion to pacifism. Daddy hated it. Not the fighting so much as the intellectual snobbery. Imagine, a garage mechanic in the International Brigade among all those poets. Took him years to get over the humiliation. I'd never quite forgiven Mother before this visit. Sorry. Not your problem, of course.'

Baxter made understanding noises.

'But it isn't just me Mother's been snapping at. She's

been dreadfully rude to everyone except Damien. Including people like Cousin Esther and Dr Finchley who've gone out of their way to offer sympathy and help. I feel quite embarrassed to remember what she's said when I'm showering at Appletrees.'

'Showering?' Baxter echoed stupidly.

'Yes. Mother's electricity's been cut off for some time, because of the roof repairs, so the Finchleys insisted she used the washing facilities at Appletrees. Uncle Rupert's gas water-heater is somewhat erratic, I understand.'

'Are you planning to take your mother away for a holiday?'

'My rule doesn't permit, and anyhow I doubt whether it'd work out. But somewhat to my surprise, she's agreed to a month at a friend's cottage in Devon, which would allow time for roof repairs.'

'By Damien Ronson and Company?'

'Goodness, no. Damien's moving out today. We're employing professionals. I've made the arrangements, and Dr Finchley has volunteered to keep an eye on progress. He's actually offered more than once, it seems, to finance the repair out of his own pocket. But there'll be no need for that, if Mother controls her generous impulses. The bank made no difficulty about an advance.'

'When is she planning to leave?'

'At eleven on Monday, if you've no objection. I'd have liked it to be sooner, but she's anxious to keep an appointment with her solicitor. I'll travel up to Town with her and see her on to the West Country train at Paddington before returning to my community in Gloucestershire. I'll be back for Uncle Rupert's funeral. Mother says she'd rather not. Funerals don't mean much to her, not being a believer.'

'No problem about this from our end, Sister, provided you can let me have your address and hers.'

'Oh, thank God! Here you are, Chief Inspector.'

Surprised by the strength of the reaction, Baxter accepted a sheet of paper on which two addresses had already been written in a neat script. 'You said your uncle's death was one reason for your wanting to get your mother away, Sister. What was the other?'

The plump fingers laced. 'I fear she's at physical risk. Oh, not just because of the hole in the roof. This business of the bicycle—'

'But Vickery's dead . . .'

'I know. But since Damien's been cleared, Mother's been chatting about it to all and sundry. And Damien's bound to talk. Sell the story to a paper, perhaps. I'm so afraid— so is Dr Finchley—that one of the other unstable youngsters Mother got involved with may attempt something similar.'

'There'll be more houseguests, I imagine?'

'No. We've had some straight talking on the subject. Genuine cooperatives are fine. You might say I live in one. But Plumtrees was never like that. When Cousin Esther and her friends told Mother the kids were exploiting her— I've heard them often—she took no notice. When I told her she'd been exploiting *them*, it seemed to make an impact.'

Sister Immaculata allowed herself a brief self-congratulatory smile. 'I suggested she should give up her rights in Plumtrees and move into a small flat. I suppose it would mean varying Grandfather's trust, but I should think the University would be delighted to get its hands on the property. Mother took to the idea quite quickly—had been thinking on similar lines herself, she said. Agreed to raise the matter with her solicitor on Monday.'

'Thus putting your mind at rest?' And Finchley's, Baxter added mentally.

Sister Immaculata shook her neatly cropped head.

'Not quite, Chief Inspector. I've another anxiety I'd like to share. I've been helping Mother sort through her belong-

ings. Not that she's much left of value—her houseguests
saw to that. But some of the junk that was moved out of
the attic when the roof was damaged could fetch good prices
in a charity shop.

'Yesterday I was going through an old cabin trunk when
I found the holster for Grandpa's service revolver—he'd
fought in the First World War, smuggled it home as a
souvenir. He showed it to me when I was seven or so, and
I'm ashamed to say I was quite impressed. Mother walked
in on the conversation—protested loudly. She was an
ardent pacifist by then. She wanted Grandfather to get rid
of the thing, but he wouldn't hear of it. Hid it where he
thought she wouldn't find it, I imagine.

'Yesterday, when I asked Mother if she'd thrown the
gun out, she said yes. But I was surprised she hadn't got
rid of the holster. And she was so flustered, so self-con-
tradictory about the circumstances when I pressed her,
that I felt sure she was lying. I was convinced it had been
stolen.'

'Why should your mother lie about that?'

'For the reason that led her to hush up the trike business.
To protect her little stray lambs—regardless of the suffering
one of them might inflict.'

'You may well be right, Sister,' Baxter said. 'I'll ask
your mother to let us have the holster—there could be
identifying marks. But my guess is that the revolver, if
stolen, was stolen for financial gain. Collectors will pay well
for pieces of that vintage, but you'd go a long way to find
suitable cartridges in usable condition.'

And yet, and yet. As he ushered out the nun, visibly
reassured, the Chief Inspector was uneasy.

Twenty minutes later he and Armstrong were about to
abandon paperwork for the cafeteria when Powers rejoined
them.

Baxter, whose stomach made trouble without regular

relining, proposed a working lunch. The cafeteria tables being too small to accommodate Powers's notebook and photocopies as well as one lasagne, one shepherd's pie and one Cornish pasty, she reported briefly from memory.

'I've been through the last five of the Institute's annual reports as printed in the *University Reporter*. Eighteen firms are named as donors of money or kind over that period, but some of the gifts were very trivial. Prizes, small pieces of equipment and so on.'

'Ignoring the tiddlers, how many firms with pharmaceutical interests?' Baxter asked.

'Three. First, Skysey Agrochemicals, who are heavily into fertilizers and foodstuffs. They've funded a research fellowship at the Parsingham, as has Findheim Firenze.'

'Implausible name,' Armstrong objected.

'But authentic.' Powers tapped her sheath of photocopies. 'FF are a Swiss-Italian conglomerate with a finger in many pies. But their sole pharmaceutical interest, from what I've checked, is in cosmetics.'

'Number three?'

'Bryce-Benson International. Mega-multinational with a clutch of pharmaceutical associates and subsidiaries. But the offshoot that caught my eye was Detoxicon, which is based in Munich and specializes in decontamination. More especially, marine decontamination.'

'That's it. That's got to be it!' Armstrong waved a gravy-dripping forkful of shepherd's pie over Baxter's lasagne.

'Too good to be coincidental,' Baxter agreed.

'Trouble is—' Powers cut open her Cornish pasty and inspected its contents—'trouble is, Bryce-Benson's contribution wasn't as generous as the other two. Five thousand a year to the Institute's equipment fund over the last three years. Would an ambitious director risk professional disgrace for that sort of money?'

'Still less, would he risk murder?' Armstrong added.

Baxter chewed thoughtfully before replying. 'It mayn't have been quite like that.'

'What's your theory, then?' Armstrong asked.

'Later. Nice work, Wendy. Write it up after lunch. But let me have your personnel list for the Bryce-Benson conglomerate right away, will you?'

Ten minutes later he rang DCI Charrington of the Metropolitan Fraud Squad.

'Keep this short, will you.' Charrington sounded as tetchy as ever. 'I'm parched, I'm hungry, I'm overdue for a briefing session.'

'OK. You're investigating Aubrey King at the instigation of the Inland Revenue. Right?'

'So?'

'I'm interested in his sources of undeclared income. Like to give me an overview?'

'High-level inquiry, old son, international ramifications. Not a squeak without a need-to-know from your CC.'

'Oh, come on, Des—'

'Go through channels. I don't make the effing rules, remember. And I can't afford to break them.'

'You can't afford to shoot yourself in the bloody foot either, can you? Listen, Des. You're in a hurry, I'm in a hurry. I'm not after something for nothing. It's give-a-little, take-a-little time.'

'So what are you giving?'

'Industrial espionage. How does that grab you?'

'Guesswork—intelligent guesswork.' Charrington's tone had changed, though. Baxter discerned curiosity behind the cynicism.

'OK, here's a name. Lord Bryce of Bryce-Benson. Am I right in thinking he did business with King?'

A long pause. 'I'm not saying he didn't. Best I can do, mate. Your turn to give. What's in it for me?'

'Something tomorrow, with luck, Des. Apply through the usual channels.'

The reply was the Charrington growl, sonorous and catarrhal, just as Baxter remembered it from his Met days. He rang off, chuckling.

Ten minutes later, as he wove his way among slow-moving clusters of tourists on the perimeter path in the First Court of Princes' College, Baxter was visited by doubts. Would Sir James Ogilvie-Walnutt, Professorial Fellow of Princes', Rhadegund Professor of Tropical Zoology, and Chairman of the Parsingham Institute, agree to see him without an appointment? Would he talk openly to a middle-ranking police officer with a Birmingham degree? Would he report his visit to Finchley?

The staircases were labelled in alphabetical sequence, starting at the Porters' Lodge, and in order to reach Ogilvie-Walnutt's stair, K, Baxter had to cover a side and a half of the square court. Had it not been for the bowler-hatted porter on traffic duty, he would have risked a diagonal short cut over the sacred turf reserved for the feet of Fellows and their escorted guests.

And, apparently, of Parsinghams. For just as Baxter passed the door labelled H, a bald, elderly man emerged from K, with a stern-faced Eve Parsingham Wells and an impassive Sister Immaculata in tow. Signalling to the porter, the don launched his guests on to the grass turf before scuttling back to base. Eve and her daughter set off at a smart trot, casting no glances in Baxter's direction.

Under cover of a trio of large Nordic tourists, he slipped up K staircase, and knocked at the worm-eaten linenfold door of K-3, Ogilvie-Walnutt's set of rooms on the first floor. The bald man answered.

He looked rather unwell, and the multicoloured shirt worn over shrunken cricketing flannels didn't flatter his beige complexion. The sight of the detective's ID didn't help either. But Ogilvie-Walnutt's 'Oh Lord!' was more resigned than astonished.

'You'd better come in, I suppose. Mind you don't step on the bones.'

CHAPTER 18

'Duck-billed dinosaur—just a baby. Reconstructive palæontology is my vacation hobby.' Ogilvie-Walnutt explained as Baxter skirted the half-assembled skeleton that occupied most of the Professor's Turkey carpet.

'Very nice.'

'Fearfully and wonderfully made, isn't it?

> *Some call it Evolution*
> *And others call it God.'*

And Ogilvie-Walnutt's bedmaker might call it something else again, Baxter surmised, as he settled on the window-seat. The Professor perched on a Regency library stool which he would have liked to examine in detail.

'No idea why you're here, Mr Baxter. No idea at all.' Ogilvie-Walnutt glanced uneasily at the ancient bones as though they had been dishonestly come by.

'Would it surprise you to know my visit concerned the Parsingham Institute?'

The faintest gasp. Then: 'Yes. Of course it would. The Parsingham is a University institution. I'm not in the habit of discussing University business with police officers.'

'Nor with Mrs Parsingham Wells?'

The Professor stiffened. 'You saw Eve leave just now, I suppose? Known her all my life—we discuss all sorts of things. Her great-grandfather was a Princes' man, you know, likewise her grandfather and late brother.'

'Whose death I am investigating.'

'Ah yes. Dreadful business. Poor Rupert. Intellectually undistinguished, but a lovely man for all that. Hard to believe anyone would want to murder him. Can you be sure—can you really be sure?'

'I'm afraid we can. It's in that connection that I want to ask you some questions about the Parsingham Institute.'

Ogilvie-Walnutt nodded, twisted his signet ring, his beige complexion fading to putty.

'Can I have your word, Sir James, that you will regard this interview as strictly confidential?'

'In the ordinary way, I should wish to make the Director privy to anything concerning the Institute.'

'The situation is extraordinary. Do I have your word?'

Ogilvie-Walnutt checked on the wellbeing of his ten stubby fingers before replying. 'Very well. Fire away. Mind you, I shan't promise to answer every question you may put.'

Baxter, who had expected tougher resistance, tried not to show his surprise.

'I should like to ask you about the Institute's dealings with Lord Bryce, Chairman of Bryce-Benson International.'

Ogilvie-Walnutt flushed muddily. 'That's all on record. Bryce-Benson was one of our benefactors.'

'Was?'

'Three-and-a-half years ago the company announced its intention of donating £5000 per annum to the Institute's equipment fund for a period of three years. The final payment was made last April.'

'But there were hopes, were there not, of something considerably more substantial?'

'I decline to answer.'

'Please, Sir James.'

'To do so would be to break my word—I see no reason for that.'

Baxter eyed the skeleton and plunged, as if into a primæ-val marsh. 'I must tell you that Lord Bryce is under suspicion of involvement in scientific espionage. That he very probably hired an agent to secure client-confidential data from the Parsingham for the benefit of his sub-sidiaries.'

'Oh my God. Did Rupert find out about this?'

'A part if not the whole. Enough, perhaps, to endanger his life.'

'Dreadful.' Ogilvie-Walnutt shook his bald head. 'Quite dreadful.'

'So I'd like you to think again, Sir James. My information suggests that two or three years ago Bryce tempted his Parsingham informant with a very attractive bait, which he withdrew this summer. Why, we've yet to establish. What was that bait?'

'You're asking *me*?' Ogilvie-Walnutt boomed. 'This is my second term as Chairman of the Board of Management. A voluntary and an unpaid post, you understand.'

'But highly regarded, no doubt.'

'Status has never meant much to me, Chief Inspector. Integrity has. Are you seriously implying that, committed as I am to the Institute's welfare, I was party to a deal that would impugn its moral reputation and my own?'

'No. I assumed the strings on the offer were tucked away where you couldn't see them. But I think all the same that the offer had to be made to you and by Bryce in person if our mole was to be persuaded it wasn't his linkman's invention.'

Ogilvie-Walnutt stared. 'Can you name the linkman?'

This was more, far more than Baxter had intended to risk. He braced himself for a second plunge. 'Off the record and confidentially?'

'Yes.'

'Aubrey King, the TV producer.'

'How sad . . . So rare, so often underrated, the talent to make science come alive. Bernal had it, Bruner and Bronowski. So had King. My grandchildren are hooked on his current series. Tell me, who was his informant?'

'I can't. Not yet.'

'In that case, I'm afraid—'

'I must ask you to trust me, Sir James. And to remember that my prime concern is a murder.'

The zoologist sighed. 'Very well. I've known Bryce slightly for almost a decade, mostly from dreary, hand-wringing conferences on the interfaces between industry and higher education. Our paths crossed at one such event about eighteen months ago. It had quite slipped my mind that he was a Parsingham benefactor—fund-raising's not really my thing. Bryce went out of his way to remind me of the fact. He went on to enthuse about the flattering reports his "spies" had given him of the Institute. Actually used the hackneyed term. Bloody cheeky, when you think of it.' Ogilvie-Walnutt thought about it for several seconds.

'Then he came out with his offer, which was for a sum sufficient to guarantee the Director's salary for a period of seven years. Been twisting his acountants' arms, he said. Money was in the pipeline. A cert, in any circumstance he could foresee. But other commitments took priority, so it wouldn't be available for a couple of years yet—i.e. next spring. His accountants wouldn't allow him to put an advance statement of intent in writing. He was sure my Board and I would understand.'

'You confided in them and the Director?'

'Orally, yes. Bryce had encouraged me to do so.'

'He would,' Baxter said dourly. 'When did he back out?'

'I'd had a sabbatical last Easter Term, delegated all my Cambridge commitments. When I returned to my Depart-

ment in early July, my secretary reported that Bryce had
made several attempts to get in touch. When I did he told
me the deteriorating economic climate had forced him to
postpone his offer indefinitely.'

'You'd no cause to doubt his reason?'

'Why should I? The recession is a fact of life. Other
sponsors were telling us much the same. The financial out-
look for the Institute was so grim that I decided to chair
the July Board meeting in person, although I was—am
still—officially on leave. A traumatic occasion.'

'So Mrs Parsingham Wells's recent gesture must have
come as a great relief.'

'You have me at a disadvantage, Chief Inspector.' The
beige face went blank.

'Sister Immaculata has given me to understand that Mrs
Parsingham Wells plans to see her solicitor on Monday
morning. I presume she has just told you what she proposes
to discuss with him. That she wishes to waive her interest
in the property held in trust for her so that it can be handed
over to the Institute.'

'No—no, Chief Inspector. Quite the contrary. Sister
Immaculata's got the wrong end of the stick—was given it,
perhaps. My conversation with Eve was in private. Her
daughter waited in the next room.'

'Then perhaps you could put me right?'

Ogilvie-Walnutt hesitated.

'May I remind you again, Sir James, that I'm investigating a murder. Another life could be in danger.'

The zoologist shivered. 'Eve's?'

'It's not impossible.'

'Very well, then.'

'Dr Finchley's not here, I'm afraid.' It being a Saturday
afternoon, Baxter and Armstrong had found the front door
of the Parsingham Institute locked against casual visitors.

It surprised the Chief Inspector a little that the receptionist was present to answer it.

'You're quite sure? When I rang him at home, his house-keeper gave me to understand—'

'He *was* here,' the receptionist conceded, shifting peppermint toffee from the right side of her mouth to the left. 'Only two or three minutes since he left. Wonder you didn't pass him. But you wouldn't, I suppose, on account of the one-way system.'

'Ask him to ring me as soon as he returns. It's urgent.' Baxter scribbled the number of the incident room on a card.

The receptionist pursed iridescent mauve lips and consulted her wristwatch. 'Mightn't be back before I left, he said. I'm doing a spot of overtime to help with the typing, you see, with Mrs Gates being off.' Baxter was relieved to hear that Valerie had accepted his advice to take leave.

'Did Dr Finchley tell you where he'd gone? Leave a contact number?'

She shook her head.

'Hazard a guess?'

'Sorry. Not as though I'm his secretary, is it? Might have gone somewhere to meet Mr Sinton, I suppose?'

'Sinton?' Baxter echoed, his skin prickling.

'Last phone call I put through was from a Clive Sinton. Dr Finchley left immediately after that.'

'Just one more. How about the Romanian elevator lady? She's sixtyish and her feet hurt.'

'N-O, Stacey. Absolutely, no. Read her yourself.' Emma Baxter scowled at her friend across Julian Otley's kitchen table. 'Four New York accents I can't do properly are more than enough. I haven't a clue what West Side Romanian sounds like.'

'Forget her goddamn accent, concentrate on her feet. Oh,

come on, Em. I don't know whether I'm writing garbage
or not till I hear someone else reading it.'

The phone rang. Stacey answered. 'You're off the hook
for a couple of minutes. It's your mother.' She handed
Emma the receiver.

'Sorry if I'm interrupting, darling. Rang Paul's flat first.
No reply.'

'I've been here since after lunch and Paul's probably at
Landers College. He'd a stack of books to return to the
college library—told me he'd probably put in a couple of
hours when he was there. Took your car, actually. You
don't mind, do you?'

'Of course not. Thing is, though, Joy Butley's broken her
ankle and I've had to take over her duty tonight. I've tried
in vain to contact your father. So I'm sorry to be a drag,
darling, but I'll have to beg back the Granada. Need it by
six-thirty.'

'Sure, Mum. Want me to run it home?'

'And miss your last show? Thanks, but no need. Joy's
son's got a Saturday job in Cambridge, and he normally
buses. You remember Alex?'

'Scruffy little kid with a squint?'

'Scruffy six-footer with a squint. If you can get the car to
Emmanuel Street by six, he'll gladly drive it here. I'll stand
you your taxi fare home unless you decide to stay over.
OK?'

'OK. Trust me, Mum. The National Health Service is
safe in our hands.'

Emma rang Landers College Library. A whispered argument ensued before the undergraduate on weekend issue
desk duty agreed to leave her post to search for Paul.

When he replied in the same library whisper, Emma
passed on Sarah's message. 'Can you rendezvous with this
Butley lad in Emmanuel Street?'

'I suppose.' Paul sounded unenthusiastic.

'But what?'

'It'll mean a detour home. Haven't got the car here.'

'Why the hell not—'

'Well, actually, I lent it to Dad.'

'You what?'

'OK, OK, Em. I'm sorry. Simply didn't occur—'

A background 'Shhh!'

'Where's Clive taken the car?' Emma asked coldly.

'Bet you what you like it's back in Mawson Road by now. Dad said he'd pop the keys through the letter-box when he returned it. He's been on a bookbuying spree. Wanted to shift his heavy gear from the hotel to a left-luggage locker at the station, save himself the hassle of finding a taxi first thing tomorrow morning.'

And the expense, Emma thought sourly. 'Huh!'

'Suppose you check at my flat,' Paul suggested. 'Ring you there in ten minutes.'

'Don't bother!' Emma slammed down the phone and picked up her cotton cardigan.

'Trouble?' Stacey asked.

'Clive Sinton trouble. Take-the-little-woman-for-granted trouble. Can I borrow your bike?'

'Yeah, sure. And don't say I didn't warn you. Anyone who's in cahoots with Eric Finchley—'

'We don't know that, Stacey. One phone message doesn't prove anything.'

But the notion niggled none the less as Emma cycled down Green Street.

There was no yellow Granada anywhere in Mawson Road. It would be a waste of time to wait for Paul's phone call, she decided. Instead, she cycled the short back-street route to the railway station. There was one H registration yellow Granada at the far corner of the station car park. Emma, who couldn't for the life of her remember the number of her mother's vehicle, pedalled over for a close inspection. The Ninja turtle inflatables and frisbees on the back seat didn't look like Sarah's playthings or Clive Sinton's.

Ten wasted minutes. Emma decided to make a circular tour of city pubs, but not before leaving a sharply worded note for Sinton at the reception desk of the University Arms Hotel. Accordingly, she cycled the humid length of Station Road and turned right into Hills Road and thickening rush-hour traffic. She was queuing at the traffic-lights at Gonville Place when she caught sight of a yellow Granada ten yards ahead. *The* yellow Granada. For that was without doubt the back of Clive Sinton's head. He carried no passengers.

Sinton had doubled his lead by the time the lights changed, but Emma managed to keep him in view throughout his stop-go progress down Regent Street and St Andrew's Street. A mandatory right-hand fork into Emmanuel Street freed the Granada from the preceding buses. When Emma followed suit, it was nowhere to be seen.

Casting a quick sideways glance into Drummer Street bus station, she chose Emmanuel Road as the likeliest available option. When she was circling the Seven Lamps roundabout, she saw that she'd guessed right. The Granada was making good speed between the rows of chestnut trees that overhung Victoria Avenue.

She lost it again before she made Victoria Bridge and Mitcham's Corner. Right or left, she asked herself as she pedalled up the hill. Left for Chesterton Lane and Appletrees. A possibility, if Stacey was right and Clive and Eric Finchley had some sort of association. But had they? Why should a Cambridge Establishment Man hobnob with a professional debunker?

Emma, sweating heavily now, turned left none the less. If, as seemed likely, she failed to find the Granada in the grounds of Appletrees, she could phone her mother from

Eve Parsingham Wells's house and advise her to make contingency transport plans.

Appletrees looked deserted, with its Venetian blinds shut against the sun, as Emma pushed her bike between the flowerless shrubs that lined the steep drive. But having followed the path to the back of the house she found a woman's cycle parked in a covered stand camouflaged by laurel bushes. And at a little distance a blue Volvo and a yellow Granada with a 'doctor on call' notice on its windscreen.

Emma retraced her steps to the front of the house and rang crossly. She was headachey now as well as hot and her nose was running. She honked into a tissue.

A small, pop-eyed woman carrying a feather duster answered more quickly than she had expected. 'Oh, thank God someone's come. Come in—do please come in.'

Standard greetings for her mother, Emma supposed. Drama she could at the present moment dispense with. Standing her ground beside a leonine doorscraper, she explained her mission.

'But I can't tell Mr Sinton nothing. Nor Dr Finchley. That's the point.'

'Sorry to be thick,' Emma said. 'But I'm not altogether with you. It's Emma Baxter, by the way.'

'June Oakes. Dr Finchley's housekeeper. Cleaning lady really, but the boss asked me to do a bit extra—get supper and that—while his wife's away. Wish to God she was here today. Clever lady. She'd have known what to do. Oh, dear. Perhaps, if you came inside, love . . .'

Emma followed her into the hall. It was cooler than she'd expected. Air-conditioned, she surmised from a background hum. 'Where can I find Dr Finchley?' she asked patiently.

'He's in his darkroom—he and the Sinton bloke. Locked in. Didn't want to be disturbed, the boss said.'

Emma's frustration yielded to curiosity. 'Been here before, this man Sinton?'

June deposited her feather duster on a console table. 'Not that I know of. Told me he'd an appointment, see, and the boss acted like he was expected. It was odd, though, the boss showing him into the darkroom.'

'Odd—why?'

'Never known him to let another soul in there. Mrs Finchley said he was worried about someone nicking his fancy cameras. Thought at first Sinton might be a salesman, might have photographic gear in that suitcase of his.'

'Sounds very likely,' Emma prevaricated. 'And I've no intention of interfering with any deals. So if you'll just show me—'

'No, wait.' As June Oakes fiddled with the top button of her shirt, Emma saw that she was goiterous. 'Couldn't have been more'n a minute, you see, before the lock clicked. I was dusting in the passage—couldn't help hearing. Funny, I thought. I mean, why bother locking themselves in, if they was just buying and selling? Then all the stuff they show on *Crimewatch* came back to me. Suppose this Sinton bloke is some kind of con man?'

'He is.' Emma had diagnosed hyperthyroidic emotionality. 'He's just conned someone into lending him my mother's car. She's a doctor. If I don't get it back to her quickly, her patients could be in deep trouble. Sorry to be blunt, Mrs Oakes, but you could be in deep trouble too unless you back off. Now, which is it to be? Do you show me to the darkroom or do I yell the house down?'

The housekeeper gripped Emma's arms. 'Shh. I'll show you. But please, *please* don't knock—not before you've had a little listen. Promise?'

Emma sighed and promised. June led the way along a corridor hung with oriental embroideries to the last of several mahogany doors. Emma applied her ear to the keyhole. She listened for almost a minute. Silence. Then a burst of dialogue, too muted to be comprehensible. The pattern repeated itself. She stood up.

'Doesn't sound right, does it?' June whispered.

Emma shook her head. She knew enough about the intonation patterns of English speech to be sure this was no mere business transaction. One man was very angry, the other very frightened.

June whispered again. 'Just suppose it wasn't cameras the Sinton bloke had in his suitcase. Suppose it was a gun.'

CHAPTER 19

Emma knocked. More silence, more mumblings.

Then: 'Later, June. I told you I didn't wish to be disturbed,' in a high, strained voice.

The two women backtracked along the corridor.

'Sounds scared, don't he?' June hissed. 'Like he was being threatened. Reckon we ought to phone the police?'

'Not yet,' Emma replied. She couldn't bring herself to believe that Clive Sinton was a killer. If he was putting the frighteners on Finchley, it must be his idea of a black joke. And she wanted to tell him in person how unfunny she had found his jokes these last few days. That he owed it to Paul to switch out of manic mode before tonight's family reunion. 'Is there another way into that room?' she asked. 'An open window?'

June shook her head. 'Boss won't allow it, not in summer. On account of the bees, you see.'

Emma didn't. 'Bloody hell.'

'There's the side door, of course.' June fumbled with a bunch of keys clipped to her waistband. 'Leads into a cloakroom off the darkroom. Boss lets me clean the cloakroom on Fridays.'

'Big deal. Let's have that key, then.'

June handed it over. 'No saying if you'll get any further, mind. Door between the cloakroom and lab's most probably locked.'

'Worth a try. Don't buzz the police or anyone else until I tell you.'

Would June comply? As she tiptoed among the tubs of dwarf conifers that surrounded the house, Emma didn't much care. She was in no mood to protect Sinton from a caution for harassment or whatever he was up to, always provided she'd got her own word in first.

The lock squeaked faintly as she let herself into the strip of a cloakroom, which had a boxed-off lavatory at one end. But the noise had probably been drowned out by the creaks, rustlings and conversation in the darkroom. She closed the outside door carefully and listened.

The door between cloakroom and darkroom was flimsy, badly fitting. There was a key in the lock, so she couldn't see anything. But she could hear what was said.

'Tell me about this one.' That was Sinton. But a new Sinton. No humour, no pretence of humour. Just cruelty.

'I can't . . . I swear I can't remember.'

'Try.'

'Seaside—I took it somewhere at the seaside.'

'That much is obvious, you bloody fool. There's sand, isn't there? There's sea. Whereabouts at the seaside?'

'I can't remember, I tell you.'

'Later then. What about this?'

'Dinner—Photographic Society dinner.'

'And the lady's name?'

'Mary—no, Marianne.'

'Marianne who?'

'Swear I can't remember.' Finchley was sobbing now.

'Does this help?' A dull clunk. The gun?

'No!' in a loud whimper. Praying that June would hear, would disobey her, Emma tried the handle of the darkroom door. It gave to her touch. She opened it, stepped inside.

'What the hell?' Clive Sinton was standing within a yard of her in front of a work-bench. His sallow face looked bloodless above his black cotton Polo. His right hand was twisted behind him as though holding something on the bench.

He's crazy, Emma thought. He's a full-blown psycho. This Cambridge visit has sent him over the edge. 'I've come for my mother's car keys,' she said quietly.

Sinton threw back his head and laughed. 'You look like an avenging bloody angel. All in good time, my love, but not quite yet. There's a queueing system.'

'Don't *my love* me, Clive. I want those keys and I want them now. If not, I'm going for help.'

'No!' Sinton's left hand gripped her shoulder. 'You're the one that's going to part with a key, Emma. The key of whatever door you came into this house by.'

'Why should I do that?' She stood very still, forcing a little smile as she mentally rehearsed her martial arts routine.

'Tell her why, Finchley.'

'The bees! The b-bloody bees.'

Sinton's right hand swung into Emma's field of vision. It held a string, from which dangled a jam-jar covered with some sort of metallic gauze. But the filter didn't stifle the buzzing.

'Do what he says, for Christ's sake.'

Emma looked for the first time at the man in the pink shirt who was seated on a lab stool further along the work-bench. At his slack, frightened face. At the several dozen faces of frightened women—in grey-and-white, sepia-and-white and full colour—that stared up from the bench in front of him.

Sickened, she handed Sinton the key. He backed out

through the cloakroom, jar in hand, to lock the side door.

'Tell me what all this is in aid of,' Emma said when he returned.

'Mrs Finchley for you, sir. Can you take the call? She rang earlier, she says.'

'Yes—yes. Put her through.'

'Glad I caught you this time round, Chief Inspector.'

'If you'd left a number . . .'

'I'd cold feet. Wasn't sure. I'm still not sure if what I'm going to tell you will do any good.'

'But?'

'But I rang Eve this morning. She told me what had been done to her trike. Said you knew who did it, and he was dead. Is that right?'

'Looks that way.'

'Worried me all the same, to think she was talking about it to all and sundry. That was why—' Dolores spoke very softly.

'Go on.'

'The first thing I want to say is . . . my husband has his problems. Problems I found it hard to come to terms with. But he's not a violent man. I can't believe he would have hurt Eve or Rupert. I've only ever heard him speak with loathing of one person—his stepsister. She died three years ago. In hospital. Cancer.' She paused as if to let the diagnosis sink in.

'I hear you. And the second thing?' Baxter prompted.

She sighed. 'I'm not sure I'd be prepared to testify to this in a lawcourt.'

'Like to hear it all the same.'

'Can't believe Eric was responsible for Rupert's death, but he might just know something. He visited Rupert on the evening he died.'

'When was this?'

'Shortly before six. I saw him go into the cottage, but he didn't know that. I was upstairs, rooting for my party dress in one of the spare rooms.'

'Did you see him come out again?'

'No. No, I didn't.'

The moment she rang off he keyed the number of the Parsingham Institute. No reply. The receptionist had presumably gone home. He tried Appletrees.

June Oakes answered. 'You again? Oh, thank God!'

'OK, OK, Mrs Oakes. Just tell me what's the matter. Take it easy. Take your time.'

'Time! There's no time. That Sinton's in the darkroom with the boss. He's a gun, I think. And the girl's in with them.'

'Girl?'

'Emma something. Sinton took her mother's car, she said.'

'Be with you right away.' It needn't be her, Baxter told himself as he buzzed Wendy. Mustn't.

'Enlighten her, Finchley.' Sinton had locked the side door and pocketed the key. He clasped both hands round the jam-jar, holding it against his stomach. There were six or seven honeybees inside, plus some white stuff. Syrup, Emma supposed.

Finchley shook his head.

Sinton smiled. 'Make the effort. Emma's a policeman's daughter.'

'Why should that worry me? There's nothing here to interest the police.'

Which was quite possibly true. The women in those photographs that lay within Emma's field of vision were neither nude nor indecently posed. All they had in common were expressions of fear, ranging from terror to mild alarm.

'You're the lawbreaker, Sinton. Forcing yourself in here, intimidating me—'

'Your housekeeper will have phoned the police by now,' Emma cut in.

'Then time's precious, Finchley.' Sinton closed up on him, swinging the jam-jar gently, like a censer. 'Tell Emma why I'm doing what I'm doing.'

The other man cowered, shielding his face with his bent left arm. 'Don't, for God's sake.'

Emma considered making a grab for the jar, but held back for fear of breaking it.

'Tell her why.'

'How can I, Sinton? How do I know how your crazy mind works?'

'Tell her what I told you.' Clive set the jam-jar down on the bench.

Eric Finchley lowered his guard, and stared at the photographs, his lopsided mouth quivering. 'He said . . . he said he wanted me to feel what she had felt.'

'She?'

'Anne. My wife—my ex-wife. Show her.'

Finchley handed Emma a faded and blurry snapshot. She stared, more embarrassed than frightened now, at a girl in a baby-doll nightdress with long, fair hair. She was sitting on the edge of a bunk bed in what looked to be the cabin of a boat or a caravan. Behind her were posters and a bookshelf. Her face was so badly focused that its expression was unreadable.

'I didn't hurt her. You're the one . . . Didn't touch her, even. I swear I didn't touch any of them. I never wanted . . .' Finchley was saying.

'You threatened her with a knife. Her and how many others?'

'Three—only three, I swear. Anne was the last. Threats never worked well. All the others are candid camera stills and video clips. Anne wasn't taken in. She knew I was bluffing. Ask her . . .'

'Crap.' But Finchley had hit home all the same. Emma felt sure of it.

The Director shifted in his seat. 'Listen, I need . . . I need to use the loo.'

Sinton jerked his head. 'Don't be too long or too noisy.' When he had shut the lavatory door behind him, Sinton sat down and Emma followed suit.

'You think I'm the pits, don't you?'

'I've nothing to say to you, Clive, till you set them free.' She indicated the bees.

He shrugged. 'As you like. Served their purpose.'

She watched him go through the cloakroom and side door. He deposited the jam-jar at the side of a brick path and loosened its cover. The bees rose crossly, confusedly into the humid air.

When he came back, Sinton added Anne's photograph to a wallet which already contained its negative. 'I'll give her these tonight. She's a right . . .'

'Will she want them after all these years?'

He shrugged. 'Her right to decide.'

'Will you tell her how you put the screws on Finchley?'

He flushed. 'No. Will you?'

'I'm not sure. It was horrible. Sick. And it's not enough to say it wasn't as bad as these.' Among the photographs, Emma had noticed several of Dolores in traditional costume. Clips from the video of a Filipino folk dance, perhaps. Systematically biased clips. *Then all smiles stopped together.*

'Tell me, Clive,' she said. 'What did Finchley mean when he said you were the one who hurt your wife?'

He grimaced. 'Anne did waitressing at various colleges when she was studying at the Tech. After the caravan incident I made her promise never to go back to Princes'— Finchley's college at that time. He was a Junior Research Fellow.'

'She knew it was Finchley who'd photographed her?'

'No. She'd known him only by sight at College, and he wore a mask for the break-in. But I knew when she imitated the first sentence he spoke: "Fond of reading, are we?" She got Eric's half-rolled r and his sneering emphasis on the *read* to perfection. And I couldn't tell her. I was too bloody ashamed to tell her.'

'Ashamed?'

'Explain later. Upshot was that I shot Anne some shitty line about the Princes' Clerk of Works reporting me to my foreman for timewasting. Said I'd been laid off the contract as a result. She didn't think that was good reason for her to chuck in an evening job there at time-and-a-half plus bonus.

'Heard from a third party that she was still working at Princes' now and then. There was a Parsingham occasion the evening I found out. Annual lecture or something, with a feast to follow. Old Rupert and Finchley were among those at High Table where Anne was serving. I marched into the hall and yanked her out. Hurt and humiliated her.

'I meant to talk to Rupert about it on Tuesday night, to justify myself.' Sinton passed a hand over his mouth as if unsaying the words.

'Could you have, if you'd had the chance?' Emma asked.

The lavatory door clicked. Finchley came back into the darkroom.

Sinton shook his head. 'Not then. Not without the intervention of my friend here. Which wasn't intended as therapy, I suspect. Show the lady a candid camera shot of me, old boy.'

Finchley stared. 'You're out of your mind.'

'Humour me.'

It was in black-and-white. An eight-by-ten blow-up. There was a panelled room, a wall lined with books. A boy with shaggy hair in sweatshirt and jeans who might have been a lefty student except for his hands, which were scarred and chalky. The right hand was reaching for a book.

'Geddit, Emma?' Sinton prompted.

She glanced at the boy's profile and then at Sinton's. 'Yourself when young?'

'In our friend's room at Princes'— sorry, Finchley—his *set* of rooms. Didn't bother me that the bedroom door was ajar that day. Usually was. I'd been working on his side of the court, you see. Repairing the ashlar work. Stage one in face masonry. Never made it to stage two. No matter. Gave me plenty of time to observe Academic Man. Stimulated the imagination, you might say.

'Got to know Finchley's little ways. Went to Hall for lunch from five to one till five to two regular as clockwork, didn't you? So how was I to know you'd taken to doubling back when I was in the Portakabin scoffing my sarnies?'

Emma turned to Finchley. 'You spied on him? You took those pictures?'

'As evidence for the police—I'd every right to protect my books.'

'Books your uncle bought, Eric. That to judge by the dust you'd never read.'

'If that were true, which it's not, it would be irrelevant. Tell her about your next visit, Sinton. Tell her how you cringed and crawled. Swore you'd pack in your job on the Princes' contract right away if I didn't turn you in to the police.'

'And you didn't? Why didn't you?' Emma asked Finchley. She thought she'd heard something outside the side door. Scufflings? A whisper? Neither of the men appeared to have noticed.

It was Sinton who answered. 'Like a fool, I'd told him I was desperate my wife shouldn't find out. You'd seen me around the place with Anne, hadn't you, Finchley? Fancied her? And you thought it would be safe to get back at me through her. The "Fond of reading?" reprise was deliberate, wasn't it? You knew she'd repeat it to me. Knew I'd rumble you, but that I wouldn't dare point the finger.'

'That's a lie.' Finchley's mouth twisted.

'It's the truth. The bloody truth that destroyed my marriage.'

'Really? On the evidence of your macho act in Hall, I'd have guessed that temper was the major factor.'

Emma turned back to Sinton. 'Your ex-wife paid twice over for your guilt feelings, didn't she? In the caravan and in Hall.'

Sinton nodded. 'I suppose.'

'And you never told her?'

'Never plucked up courage. Bloody stupid, that. Tonight I just might, though. Our friend here showed me how stupid I'd been when he proposed his trade-in the other day.'

'Trade-in? There was no trade-in. He's fantasizing.'

'What big words you use, Mr Wolf. Believe it or not, Emma, I'm here today because our friend promised to hand over these old pics.'

'For a price?'

'Oh yes. The price was an alibi. An alibi for Rupert Parsingham's murder.'

'My God.'

'Concentrates the mind wonderfully, murder. Forces you to revise your priorities. No, you don't, Finchley!' He lunged to wrest a matchbox from the other man's hands.

'Lies—it's all lies.'

'My son took your phone message,' Sinton said.

'Stacey Caldwell recognized your number on the note,' Emma added.

A loud knock at the side door. 'Police!'

'Sounds like your dad, Emma. Best not wind him up, eh?' Sinton dug in the hip pocket of his shorts and tossed her the house and car keys.

She hurried to the door.

CHAPTER 20

Baxter and Wendy Powers faced Finchley across one of the work-benches. Clive Sinton had left in a police car to make a revised statement at District HQ. Emma had promised to call there after delivering her mother's Granada.

'You know what Sinton's going to say, don't you?' Baxter began.

Finchley shrugged.

'I think he's going to talk about blackmail, don't you? Not a pretty word.'

'It never happened. Sinton's lying.'

'You rang him on Thursday, he said. My daughter and her friend heard his son give him your message.'

'All right—I rang him, for old time's sake. I'd seen him in the swimming-pool on Tuesday evening, half-recognized him. It wasn't until I read a piece about *Spin City* in the *News* the next day that I knew he was Paul Sinton's father. And on a trip to Cambridge. It seemed like an opportunity to heal old wounds.'

'And to reminisce about old photographs?'

'That was Sinton's doing. Ask your daughter. He forced himself in here. Threatened me—'

'With a weapon?'

'With a jam-jar full of bees. I see that amuses you, Sergeant.'

Wendy flushed. 'Sorry, I didn't—'

'Ever been poisoned, Sergeant? Badly? Ever had a serious bout of asthma or giddiness? No? Add the lot together, multiply by ten and you'll have some idea of what bees do to me before I pass out. Sinton knew. Imagination's his business, isn't it? Anne must have told him about the allergy. There were flowers in the caravan that night. Something buzzing. That's why I left in a hurry, why the picture was spoilt.'

Baxter was puzzled, but this was no time to pursue irrelevant hares. 'According to what you told DS Powers, you returned home around five last Tuesday. Spoke to your wife, changed and showered. Left on your bicycle at about five-forty, spent the hour between five forty-five and six forty-five in Parkside swimming-pool. Right?'

'Right. And what's more, Sinton knows it's right. He was in the pool when I arrived.'

'I must ask you to think again, Dr Finchley. We've evidence to the contrary from the landlord of the Signal Box and one of his customers.' No need to rely on Emma's testimony, thank God.

'I—really? I slipped in here for a bit—may have got my departure time a few minutes wrong.'

'More than that, according to our evidence.'

'Yes? Well—what does it matter, for Christ's sake?' Finchley blustered. 'I'd other things on my mind—have. Professional concerns. This nitpicking is such a waste of time, so unnecessary.'

'You've made it necessary, Dr Finchley. You talked to Mrs Parsingham Wells on Wednesday morning, didn't you? Learnt from her that her brother had had his five o'clock tea and cleared up before he died. Realized that it would be desirable to have an alibi from five-forty onwards—'

'No! It wasn't like that.' Finchley ran a finger inside his shirt-collar. 'It's bloody embarrassing, actually. Dolly was upstairs having her bath when I called out that I was leaving. To be honest, I came in here. For how long, I'm not sure. This isn't something I want to come out in court—so distressing for Dolly, so humiliating.'

'And damaging for your career prospects?'

Finchley nodded. 'I shan't deny it. I—I needed to be here, you see. It had been a rough day at work. You wouldn't understand—you don't have to understand, Chief Inspector.'

No, thank God. But Finchley was determined that he should listen. 'It started when I was twelve or so, when my stepsister Laura was bullying me, teasing me. She was fifteen then. A big girl, attractive. She could twist my stepfather round her little finger—almost. She wasn't able to stop his remarriage and she never came to terms with it. No one listened when I complained about her, so I gave up complaining. The worst sting reaction I ever had was Laura's doing. At a picnic, she . . .' His voice broke. 'Sorry. Even after all these years, I can't bear to think of it.'

'There's no need—' Baxter tried in vain to stem the flow.

'It was in hospital afterwards, looking at a picture like this in someone else's holiday brochure—' Finchley pointed to a shot of an O-mouthed, goosepimpled teenager leaping into turquoise waves. 'That's when I found my way of getting my own back. I used cuttings at first, before I went into photography. They're all her underneath, you see. They're all Laura.' Flushed now, and sweating, he shoved the prints aside, out of his sight.

But Laura had won in the long run. She'd hung in to obsess him. Poor bastard. Poor disgusting bastard. And also, very likely, a murderer. 'We're not here to plumb the depths of your fantasy life,' Baxter said crisply. 'We're investigating Rupert Parsingham's death.'

'But I've told you—'

'Not quite everything. Not why you visited Mr Parsingham on Tuesday evening.' Finchley's head jerked back briefly, then steadied. 'Or why you concealed the fact from DS Powers.'

'It's a lie . . . fabrication.'

'I must warn you . . .' Baxter administered the formal

caution. 'You were seen going into the cottage, Dr Finchley, but not coming out.'

A shake of the heavy head.

'Let me help. You'd had a rough day, you said. More specifically, I'd guess, a rough Board meeting.'

'Nothing to do with the case.'

'No? According to our information the announcement of the Bryce-Benson back-off hit the Chairman and his colleagues pretty hard. You'd seen it coming as long as last May, hadn't you? That night in the Ruffled Feathers—'

'Aubrey King.' The pale eyes widened. 'What's Aubrey been saying?'

'Lots—or he will, soon as the Fraud Squad sink their teeth in. From what I hear, King would ditch any dirt anywhere to further his interests.'

Tears gathered in Finchley's eyes. 'The glitterati circuit . . . money. I didn't need things like that. Anything I did I did for the Institute. And her.'

'Her?'

'My mother.'

His stepsister . . . his mother. Was his wife a poor third or nowhere, Baxter asked himself.

'Don't judge me by these.' Finchley gestured towards the photographs. 'Mother had no idea. She always wanted the best for me. That's why she remarried—to give me a good schooling, a good start. When my stepfather died, it was almost the way it had been. She was so proud the first time I showed her over the Institute, soon after I became Director. She died soon after, but I always think of it as her place. The place where I can be the son she wanted, where I can still talk to her. That matters to me, don't you see? That matters more than anything else in the world. I couldn't let it go without a struggle.' He blew his nose.

'Detoxicon,' Baxter said quietly. 'You passed Otley's Pacific pollution data to Detoxicon?'

The soft mouth opened and closed soundlessly.

'It's too late, Finchley. I've spoken to Sir James.'

Tears welled up in his pale eyes. 'All right. It didn't come off, but I'm not ashamed of trying. What difference will it make in the long run? What chance does a Third World scratch team stand against the multinationals?'

'Less, because of you and the likes of you,' Wendy Powers muttered.

Finchley made a despairing gesture, let the tears trickle down the furrows of his slack face.

'Rupert and his sister were your last chance, weren't they?' Baxter prompted. 'With them out of the way, the trust capital and property—'

'No. I never thought like that, never allowed myself . . . Besides, it wasn't necessary. Plumtrees is too much for those two old people to manage—has been for years. The sensible thing would be for them to relinquish their rights in favour of the University. In exchange for an inflation-proofed annuity which I'd have been glad to supplement from my own pocket. Discreetly, of course.'

Finchley allowed himself a wry self-congratulatory smile, as if denying his dealings with King and the implications of their exposure.

'Of course. But you'd put this proposal to Mrs Parsingham Wells, hadn't you, and had it rejected?'

At that time, yes.' Again, the smug smile. So Eve, that downy old bird, had fooled Finchley as she had fooled her daughter. 'It occurred to me on Tuesday evening that an approach to Rupert might yield fruit. That he might be able to persuade his sister.'

'An unlikely scenario, surely, given their respective characters?' Baxter retorted.

Finchley shrugged and sighed. 'Rupert said he would speak to her. Perhaps he did. Perhaps that accounted for her change of tune.' A joyless smile, this time. The hopelessness of his situation had struck home. Even if—as he obviously believed—the Institute's future had been secured, his own career there was finished.

'What else did Mr Parsingham say?' Baxter asked.

'Oh, I don't know. Small talk.' The words came slowly now, painfully. 'I apologized for disregarding his notice and he said it was aimed at the partygoers. I asked him if his virus trouble had cleared up. He said he still felt rather tired. Then I spoke about the Institute's financial crisis, told him a major sponsor had backed off.'

'You didn't name names?'

'No. Rupert was discreet, but Eve isn't. I was afraid he'd pass Bryce's name to her. It could have prejudiced future relationships with the corporation if the episode had been publicized outside the Institute.'

'Did he speak of suicide?'

'No. But he wouldn't, I suppose. We were never what you would call close. Dolly—Dolores—knew him much better than I.'

There was no hint of jealousy in the statement.

'How long were you in the cottage?'

'What does it matter? What does any of this matter?'

'To us it does, Dr Finchley.'

A shrug. 'Fifteen minutes, perhaps. I put my case briefly, because Rupert was yawning a bit. I thought perhaps he was ready for a nap.'

'OK. You came back here. Did you speak to your wife?'

'No. The car was gone, so I assumed Dolly had used it to transport food to Plumtrees or to do last-minute shopping. She came back later, though. She was in the house when I left for the Parkside Pool.'

'When did she return?'

'No idea.'

'But surely you must have seen or heard the car?'

Finchley shook his head. 'Wouldn't have seen it from

here with the blinds drawn. As for hearing. Well, to be frank, when my mind's on other things—' He flushed, letting his eyes stray to the photographs.

'Did you speak to your wife after she returned?'

'No.'

'Then how—?'

'Heard her start up the washing-machine in the basement. That's when I looked at my watch, decided I'd better get going soon.'

Baxter had a sudden vision of clothes rotating in a washing-machine.

Dirty clothes—oily clothes?

'What time was this?' he asked.

'Six twenty-five. I remember checking. You're not suggesting that Dolly . . .? No, I'm sure she's not capable. Unless Rupert, unless he's tried . . .' The words trailed off helplessly.

'Notice your car as you left?'

'No, but I went out by the side door. And as you saw, the turning space and garage are at the back.'

'Very well.' Baxter stood up.

'You've finished with me?' Finchley asked dully.

'Personally, yes. For the moment.' Baxter used his radio to summon the second pair of uniformed constables and to liaise with Armstrong. 'You've no objection, I take it, to providing my colleagues with a fuller account of your dealings with Mr King? There's a car waiting to run you to the police station.'

Finchley raised his large hands and let them fall. He got up awkwardly.

June Oakes had given up all pretence of dusting when Baxter and Powers joined her in the hall. 'Washing? Yes. Did a load yesterday morning.'

Baxter cursed silently.

'Anyone other than yourself been in there recently?'

'Since Mrs Finchley went to London? Only Mrs Parsingham Wells and Sister Imm—whatever she calls herself. Mrs PW has been showering and laundering here ever since the power was cut next door. Her poor old brother didn't have much in the way of mod. cons., I suppose. I bumped into her here yesterday lunch-time, as a matter of fact, on her way down to the utility room. Odd, really.'

'What was odd?'

'Oh, just that she didn't ring the doorbell. Mrs F. had given her a key so she could let herself in, but she and her daughter had always rung first, all the same, any time I was around. Didn't want me to come down with her yesterday. Bit short about it, but you make allowances, don't you, after a bereavement? I insisted on coming, of course.'

'To help carry her laundry bag?'

'Oh no. She didn't have a laundry bag. She was looking for a sock her daughter had left behind from her last load, she said. Horrible thick greyish things, Mrs PW wears. We searched all over. No joy. The old girl wasn't too put out. Said she'd have another look at home. That she'd lose her head next time round.'

Baxter edged towards the basement staircase.

'Mustn't witter, must I? Like me to show you the way?'

Baxter declined as politely as his growing excitement would allow.

'Right-oh. Straight ahead at the bottom. Can't miss it.'

Nor could they. The large utility room and two small cellars comprised the whole of the basement.

The washing-machine sparkled inside and out. So too the tumble-drier. Who'd use a tumble-drier in this heat? Unless . . . He squatted to inspect the filter. Unless they were in a hurry.

'See what I see?' He made way for Powers.

'Lint—some of it's blue.'

No sight or smell of oil, but he poked the filter out all the same. 'Wrap it up, will you, Wendy? And let's keep looking.'

'For a sock?'

'Anything but that, I fancy. Anything that looks out of place.'

Dodging between clothes-airers and an ironing-board, Baxter opened one of the roomy cupboards that lined two of the walls. Powers followed his example. The contents comprised cleaning equipment and detergents, large cooking receptacles and items of china which were presumably not in daily use.

It was in a copper fish-kettle that Powers found the revolver.

Baxter made a quick inspection. 'Webley Mark 4.'

'First World War vintage?'

'That's right.' He sniffed and squinted. 'Unloaded. No sign of recent use.'

'It's inconvenient. Tell them it's bloody inconvenient, Ginnie!' Eve Parsingham's protest resonated down the dusty front staircase of Plumtrees.

A murmured dialogue ensued. Sister Immaculata materialized, frowning, and descended. 'Could you possibly come back at another time, Chief Inspector? Mother suggests Monday at eleven, but perhaps tomorrow? She's really quite exhausted.'

'*Really?*' Baxter raised a quizzical eyebrow.

'Emotionally if not physically,' Immaculata amplified. 'It's taken its toll, sorting out Uncle Rupert's belongings.' She indicated two black polythene sacks just inside the front door.

Baxter read the labels. *Oxfam, Jumble Sale.* 'Clothes, I take it, Sister? All your uncle's?'

'Plus a few items of my mother's that she'd been meaning to dispose of.'

'All washed or drycleaned, I presume?'

'Naturally!' Immaculata bridled, clutching her crucifix. A pious alternative, perhaps, for counting ten backwards? 'What's this all about, may I ask? Why the cross-examination?'

'I've reason to believe one or both sacks may contain items relevant to our investigation. I propose to remove them for detailed examination.'

'I can't think what Mother . . . we understood from the Scenes of Crime officer that the police had no further interest—'

'Sorry, Sister. New circumstances have arisen. A careful inventory will be made. Meanwhile, there's a question I want to ask you. Have you used the washing-machine in Appletrees in the course of this visit?'

Her forehead puckered. 'Yes, I thought I'd already told you. Mother had *carte blanche*.'

'And the tumble-drier?'

'In this weather? Good gracious, no. I hung the spun clothes out for an hour or two before taking them back for ironing. But what possible interest—?'

'Sorry, Sister. Now I need to talk to your mother. Yes, now, I'm afraid. Would you ask whether she would prefer to see us upstairs or downstairs?'

Immaculata obeyed without further argument, asking them to wait in the large front room which Baxter had seen on his last visit. In her absence, he sent Powers to stow the sacks in the boot of his car. A minute or two after her return, Eve bustled in.

'I resent this, Chief Inspector. I resent it wholeheartedly.' Eve's chain-hung glasses glinted against her plaid housecoat as she threw herself into a tub-chair and fixed him with a Churchillian glare.

'I regret it, Mrs Parsingham Wells,' Baxter said soberly. 'But I've more questions to ask. You currently use the laundry facilities at Appletrees, I understand.'

Eve nodded.

'When did you last use them?'

'I—I—can't remember.' She clutched at her spectacles.

'Would it surprise you to know that you had been heard washing clothes last Tuesday? When Mrs Finchley was out shopping at the supermarket? We won't have difficulty in checking out her story, I imagine. Filipinas aren't thick on the Cambridge ground.'

'Possibly. I really can't—yes, I did a load last Tuesday.'

'In the midst of your party preparations?'

'Found out at the last minute that my caftan—only thing I had fit to wear—was grubby. Shoved in a few other garments as makeweights.'

'Did you use the tumble-drier?'

'No—yes, I believe so. Ecologically improper, but it saved me from ironing the caftan.' She made a business of polishing her glasses. 'Eric Finchley was snooping about, I take it? Reporting on the noises off? Well, if that's all—' She started to rise.

'Not quite. Why, for example, didn't you tell me about this sooner?'

'Slipped my mind. Effects of shock, I dare say. Don't they teach you people things like that?'

'Shall I tell you what I think? I think one or more of the garments you washed and dried is now bagged up for charity.'

'So what?' Eve clasped her hands tightly. To stop them shaking?

'The filter, if you please, Sergeant.'

Powers held it up, sheathed in polythene.

'I've a hunch the forensic scientists will be able to match fibres from this gunge with garments in your charity bags.

I've a hunch they'll find traces of petrol and or motor oil.'

'So what?' It came fainter this time.

'Let's talk about your sock, now.'

'Sock?' A barking laugh.

'The one you lost, remember? The one Mrs Oakes tried to help you find.' He signalled to Powers, who held up the revolver.

Eve thumped on the arm of her chair. 'Monday! Why couldn't you wait until Monday? Now you've buggered up everything.' She wept noisily, like an elderly toddler.

CHAPTER 21

'You'd hoped to defer this encounter until you were on your way to Devon, had you?' Baxter asked. 'Was it really to be Devon or somewhere farther afield?'

Eve lifted her chin. 'Neither. I agreed to the Devon scheme to shake off Ginnie—Immaculata. I'd every intention of leaving the train at Bishop's Stortford and doubling back. Seeing Harrison Garbutt is what mattered. Matters.' Her voice strengthened. 'Sorry, Chief Inspector. I've no intention of helping you further until I've spoken to Harrison.'

'Couldn't his brother Goronway serve your purpose? Or their partner?'

Eve snorted. 'That pair of twisters! Wouldn't trust either of them as far as I could throw them.'

'But presumably you've a higher opinion of Professor Ogilvie-Walnutt? I gather you showed him your hand this afternoon.'

'James passed on what I told him in confidence to you? To a policeman? I don't believe it. I refuse to believe it.'

'Correct me if he misled me, then. He told me you wished

to renounce your interest in the trust created by your father's will in favour of the University. You made a proviso, however. If your legal application succeeded, none of the capital thus released to finance tropical scientific studies was to be assigned to the Parsingham Institute.'

'James really did tell you all this? He'd no right—'

'I'd placed other facts before him. No doubt he felt grateful. He added that your wishes would be respected.'

'Oral assurances aren't enough. I confided in James as a precautionary measure—in case I was struck down by the proverbial bus. But I shan't be happy until I've conveyed my written directions to Harrison in person.'

'That could still be arranged,' Baxter said quietly.

She shot him a 'Promise?'

'I promise. Please put that on record, Sergeant.' Powers made a note.

Eve sighed. 'Very well.'

Baxter administered the caution.

She grimaced. 'Ginnie had a soft spot for her uncle. I'd rather she were miles away.'

'To learn from the media that you'd been arrested for his murder?'

'You won't let up, will you?'

'Not now.'

She grimaced. 'Better get it over quickly, then. Like brimstone and treacle. Which was before your time, I suspect?'

He nodded.

'Cure for hives, as I remember. Sulphurous taste stuck to the tongue for ages. Bear—Rupert—made a tremendous fuss about swallowing his. Made such a fuss about everything when it came to the bit. Even dying.'

'You were there?'

'You know I was there, doing what he'd asked me to do. Doing my duty. It was difficult. Bear made it so damn difficult.' Eve's brown eyes refilled with angry tears.

'You don't have to distress yourself,' Baxter said quietly. 'The facts will do.'

'No, they bloody well won't. I put them on paper on Wednesday night, actually, soon as I'd got Esther off the premises. Right-hand top drawer of my dressing-table, in case you're interested. Never intended to let anyone else take the rap, once you'd twigged it wasn't suicide. Hard to get one's motives into writing, though. So you two are going to hear them—you're damn well going to hear them.' Her eyes zigzagged between the detectives' faces.

'We'd a pact, Rupert and I, that we'd help each other end our lives if help was needed. An unlikely contingency in my case, total physical incapacity always excepted. But he was always the weaker vessel. Loathed boarding-school twice as much as I did, but I was the one who ran away. Three times,' she recalled with evident satisfaction.

'Rupert professed pacifism in nineteen-thirty-nine, which I could have respected if he'd gone to prison instead of signing up for the Ambulance Corps.'

'Let's talk about last Tuesday.' Baxter's ulcer was pricking. He helped himself to a sodamint.

Eve made no acknowledgement of the interruption. 'My brother reminded me of our pact the day he'd been warned that his driving licence wouldn't be renewed. He told me he wanted to die immediately his work at the Garden Centre ended. That he'd like to gas himself—and quickly—in his garage, where I would almost certainly be the first to find him. He added that the arthritis in his wrists was worse on some days than others, so he might need help in fixing a hose to the exhaust pipe.' Eve paused, blew her nose again.

'We argued. I was distressed. I wish you to understand that I was distressed. And angry. If he had been terminally ill . . . But giving up driving was such a little thing, which so many—myself included—have done voluntarily. From principle. But my poor dear brother was never what I would call a principled person. Mother and Father were away a great deal when he was small, you see. Grandfather was over-indulgent. Our suffragette aunt died too soon to be a major influence.'

Baxter cleared his throat.

Eve surveyed him with grim amusement. 'Patience, Chief Inspector. I am now proceeding in a forwardly direction. I was distressed, as I said, at the prospect of losing my brother for such a trivial reason. And angry when I thought of the causes crying out for supporters to which he could have put his talents. But having said my say, I gave in. We agreed that we wouldn't discuss the matter further, but that I'd honour our longstanding agreement. Do what he'd asked on the evening of his retirement.'

'Had he asked for that?' Baxter pointed to the revolver.

Eve's colour rose. 'Not in so many words—but he'd said: "Keep me to it, won't you, Pudding? Don't let me cop out." It seemed the best way. Grandfather took us duck-shooting in the Fens once or twice when we were kids. Rupert hated it—he was terrified of guns, even then.' Her voice broke.

'When I saw the notice on his door on Tuesday afternoon I took it as confirmation. Dolly Finchley was the only person who might have disregarded it, but I kept her busy with preparations for the garden-party.'

'An odd day for you to give a party.'

'I knew I'd need distraction, don't you see? I'd need it desperately. I asked Dolly to do some last-minute shopping for drink and nibbles that would entail a trip down-town and another to the Milton Tesco's and give me half an hour to play with. I felt sure she'd wait until after the rush-hour, which she did. I fiddled about in the garden, listening out for her. As soon as I heard her drive off, I took the revolver from the kitchen drawer where I'd temporarily stowed it.

'I felt worse, so much worse than I'd expected. I had to force myself to take every step. Rupert looked ghastly when he came to the door. He'd been off form for a couple of weeks, but I'd never seen him like that. Greyish.' Eve stared as if he had returned to her.

'He started to make difficulties the minute I was in the cottage. Said he still wanted to die, but he wasn't quite ready. He'd things to do—people to talk to. Couldn't we put it off for twenty-four hours?

'But I couldn't face that, don't you see?' Eve's plump hands fisted. 'Couldn't have gone through all that again, even if I believed he had good reason. Which I didn't. I thought—think—he was making excuses. So I brought out the pistol. It wasn't loaded—you'll have seen—'

'Not when we found it,' Baxter conceded.

'Not on Tuesday either. But Rupert never guessed. I told him that if he didn't keep his word I'd shoot him and then me. I asked him if he'd want Dolly to find us—that struck a chord.' There was a note of malice in the phrase.

'Didn't he attempt to disarm you?'

'Didn't dare, I imagine. I've always been fitter, though I was female and four years older. Besides, with his wrists and his eye-trouble . . . He caved in when I mentioned Dolly. Picked up a notepad for the suicide note. My suggestion. Went ahead of me into the garage.

'I'd plastic gloves on. I'd thought out beforehand what must be done to cover my tracks.'

'That was important to you?'

'Of course. As I've told you, I've views on voluntary assisted euthanasia—'

'*Voluntary*,' Powers echoed ironically.

'Which if Hardy came to Hardy, I'd have defended in court. But Deep Green takes priority, and there are limits to what one can contribute to a movement from behind

bars. I'd thought everything through in detail. Rupert
obeyed my suggestions silently, shakily. I told myself it was
teaching him to swim all over again. Had to make light of
it to myself, don't you see?'

Baxter thought of the frightened old man and grunted.

'He wrote the note from the driving-seat. I'd retreated to
the door of the garage by then. Couldn't see which hand
he was using, and it didn't occur to me to wonder. When
he'd finished, I told him to switch on. He'd two things to
ask of me first, he said. It was horrible, the way he said it.
As if I were his executioner.'

'Which you were, weren't you?' Powers said so softly that
Eve seemed not to hear.

'Rupert said Eric Finchley had called on him very
recently. Pushed the line he'd tried on me and failed. The
Institute was in desperate straits, Finchley had said. He'd
found generous sponsors in the past—could find more,
given time. But the University wouldn't give him time without an early and substantial cash injection. Rupert and I
were his only hope.

'Rupert had agreed to raise the matter with me, but only
to warn me. Finchley was unfit to be Director, he said. He
should be sacked. I agreed. I'd always disliked the man.
Dr Fell thing—the reason why I could not tell. Rupert was
more specific—said Finchley had treated his staff abominably, that he had almost certainly used illicit methods to
raise finance.'

'How'd your brother know this?'

'Through Stacey and Julian, I guessed. But Rupert
wouldn't say, and I didn't ask. It didn't matter. If the
Institute folded, the directorship was a non-issue. Didn't
say a word to Rupert, but I'd taken soundings in the weeks
since Finchley had approached me. I'd already decided the
place had become an absurd anachronism, an insult to my
great-grandfather's memory. He was a rebel, you know, a

Darwinian when Darwinism was a heresy. He looked to the
future, as we must all look to the future!'

Baxter belched discreetly. It was an odd experience to
be preached at by a murderer. 'Your brother had a second
message, you said?'

'Said he'd stowed some cash savings in a desk drawer,
which he'd intended to give to Dolores Finchley. He didn't
mention a sum. A few hundreds, I suppose. I promised to see
to it later, after the police had been. Never dreamt you people
were going to turn the place upside down. Now I shan't be in
a position . . . That money must go to Dolores the minute
you've finished with it. I shall speak to Harrison.'

'In view of its likely origins, that may not be possible.'

'Origins? Explain yourself, Chief Inspector.'

To his surprise, he heard himself obeying. Eve's sombre
face dissolved in laughter. 'The old slyboots. Might have
let me in on it. Nice to think his last summer wasn't just
doom and gloom, all the same.'

'You promised you'd see Mrs Finchley got the money.
What then?' Baxter prompted.

Eve reverted with evident distress to the scene in the
garage. 'Rupert made . . . made more difficulties. Repeated
that he wanted to say goodbye to Dolores. I said better
not, for both their sakes. I threatened to shoot myself. He
switched on the ignition soon after that, started up the
engine. I waited until the fumes were quite bad, four or five
minutes, perhaps. I said: "'Night, Bear."

'Then I left, handling the lock as little as I could, so as
not to spoil Rupert's prints. I listened outside for a little.
Nothing but the engine. Hurried home to change, then took
my bag of laundry to Appletrees. Ran it through a short
cycle. Not long enough, but I didn't want Dolores to come
back when I was unloading. In fact, she brought the booze
straight back to Plumtrees.

'She was setting out chairs in the garden when I sneaked

back, so she didn't spot me or the laundry bag. Just told her I'd been bathing at her place. Everything would have worked out very well, you see, if it hadn't been for Inspector Armstrong. Except for the money, perhaps.'

'She might have found it an embarrassment.'

'Perhaps you're right. I've been unfair to Dolly at times, I admit. Bear had this thing about young women, ever since his young wife died. I thought Dolly was taking advantage. Didn't know about the OU course, until she told me over the phone the other day. Might do something academic myself, I suppose, in the slammer. Ecology perhaps . . . Time for us to be on the move, isn't it? But first I'll have to break the news to poor Ginnie.' She sighed.

'Unless you'd rather—'

'No, no. Buck stops here and all that. Who said that? Roosevelt? Eisenhower?'

At four o'clock next morning Baxter woke from a dream of Eve. Was she dreaming in her cell, he asked himself? As much to exorcize her image as from personal curiosity, he padded downstairs to his dining-room to consult the *Penguin Dictionary of Modern Quotations*.

So the proverbial buck had stopped with little old Harry S. Truman. Who'd have thought it? A man gone and almost forgotten. As Rupert Parsingham soon would be. But neither of them would vanish as completely as the anonymous maker of the miniature chest-of-drawers that awaited his daughter's descent.

He untied the fancy wrappings that Sarah had found for it and made a final inspection. The front curved sweetly, the crossbanding was finely wrought. The mahogany had been thoroughly waxed and buffed, as well it might. Jo Mercier's London overheads obliged her to charge her friends something approaching London prices. He lifted each drop handle in turn, and found spots of tarnish on the undersides of two of them. He went into the kitchen for brass polish. Retrieving it from a high shelf in the cleaning cupboard, he dislodged a squeegee mop with his sleeve and sent it clattering across the tiled floor.

A thump overhead. Bare feet padding on the stairs. 'OK, Sarah,' he yelled as he grabbed the mop, then remembered she was out on a call.

Emma was on the threshold in one of her oversize night-shirts, laughing. 'What's all this? Dad's Army drill?' As he stowed the squeegee, she caught sight of the tin of polish. 'Kit inspection? Got it bad, haven't you?'

'Looking for a light bulb,' Baxter fibbed. 'Bedside lamp's conked out. Sorry I woke you, love.'

'You didn't, I couldn't get over. Too much black coffee after supper, I suppose.'

'Uh-huh?' He retrieved the box of light bulbs. 'Weren't driving, were you?'

'No. Taxi at Mum's expense. Reckoned I owed it to Paul, though. Hard to say goodbye nicely if you're canned, don't you think?'

'You and he've split? Oh, I'm sorry.' Baxter absent-mindedly replaced the bulb box unopened.

'Me too, a smidgin. Well, more than a smidgin. Tough on Paul too, just when it looks like his parents might get something going again. Right decision to me, but you know how it is.'

'I know.'

'Mind if I talked about it for a bit, Dad, seeing as you're here?'

''Course not, Em. Take a pew. I'll make us—'

'Whisky and soda for me, thanks. Help myself from the sideboard. Can I tempt you?'

'Wait!'

But he was too late to intercept her dive into the dining-room.

'Oh, Dad! For me?' She was standing by the chest-of-drawers when he caught up with her.

'Happy birthday, Em.' He kissed her awkwardly. 'If you don't like it, you can have the cash. No problem.'

She opened each drawer in turn.

'Just because you wanted something as a kid doesn't mean you have to . . .' he gabbled. 'Don't think I'm trying to turn the clock back, trying to make up . . .' But half of him was, of course. He poured them both whiskys.

She hugged him when he came back. 'I love it. I want it. Truly. Only thing . . . You were going to polish it just now, weren't you?'

'Two of the handles. Little spots of verdigris underneath. There and there, see?'

'Thing is, darling. Way I'll be living in London, I'll do my best, but I can't promise to take such good care of it as you would. I can't even promise no one'll never put a beer-mug on it. OK?'

He swallowed. 'OK, love. You wanted to talk?' He handed her a glass.

'That'd be good.' She followed him back to the kitchen table. 'And afterwards, if you liked, you could tell me about that case of yours.'

That would be good too. He took his first sip of whisky.

THE END